You are cordially invited to the weddings
of Lord Ratliffe's three daughters
as they marry their courageous heroes

A captain, a surgeon in the Royal Navy and a
Royal Marine prove true husband material in
his stirring Regency trilogy from Carla Kelly

MARRYING THE CAPTAIN
THE SURGEON'S LADY
MARRYING THE ROYAL MARINE

MARRYING THE
ROYAL MARINE

Carla Kelly

First published in Great Britain 2012
by Mills & Boon, an imprint of Harlequin (UK) Limited.
Harlequin (UK) Limited, Eton House, 18-24 Paradise Road,
Richmond, Surrey TW9 1SR

© Carla Kelly 2010

ISBN: 978 0 263 89229 1

Harlequin (UK) policy is to use papers that are natural, renewable and recyclable products and made from wood grown in sustainable forests. The logging and manufacturing process conform to the legal environmental regulations of the country of origin.

Printed and bound in Spain
by Blackprint CPI, Barcelona

Carla Kelly has been writing award-winning novels for years—stories set in the British Isles, Spain, and army garrisons during the Indian Wars. Her speciality in the Regency genre is writing about ordinary people, not just lords and ladies. Carla has worked as a university professor, a ranger in the National Park Service, and recently as a staff writer and columnist for a small daily newspaper in Valley City, North Dakota. Her husband is director of theatre at Valley City State University. She has five interesting children, a fondness for cowboy songs, and too many box elder beetles in the autumn.

Novels by the same author:

BEAU CRUSOE
CHRISTMAS PROMISE
   (part of *Regency Christmas Gifts* anthology)
MARRYING THE CAPTAIN*
THE SURGEON'S LADY*

*linked by character

MARRYING THE ROYAL MARINE features characters you will have met in MARRYING THE CAPTAIN and THE SURGEON'S LADY

**Did you know that some of these novels
are also available as eBooks?
Visit www.millsandboon.co.uk**

To Lynn and Bob Turner, former U.S. Marines.
Semper Fi to you both.

Prologue

Stonehouse Royal Marine Barracks,
Third Division, Plymouth—May 1812

Black leather stock in hand, Lieutenant Colonel Hugh Philippe d'Anvers Junot, Royal Marine, stared into his mirror and decided his father was right: he was lonely.

Maybe early symptoms were the little drawings that deckled Hugh's memorandum tablet during endless meetings in the conference room at Marine Barracks. As Colonel Commandant Lord Villiers covered item after item in his stringent style, Hugh had started drawing a little lady peeking around the edge of her bonnet. During one particularly dull budget meeting, he drew a whole file of them down the side of the page.

Hugh gazed more thoughtfully into the mirror, not bothered by his reflection—he knew his height, posture, curly brown hair, and nicely chiselled lips met the demands of any recruiting poster—but by the humbling knowledge that his father still knew him best.

He had written to his father, describing his restlessness and his dissatisfaction with the perils of promotion. While flattering, the promotion had bumped him off a ship of the line and into an office. *I know I should appreciate this promotion*, he had written, *but, Da, I am out of sorts. I'm not sure what I want. I'm sour and discontented. Any advice would be appreciated. Your dutiful, if disgruntled, son.*

A week later, he had read Da's reply over breakfast. He read it once and laughed; he read it again and pushed back his chair, thoughtful. He sat there longer than he should have, touched that his father had probably hit on the matter: he was lonely.

Damn this war, he had thought then. The words were plainspoken as Da was plainspoken: *My dear son, I wrote a similar letter to your grandfather once, before I met your mother, God rest her soul. Son, can ye find a wife?*

'That takes more time than I have, Da,' he had said out loud, but Da was probably right. Lately, when he attended the Presbyterian church in Devonport, he found himself paying less attention to the sermon and more attention to husbands, wives, and children sitting in the pews around him. He found himself envying both the comfortable looks of the couples married longest, and the shy hand-holdings and smouldering glances of the newly married. He tried to imagine the pleasure of marrying and rearing children, and found that he could not. War had ruined him; perhaps Da wasn't aware of that.

It was food for thought this May morning, and he chewed on it as he took advantage of a welcome hiatus from a meeting—the Colonel Commandant's gout was dictating a start one hour later than usual—and took himself to Stonehouse Naval Hospital. He had heard the jetty bell clanging late last night, and knew there would be wounded Marines to visit.

The air was crisp and cool, but threatening summer when he arrived at Block Four, where his friend Owen Brackett worked his surgeon's magic on the quick and nearly dead. He found Owen on the second floor.

The surgeon turned to Hugh with a tired smile. 'Did the jetty bell wake you?'

Hugh nodded. 'Any Marines?'

'Aye. If you have a mind to visit, come with me.'

Hugh followed Brackett down the stairs into

another ward. With an inward sigh, he noted screens around several beds.

'There was a cutter returning from Surgeon Brittle's satellite hospital in Oporto. The cutter was stopped at sea by a frigate with some nasty cases to transfer,' Owen said. 'Seems there was a landing attempted farther north along the Portuguese coast. Sit.'

He sat, never used to ghastly wounds, and put his hands on the man's remaining arm, which caused the Marine's eyes to flicker open.

'Meet Lieutenant Nigel Graves, First Division,' Brackett whispered before leaving.

'From Chatham?' Hugh asked, putting his lips close to the man's ear.

'Aye, sir. Serving on...*Relentless*.' It took ages for him to get out the words.

'A regular mauling?' he asked, his voice soft. 'Take your time, Lieutenant. We have all day.' He didn't; the Lieutenant didn't. It was a serviceable lie; both knew it.

Lieutenant Graves tried to sit up. Hugh slipped his arm under the young man's neck. 'What were you doing?'

'Trying to land at Vigo.'

'A one-ship operation?'

'Four ships, sir.' He sighed, his exasperation obvious. 'We didn't know each other! Who was in charge when the Major died?' He closed his eyes. 'It was a disaster, sir. We should have been better.'

Hugh could tell he wanted to say more, but Lieutenant Graves took that moment to die. Hugh gently lowered him to the cot. He was still sitting there when Owen Brackett returned, enquired about the time of death from him, and wrote it on the chart.

'A botched landing at Vigo,' Hugh said. 'Uncoordinated Marines working against each other, when all they wanted to do was fight! I've heard this before.'

'It makes you angry,' Owen said.

'Aye.' Hugh smoothed down the Lieutenant's hair. 'Each company on each vessel is a well-oiled machine, because we train them that way. Put one hundred of them on a ship of the line, and you have a fighting force. Try to coordinate twenty-five here or fifteen there from three or four frigates operating in tandem, and it can be a disaster.'

The surgeon nodded. 'All they want to do is their best. They're Marines, after all. We expect no less.'

Hugh thought about that as he took the foot-bridge back over the stream to the administration building of the Third Division. He was never late to anything, but he was late now.

The meeting was in the conference room on the first floor. He stopped outside the door, hand on knob, as a good idea settled around him and blew away the fug. Why could someone not enquire of the Marines at war how they saw themselves being used in the Peninsula?

'You're late, Colonel Junot,' his Colonel Commandant snapped.

'Aye, my lord. I have no excuse.'

'Are those *stains* on your uniform sleeve?'

Everyone looked. Hugh saw no sympathy. 'Aye, my lord.'

Perhaps it was his gout; Lord Villiers was not in a forgiving mood. 'Well? Well?'

'I was holding a dying man and he had a head wound, my lord.'

His fellow Marine officers snapped to attention where they sat. It might have been a tennis match; they looked at the Commandant, as if on one swivel, then back at Hugh.

'Explain yourself, sir,' Lord Villiers said, his voice calmer.

'I visited Stonehouse, my lord.' He remained at attention. 'Colonel, I know you have an agenda, but I have an idea.'

Chapter One

Lord Villiers liked the idea and moved on it promptly. He unbent enough to tell Hugh, as he handed him his orders, 'This smacks of something I would have done at your age, given your dislike of the conference table.'

'I, sir?'

'Belay it, Colonel Junot! Don't bamboozle someone who, believe it or not, used to chafe to roam the world. Perhaps we owe the late Lieutenant Graves a debt unpayable. Now take the first frigate bound to Portugal before I change my mind.'

Hugh did precisely that. With his dunnage stowed on the *Perseverance* and his berth assigned—an evil-smelling cabin off the wardroom—Hugh had dinner with Surgeon Brackett

on his last night in port. Owen gave him a letter
for Philemon Brittle, chief surgeon at the Oporto
satellite hospital, and passed on a little gossip.

'It's just a rumour, mind, but Phil seems to
have engineered a billet for his sister-in-law, a
Miss Brandon, at his hospital. He's a clever man,
but I'm agog to know how he managed it, if the
scuttlebutt is true,' Brackett said. 'Perhaps she
is sailing on the *Perseverance*.'

'Actually, she is,' Hugh said, accepting tea
from Amanda Brackett. 'I've already seen her.'

'She has two beautiful sisters, one of whom
took leave of her senses and married Phil Brittle.
Perhaps your voyage will be more interesting
than usual,' the surgeon teased.

Hugh sipped his tea. 'Spectacles.'

'You're a shallow man,' Amanda Brackett
said, her voice crisp.

Hugh winced elaborately and Owen laughed.
'Skewered! Mandy, I won't have a friend left in
the entire fleet if you abuse our guests so. Oh.
Wait. He's a Royal Marine. They don't count.'

Hugh joined in their laughter, at ease with
their camaraderie enough to unbend. 'I'll have
you know I took a good look at her remarkable
blue eyes, and, oh, that auburn hair.'

'All the sisters have it,' Amanda said. 'More
ragout?'

'No, thank you, although I am fully aware

it is the best thing I will taste until I fetch the Portuguese coast in a week or so.' He set down his cup. 'Miss Brandon is too young to tempt me, Amanda. I doubt she is a day over eighteen.'

'And you are antiquated at thirty-seven?'

'I am. Besides that, what female in her right mind, whatever her age, would make a Marine the object of her affection?'

'You have me there, Colonel,' Amanda said promptly, which made Owen laugh.

She did have him, too, Hugh reflected wryly, as he walked from Stonehouse, across the footbridge, and back to the barrack for a final night on shore. *Perhaps I am shallow*, he considered, as he lay in bed later. Amanda Brackett was right; he was vain and shallow. Maybe daft, too. He lay awake worrying more about his assignment, putting Miss Brandon far from his mind.

Hugh joined the *Perseverance* at first light, the side boys lined up and the bosun's mate piping him aboard. His face set in that no-nonsense look every Marine cultivated, and which he had perfected, he scanned the rank of Marines on board. He noted their awed recognition of his person, but after last night's conversation, he felt embarrassed.

He chatted with Captain Adney for only a brief minute, knowing well that the man was too busy for conversation. Out of the corner of his eye, he noticed Miss Brandon standing quietly by the binnacle, her hands clasped neatly in front of her, the picture of rectitude, or at the very least, someone just removed from the schoolroom herself. Amanda Brackett had said as much last night. She was a green girl.

He had to admit there was something more about Miss Brandon, evidenced by the two Midshipmen and Lieutenant grouped about her, appearing to hang on her every word. She had inclined her head to one side and was paying close attention to the Lieutenant. Hugh smiled. He could practically see the man's blush from here on the quarterdeck.

Miss Brandon, you are obviously a good listener, he thought. *Perhaps that compensates for spectacles.* The moment the thought swirled in his brain, he felt small again. *What a snob I am,* he concluded, turning his attention again to Captain Adney.

'...passage of some five days, Colonel, if we're lucky,' he was saying. 'Is it Oporto or Lisbon for you?'

It scarcely mattered, considering his *carte blanche* to wander the coastline on his fact-finding mission. Perhaps he should start at Lisbon. 'Oporto,' he said. He knew he had a letter for Surgeon Brittle, Miss Brandon's brother-in-law, but he also knew he could just give it to her and make his way to Lisbon, avoiding Oporto altogether. 'Oporto,' he repeated, not sure why.

'Very well, sir,' Captain Adney told him. 'And now, Colonel, I am to take us out of harbour with the tide. Excuse me, please.'

Hugh inclined his head and the Captain moved towards his helmsman, standing ready at the wheel. Hugh watched with amusement as the flock around Miss Brandon moved away quickly, now that their Captain was on the loose and prepared to work them.

Hardly knowing why, Hugh joined her. He congratulated himself on thinking up a reason to introduce himself. He doffed his hat and bowed. 'Miss Brandon? Pray forgive my rag manners in introducing myself. I am Lieutenant Colonel Hugh Junot, and I have some business you might discharge for me.'

She smiled at him, and he understood instantly why the Lieutenant and Midshipmen had been attracted to her like iron filings to a magnet. She had a direct gaze that seemed to block out everything around her and focus solely on the object of her interest. He felt amazingly flattered, even though she was doing nothing more than giving him her attention. There was nothing coy, arch or even flirtatious about her expression. She was so completely *present*. He couldn't describe it any better.

She dropped him a deep curtsy. Considering that it was high summer and she wore no cloak, this gave him ample opportunity to admire her handsome bosom.

'Yes, Colonel, I am Miss Brandon.'

As he put on his hat again, her eyes followed it up and she did take a little breath, as though she was not used to her present company. He knew she must be familiar enough with the Royal Navy, considering her relationship to a captain and a surgeon, but he did not think his splendid uniform was ringing any bells.

'I am a Marine, Miss Brandon,' he said.

'And I am a hopeless landlubber, Colonel,' she replied with a smile. 'I should have known that. What can I do for you?'

What a polite question, he thought. *It is almost as if I were infirm. She is looking at me as though I have a foot in the grave, no teeth, and more years than her brothers-in-law combined. What an ass I am.*

Feeling his age—at least every scar on his body had not started to ache simultaneously—he nodded to her. 'Miss Brandon, I have been charged by Surgeon Owen Brackett to take a letter to your brother-in-law in Oporto. I suppose that is why I sought to introduce myself, rather than wait for someone else—who, I do not know—to perform that office.'

That is marvellously lame, he thought sourly, thinking of the gawking Midshipmen who had so recently claimed her attention, and mentally adding himself to their number.

The deferential look left her face. 'Taking a letter to my brother-in-law is a pleasant assignment, sir. I am headed to the same place. Do you know Surgeon Brittle?'

'Not yet.'

'If you are too busy to discharge your duty, I can certainly relieve you of the letter, Colonel,' she told him.

'I am going there, too.'

He could think of nothing more to say, but she didn't seem awkwardly waiting for conversation. Instead, she turned her back against the rail to watch the foretopmen in the rigging, preparing to spill down the sails and begin their voyage. It was a sight he always enjoyed, too, so he stood beside her in silence and watched. Although he had scarce acquaintance with the lady beside him, he felt no urge to blather on, in the way that newly introduced people often do.

The *Perseverance* began to move, and he felt his heart lift, so glad he was to be at sea again and not sitting in a conference room. He would range the coast, watch his Marines in action, interview them, and possibly formulate a way to increase their utility. With any luck, he could stretch his assignment through the summer and into autumn.

'I have never sailed before,' Miss Brandon said.

'You'll get your sea legs,' he assured her, his eyes on the men balancing against the yardarms. He hoped it wasn't improper to mention legs to a lady, even the sea kind.

In a few more minutes, she went belowdeck. He watched Marines working the capstan with the sailors, and others already standing sentry by the water butt and the helm. He nodded to the Sergeant of Marines, who snapped to attention, and introduced himself as the senior non-commissioned officer on board. A thirty-six-gun frigate had no commissioned officer. Hugh explained his mission and told the man to carry on.

He stayed on deck until the *Perseverance* tacked out of Plymouth Sound and into the high rollers of the Channel itself. He observed the greasy swell of the current and knew they were in for some rough water. No matter—he was never seasick.

He went belowdeck and into his cabin, a typical knocked-together affair made of framed canvas, which was taken down when the gun-deck cleared for action. His sleeping cot, hung directly over the cannon, was already swaying to the rhythm of the Atlantic Ocean. He timed the swell and rolled into the cot for a nap.

Because Miss Brandon had admitted this was her first sea voyage, Hugh was not surprised when she did not appear for dinner in the wardroom. Captain Adney had the good sense to give her the cabin with actual walls, one that probably should have gone to a Lieutenant Colonel of Marines, had a woman not been voyaging. The Sergeant had posted a sentry outside her door, which was as it should be. There were no flies growing on this little Marine detachment, and so he would note in his journal.

There was no shortage of conversation around the wardroom table. The frigate's officers let him into their conversation and seemed interested in his plan. Used to the sea, they kept protective hands around their plates and expertly trapped dishes sent sliding by the ship's increasingly violent motion. When the table was cleared and the steward brought out a bottle, Hugh frowned to hear the sound of vomiting from Miss Brandon's cabin.

The surgeon sighed and reached for the sherry as it started to slide. 'Too bad there is no

remedy for *mal de mer*,' he said. 'She'll be glad
to make land in a week.'

They chuckled, offered the usual toasts,
hashed over the war, and departed for their
own duties. Hugh sat a while longer at the table,
tempted to knock on Miss Brandon's door and
at least make sure she had a basin to vomit in.

She didn't come out at all the next day,
either. *Poor thing*, Hugh thought, as he made
his rounds of the Marine Privates and Cor-
porals, trying to question them about their
duties, taking notes, and wondering how to make
Marines naturally wary of high command understand that all he wanted was to learn from
them. Maybe the notion was too radical.

Later that night he was lying in his violently
swinging sleeping cot, stewing over his plans,
when someone knocked on the frame of his canvas wall.

'Colonel, Private Leonard, sir.'

Hugh got up in one motion, alert. Leonard
was the sentry outside Miss Brandon's door. He
had no business even crossing the wardroom,
not when he was on duty. *Your Sergeant will
hear from me, Private*, he thought, as he yanked
open his door.

'How dare you abandon your post!' he snapped.

If he thought to intimidate Private Leonard, he was mistaken. The man seemed intent on a more important matter than the potential threat of the lash.

'Colonel Junot, it's Miss Brandon. I've stood sentinel outside her door for nearly four hours now, and I'm worried.' The Private braced himself against the next roll and wiggle as the *Perseverance* rose, then plunged into the trough of a towering wave. 'She was puking and bawling, and now she's too quiet. I didn't think I should wait to speak until the watch relieved me, sir.'

Here's one Marine who thinks on his feet, Hugh thought, as he reached for his uniform jacket. 'You acted wisely. Return to your post, Private,' he said, his voice normal.

He had his misgivings as he crossed the wardroom and knocked on her door. Too bad there was not another female on board. He knocked again. No answer. He looked at Private Leonard. 'I go in, don't I?' he murmured, feeling suddenly shy and not afraid to admit it. There may have been a great gulf between a Lieutenant Colonel and a Private, but they were both men.

'I think so, sir,' the Private said. 'Do you have a lamp?'

'Go get mine.'

He opened the door and was assailed by the stench of vomit. 'Miss Brandon?' he called.

No answer. Alarmed now, he was by her sleeping cot in two steps. He could barely see her in the gloom. He touched her shoulder and his hand came away damp. He shook her more vigorously and was rewarded with a slight moan.

No one dies of seasickness, he reminded himself. 'Miss Brandon?' he asked again. 'Can you hear me?'

Private Leonard returned with his lantern, holding it above them in the tiny cabin. The light fell on as pitiful a specimen of womanhood as he had ever seen. Gone was the moderately attractive, composed young lady of two days ago. In her place was a creature so exhausted with vomiting that she could barely raise her hands to cover her eyes against the feeble glow of the lantern.

'I should have approached you sooner, sir,' Private Leonard said, his voice full of remorse.

'How were you to know?' he asked. 'We officers should have wondered what was going on when she didn't come out for meals. Private, go find the surgeon. I am relieving you at post.'

'Aye, aye, Colonel.'

Uncertain what to do, Hugh hung the lantern from the deck beam and gently moved Miss Brandon's matted hair from her face, which was dry and caked. She didn't open her eyes, but ran her tongue over cracked lips. 'You're completely parched,' he said. 'Dryer than a bone. My goodness, Miss Brandon.'

She started to cry then, except she was too dehydrated for tears. Out of his element, he didn't know how to comfort her. Was she in pain? He wished there was a porthole he could open to let in some bracing sea air and banish the odour. Poor Miss Brandon was probably suffering the worst kind of mortification to be so discovered by a man she barely knew. If there was a better example of helplessness, he had never encountered it.

Private Leonard returned. Hugh looked behind him, but there was no surgeon.

'Sir, the surgeon and his mate are both tending to a foretopman who fell from the rigging.' Private Leonard made a face. 'He reminded me that no one dies of seasickness and recommended we get some water and vinegar so she can clean herself up.'

'Private, she can't clean a fingernail in her condition,' he said. He stood there a moment, looking down at Miss Brandon, then at the Private. 'Go get a quart or two of vinegar from Cook and a gallon of fresh water. If anyone gives you any grief, tell them they don't want to know how bad it will be if I have to come up and do it myself!'

The Private stood even straighter. 'Aye, aye, sir. Should I get some cloths, too?'

'As many as you can gather. Good thinking.'

He closed the door behind the Private, who pounded up the companionway, obviously glad to have a purpose. He found a stool and pulled it close to the sleeping cot, which was swaying to the ship's roll. He tried to keep his tone conversational, knowing that nothing he was going to do in the next hour would be pleasing to a modest lady. 'Miss Brandon, the surgeon cannot come, but he has declared that no one dies of seasickness. You will not be the first, and certainly not on my watch.'

'I. Would. Rather. Die.'

At least she was alert. 'It's not allowed in the Royal Navy, my dear,' he told her kindly. 'When Private Leonard returns, I am going to tidy you, find you another nightgown, and put you in my sleeping cot, so I can swab down this one.'

She started to cry in earnest then, which was a sorry sight, since there were no tears. 'Leave me alone,' she pleaded.

'I can't leave you alone. I would do anything to spare you embarrassment, Miss Brandon, but you must be tended to.'

'The surgeon?'

'Busy. My dear, you'll just have to trust me, because there is no one else.'

She hadn't opened her eyes in their whole exchange, and it touched him to think how embarrassed she must be. She was obviously well educated and gently reared, and this was probably the first time in her whole life she had ever been alone with a man who wasn't a relative. He wasn't sure what to do, but he put his hand against her soiled cheek and held it there until she stopped her dry sobbing.

Private Leonard returned with the vinegar and water. He had tucked clean rags under his arm, and removed them when he set down the bucket. 'I'll get some sea water, too, Colonel,' he said. 'That fresh water isn't going to go far, and you can swab her down with salt water.'

'Do it, Private. When you return, close the door and resume your sentry duty. If there are two of us trying to help Miss Brandon, it'll be too much for her.'

He could see that Private Leonard was relieved by that order. He came back soon with two buckets of sea water; God knows there was plenty of it to spare on a frigate in a squall. Private Leonard closed the door quietly.

Miss Brandon tried to sit up and failed. 'If

you leave the water, I can do this myself,' she managed to say.

'Begging your pardon, Miss Brandon, but I don't think you even have the strength to scratch your nose right now,' he told her. 'I am so sorry that no one knew the extent of your extremity, or believe me, it would not have come to this.'

She opened her eyes then, and he saw all the shame, embarrassment, and humility in the world reflecting from them. All she could do was shake her head slowly and put up her hands to cover her chest.

It was such a defensive gesture that his heart went out to her. She was soiled and smelly and more wretched that the worst drab in the foulest slum in the rankest seaport he had ever visited. The last thing he wanted to do was violate her dignity, which was all she had remaining. He rested his hands gently on hers. 'Whatever I do for you, I do out of utter necessity, Miss Brandon. I can do no less because I never back down from a crisis.' He smiled at her. 'My, that sounds top-lofty, but it is true. Take a leap of faith, Miss Brandon; trust me to be kind.'

She was silent a long while, her hands still held stubbornly in front of her. 'I have no choice, have I?' she said finally.

'No, you don't. Take that leap, Miss Brandon. I won't fail you.'

Chapter Two

Miss Brandon didn't say anything, but her hands relaxed. Hugh did nothing for a moment, because he didn't know where to begin. He looked closer in the dim light. She was wearing a nightgown, which chastely covered most of her, so his task was not as uncomfortable yet as it was going to get. He opened the door.

'Private, go in my cabin. Bring my shaving basin, plus the silver cup next to it.'

He was back in a moment with the items. Hugh put his hand behind Miss Brandon's back and carefully raised her upright. He dipped the cup in the fresh water Private Leonard had brought, and put it to her lips.

'It will only make me vomit,' she protested weakly.

'Just swirl it around in your mouth, lean over the edge of the cot and spit it out.'

'On the *floor*?' she asked, aghast.

'Yes, ma'am. The deck—the floor—has suffered some ill usage. I'll never tell.'

She sighed. He held the cup to her parched lips and she took a small sip, doing what he said and spitting on the deck.

'Try another sip and swallow it this time.'

She started to protest, but gamely squared her shoulders and did as he said. 'My throat is on fire,' she said, her voice a croak.

'I imagine it is raw, indeed, Miss Brandon, considering the ill treatment it has suffered for nearly two days.' It smote him again how careless they had all been not to check on her. 'Try another sip. Just a small one.'

She did, then shook her head at more. They both waited, but she kept it down.

'I'm encouraged. Just sit here,' he told her. 'I'm going to mix some vinegar in this little bit of fresh water and wipe your face and neck. I'll see what can be done with your hair.'

Silent, she let him do what he wanted, turning her head obediently so he could swab around her eyes and nostrils. 'Soon I'll have you smelling like a pickle, Miss Brandon,' he joked, trying to lighten the mood. She did not indicate any amusement, which hardly surprised him. When her face was as clean as he could manage, he added more vinegar to the bucket of sea water and wiped her neck and ears.

Her hair took much longer, as he pulled a few strands at a time through the vinegar-soaked cloth between his fingers, working as quickly and gently as he could. He had to stop for a while when the ship began to labour up and down steeper troughs, as the storm intensified. She moaned with the motion, so he braced the sleeping cot with his body so it would not swing. As he watched her face, it suddenly occurred to him that part of her problem was fear.

'Miss Brandon, I assure you that as bad as this seems, we're not going to sink,' he said. He spoke loud enough to be heard above the creaking and groaning he knew were normal ship noises in a storm. 'Ships are noisy. The sea is rough, I will grant you, but that is life in the Channel.'

She said nothing, but turned her face into his shoulder. Hugh kept his arms tight around her, crooning nothing that made any sense, but which seemed to calm her. He held her close as she clung to him, terrified.

When the waves seemed to subside, he released her and went back to cleaning her long hair. When he felt reasonably satisfied, he knew he could not avoid the next step. 'Miss Brandon, do you have another nightgown in your luggage?'

She nodded, and started to cry again.

'I'd happily turn my back and let you manage this next part by yourself, my dear, but I don't think you're up to it. You can't stay in this nightgown.'

After another long silence during which he made no attempt to rush her, her hands went to the buttons on her gown. She tried to undo them, but finally shook her head. Without a word, he undid her buttons. 'Where's another nightgown?' he asked quietly.

She told him and he found it, fragrant with lavender, in her trunk. Taking a deep breath, Hugh pulled back the sheet. Her hand went to his wrist, so he did nothing more until she relaxed her grip.

'I'm going to roll up your nightgown, so we can best keep the soiled part away from your face and hair when I pull it over your head. Miss Brandon, I regret the mortification I know I am causing you,' he said.

She was sobbing in good earnest now, and the parched sound pained him more than she possibly could have realised. Not only was he trampling on her female delicacy now, but jumping up and down on it.

'No fears, Miss Brandon, no fears,' he said

quietly, trying to find a balance between sympathy and command.

Maybe she finally realised he was an ally. He wasn't sure he would have been as brave as she was, considering her total helplessness to take care of herself. Feeling as stupid and callow as the merest youth, he couldn't think of a thing to say except, 'I mean you no harm. Not ever.'

He wondered why he said that, but his words, spoken quietly but firmly, seemed to give Miss Brandon the confirmation she needed of his utter sincerity. She stopped sobbing, but rested her head against him, not so much because she was tired now, but because she needed his reassurance. He could have been wrong, but that was what the moment felt like, and he wasn't one to quibble.

Without any talk, he continued rolling up her nightgown as she raised her arms. His fingers brushed against her bare breast, but they were both beyond embarrassment. Even though the night was warm, she shivered a little. He quickly popped her into the clean nightgown, pulling it down to her ankles, then helped her lie back. She sighed with relief and closed her eyes.

The winds picked up and the ship began another series of torturous swoops through the waves. He braced the cot against his hip and kept his arms tight around Miss Brandon as she clung to him and shivered.

'I don't know how you do this,' she said finally, when the winds subsided.

'It comes with the job,' he replied and chuckled.

'Are you never seasick?'

'No.'

'Are you lying?'

He wasn't, but he wanted her to laugh. 'Yes.' He knew nothing in the rest of his life would ever put him at ease more than the slight sound of her laugh, muffled against his chest.

Since his arms were around her, he picked her up. She stiffened. 'I'm going to carry you across the wardroom to my pathetic cabin, and put you in my cot. You're going to promise me you won't be sick in it, and you're going to go to sleep. I'll come back in here and clean up everything.'

'A Lieutenant Colonel in the Royal Marines,' she murmured, and Hugh could hear the embarrassment in her voice again.

'I can't help that,' he told her, and was rewarded with another chuckle. 'I've swabbed a deck or two in my earlier days.' He wasn't going to tell her how unpleasant that had been, cleaning up a gun deck after a battle. Nothing in her cabin could ever compare with that, but he wasn't going to enlighten her further.

He was prepared to stay with her in his cabin until she felt easy, but she went to sleep almost before he finished tucking his blanket around her. He looked down at her, smelling of vinegar now, but as tidy as he could make her, in his clumsy way. He looked closer. There was something missing. He gave her a slight shake.

'Miss Brandon, where are your spectacles?'

She opened her eyes, and he saw nothing but remorse. 'I…I fear they landed in that basin by the cot, when I vomited.'

She started to laugh then, which must have hurt because her hand went to her throat. 'Don't look so stunned, Colonel,' she told him. 'I am quizzing you. They're in my trunk, next to my hair brush.'

He grinned at her, relieved that she could make a joke. 'I'll get you for that.'

'You and who…?' she began, then drifted to sleep.

He stood there another long moment, watching her sleep, dumbfounded by her resiliency, and not totally sure what had just happened. 'I'd have looked for them in that foul basin, I hope you know,' he whispered, then left his cabin.

He spent the next hour cleaning Miss Brandon's cabin. Before Private Leonard went off duty and was replaced by another sentry, he swore him to utter secrecy on what had passed this evening.

'Sir, I would never say anything,' the Private assured him. 'She's a brave little trooper, isn't she?'

Hugh would have spent the night in her cot, except that it was wet with vinegar and he didn't relish the notion. He could put his greatcoat on the floor in his cabin and not disturb Miss Brandon at all. He put her nightgown to soak in the bucket with sea water, and poured in the remaining vinegar. He found his way to the orlop deck, where the surgeon, eyes bleary, was staring at a forefinger avulsion that gave Hugh the shivers.

'He caught it on a pump, if you can imagine,' the surgeon murmured. He patted the seaman who belonged to the finger. 'Steady, lad, steady. It looks worse than it is, as most things do.'

While the seaman stared at his own finger, Hugh took the surgeon aside and explained what had happened to Miss Brandon.

'Poor little lady,' the surgeon said. 'I hope you were gentle with her, Colonel.'

'I did my best.'

The surgeon shook his head. 'Only two days out, and already this voyage is more than she bargained for, I'm certain. All's well that ends. Give her some porridge tomorrow morning and a ship's biscuit, along with fortified wine, and all the water she will drink. That should take care of the dehydration.'

Hugh walked thoughtfully back to his deck, after looking in on the unconscious foretopman, with the surgeon's mate sitting beside him. A howl from the orlop told him the surgeon had taken care of the avulsion. *Give me Miss Brandon and her troublesome seasickness any day*, he thought with a shudder.

Counting on his rank to mean something to one of the captain's young gentlemen, he asked for and received a blanket and returned to his cabin. He looked down at her, asleep in his gently swaying cot. *Poor little you. The surgeon was right; you didn't bargain on this*, he thought.

Surprisingly content with his lot, Hugh spread his overcoat and pulled the blanket over him. He woke up once in the night to check on her, but she was breathing deeply, with a small sigh on the exhalation of breath that he found childlike and endearing. Feeling charitable, he smiled down at her, and returned to his rest on the deck.

A fierce and nagging thirst woke Polly at sunrise, rather than the noise of a ship that she had feared last night would sink at any minute. She stared at the deck beams overhead, wondering where she was, then closed her eyes in total mortification when she remembered. *Maybe if I keep my eyes closed, the entire world will move back four days. I will remain in Torquay with my sister Nana and none of what I know happened will have taken place*, she told herself.

No such luck. She smelled of vinegar because she had been doused in it, then pulled from her nightgown and—horror of horrors—been set right by a Royal Marine of mature years who would probably rather have eaten ground glass than done any of the duties her care had required.

If she could not forget what had happened, perhaps Lieutenant Colonel Junot had transferred during the night to another vessel, one sailing to Australia. Failing that, hopefully he had suffered amnesia and remembered nothing past his tenth birthday. No such luck. She could hear someone snoring softly, so she rose up carefully on her elbow and peered over the edge of the sleeping cot.

There lay her saviour, a mature man—not a Midshipman—with curly dark hair going a bit grey at the temples, a straight nose, and chiselled lips that had caught her attention a few days ago, when she was still a reasonable being. He lay on his back and looked surprisingly comfortable, as though he had slept in worse places. He had removed his shoes, unbuttoned his dark trousers, and unhooked his uniform tunic, so a wildly informal checked shirt showed through. The gilt gorget was still clasped around his neck, which made her smile in spite of her mortification, because he looked incongruously authoritative.

He opened his eyes suddenly and he smiled at her, because she must have looked even funnier, peering at him over the edge of the sleeping cot like a child in a strange house.

'Good morning, Miss Brandon. See? You're alive.'

If he had meant to put her at her ease, he had succeeded, even as he lay there all stretched out. He yawned, then sat up, his blanket around him again.

'Would you like some water?' he asked.

She nodded, then carefully sat up, which only made her lie down again, because the room was revolving.

He was on his feet in an instant, turning his back to her to button his trousers, then stretching his arm up to grasp the deck beam as he assessed her. 'Dizzy?'

She nodded, and wished she hadn't. 'Now the ship is spinning,' she groaned.

'It will stop.' He brought her a drink in a battered silver cup that looked as if it had been

through a campaign or two. His free arm went
behind her back and gently lifted her up just
enough to pour some water down her sorely
tried throat. 'Being as dried out as you are plays
merry hell with body humours, Miss Brandon.
You need to eat something.'

'Never again,' she told him firmly. 'I have
sworn off food for ever.'

'Take a chance,' he teased. 'You might be
surprised how gratifying it is to swallow food,
rather than wear it. Another sip now. That's a
good girl. Let me lay you down again.'

After he did so, he tucked the blanket up to
her chin again. 'You'll do, Brandon,' he told her
in a gruff voice, and she knew that not a kinder
man inhabited the entire universe, no matter if he
was a Marine and fearsome. 'Go back to sleep.'

She closed her eyes dutifully, certain she
wouldn't sleep because she was so embarrassed, except that the Colonel yawned loudly.
She opened her eyes at such rag manners, then
watched as he stretched and slapped the deck
beam overhead, exclaiming, 'I love a sea voyage, Brandon. Don't you?' which made her
giggle and decide that perhaps she would live,
after all.

When she woke again, it was full light and
the Colonel was gone. She sat up more cau-

tiously this time, pleased when the ship did not spin. She wasn't sure what to do, especially without her spectacles, except that there they were in their little case, next to the pillow. *What a nice man*, she thought, as she put them on.

She looked around. He had also brought over her robe, which she had originally hung on a peg in her cabin. *I think he wants me gone from his cabin*, she told herself, and heaven knew, who could blame him?

As for that, he didn't. Colonel Junot had left a folded note next to her robe on the end of the cot, with 'Brandon' scrawled on it. She couldn't help but smile at that, wondering why on earth he had decided to call her Brandon. All she could assume was that after the intimacy they had been through together, he thought Miss Brandon too formal, but Polly too liberal. Whatever the reason, she decided she liked it. She could never call him anything but Colonel, of course.

She read the note to herself: *Brandon, a lob-lolly boy is scrubbing down your cabin and will light sulphur in it. The stench will be wicked for a while, so I moved your trunk into the ward-room. Captain Adney's steward will bring you porridge and fortified wine, which the surgeon insisted on.*

He signed it 'Junot', which surprised her.

When he introduced himself, he had pronounced his name 'Junnit', but this was obviously a French name. That was even stranger, because he had as rich a Lowland Scottish accent as she had ever heard. 'Colonel, Brandon thinks you are a man of vast contradictions,' she murmured.

She climbed carefully from the sleeping cot, grateful the cannon was there to clutch when the ship shivered and yawed. *I will never develop sea legs*, she told herself. *I will have to become a citizen of Portugal and never cross the Channel again.* When she could stand, she pulled on her robe and climbed back into the sleeping cot, surprised at her exhaustion from so little effort. She doubled the pillow so she could at least see over the edge of the sleeping cot, and abandoned herself to the swaying of the cot, which was gentler this morning.

She noticed the Colonel's luggage, a wooden military trunk with his name stenciled on the side: Hugh Philippe d'Anvers Junot. 'And you sound like a Scot,' she murmured. 'I must know more.'

Trouble was, knowing more meant engaging in casual conversation with a dignified officer of the King's Royal Marines, one who had taken care of her so intimately last night. He had shown incredible aplomb in an assignment that would have made even a saint look askance. No. The *Perseverance* might have been a sixth-rate and one of the smaller of its class, but for the remainder of the voyage—and it couldn't end too soon—she would find a way to avoid bothering Colonel Junot with her presence.

In only a matter of days, they would hail Oporto, and the Colonel would discharge his last duty to her family by handing her brother-in-law a letter from his former chief surgeon. Then, if the Lord Almighty was only half so generous as both Old and New Testaments trumpeted, the man would never have to see her again. She decided it wasn't too much to hope for, considering the probabilities.

So much for resolve. Someone knocked on the flimsy-framed door. She held her breath, hoping for the loblolly boy.

'Brandon? Call me a Greek bearing gifts.'

Not by the way you roll your r's, she thought, wondering if Marines were gluttons for punishment. She cleared her throat, wincing. 'Yes, Colonel?'

He opened the door, carrying a tray. 'As principal idler on this voyage, I volunteered to bring you food, which I insist you eat.'

If he was so determined to put a good face on all this, Polly decided she could do no less. 'I told you I have sworn off food for the remainder of my life, sir.'

'And I have chosen to ignore you,' he replied serenely. 'See here. I even brought along a basin, which I will put in my sleeping cot by your feet, should you take exception to porridge and ship's biscuit. Sit up like the good girl I know you are.'

She did as he said. As congenial as he sounded, there was something of an edge in his imperatives. This was something she had already noticed about her brother-in-law Oliver, so she could only assume it had to do with command. 'Aye, sir,' she said, sitting up.

He set the tray on her lap. To her dismay, he pulled up a stool to sit beside the cot.

'I promise to eat,' she told him, picking up the spoon to illustrate her good faith, if not her appetite. 'You needn't watch me.'

He just couldn't take a hint. 'I truly am a supernumerary on this voyage, and have no pressing tasks. The Midshipmen, under the tender care of the sailing master, are trying to plot courses. I already know how to do that. The surgeon is pulling a tooth, and I have no desire to learn. The Captain is strolling his deck with a properly detached air. The foretopmen are high overhead and I wouldn't help them even if I could. Brandon, you are stuck with me.'

It was obviously time to level with the Lieutenant Colonel, if only for his own good. She set down the spoon. 'Colonel Junot, last night you had to take care of me in ways so personal that I must have offended every sensibility you possess.' Her face was flaming, but she progressed doggedly, unable to look at the man whose bed she had usurped, and whose cabin she occupied. 'I have never been in a situation like this, and doubt you have either.'

'True, that,' he agreed. 'Pick up the spoon, Brandon, lively now.'

She did what he commanded. 'Sir, I am trying to spare you any more dealings with me for the duration of this voyage.'

His brown eyes reminded her of a spaniel given a smack by its owner for soiling a carpet. 'Brandon! Have I offended you?'

She didn't expect that. 'Well, n…no, of course not,' she stammered. 'I owe you a debt I can never repay, but—'

'Take a bite.'

She did, and then another. It stayed down, and she realised how ravenous she was. She ate without speaking, daring a glance at the Colonel once to see a pleased expression on his handsome face. When she finished, he moved aside the bowl and pointed to the ship's biscuit, which she picked up.

'Tell me something, Brandon,' he said finally,

as she chewed, then reached for the wine he held out to her. 'If I were ever in a desperate situation and needed your help, would you give it to me?'

'Certainly I would,' she said.

'Then why can't you see that last night was no different?'

He had her there. 'I have never met anyone like you, Colonel,' she told him frankly.

He didn't say anything for a long moment. She took another sip of the wine, then dipped the dry biscuit in it, which made him smile.

'Look at it this way, Brandon. You have a friend.'

What could she say to that? If the man was going to refuse all of her attempts to make herself invisible for the remainder of the voyage, she couldn't be little about it.

'So do you, Colonel Junot.'

Chapter Three

'Excellent!' he declared. 'If you're up to it, I recommend you dress and go on deck. The surgeon found quite a comfortable canvas chair—I tried it out—and moved it to the quarterdeck. Believe it or not, it's easier to face an enemy, which, in your case, is the ocean. We can't have that, Brandon. Fearing the ocean is scarcely patriotic, considering that we are an island nation.'

'I believe you are right, Colonel,' she said, amused.

He lifted her out of the sleeping cot, set her on her bare feet, and walked next to her, his hand warm on the small of her back to steady her, across the short space between his door and the door to her cabin. She could smell sulphur fumes behind the door, and was glad he had moved her trunk into the wardroom.

She shook her head when he offered further assistance, even though she did have trouble standing upright.

'You'll learn,' he assured her, then bowed and went up the companionway.

She took what clothing she needed from her trunk, pausing a time or two to steady herself against the ship's movement. She hadn't even crossed the small space back to Colonel Junot's cabin when a Marine sentry came down the companionway, the same Marine who had stood sentinel last night.

'I want to thank you, Private, for alerting the Colonel to my predicament last night,' she told him.

'My job, ma'am,' he replied simply, but she could tell he was pleased.

That was easy, Polly thought, as she went into the cabin and dressed. Her hair was still a hopeless mess, but at least it smelled strongly of nothing worse than vinegar. 'My kingdom for enough fresh water to wash this tangle,' she murmured.

She cautiously made her way up the companionway to the deck, where she stood and watched the activity around her. No part of England is far from the sea, but she had spent most of her eighteen years in Bath, so she felt herself in an alien world. It was not without its fascination, she decided, as she watched the Sergeant drilling his few Marines in a small space. Close to the bow, the sailing master was schooling the Midshipmen, who awkwardly tried to shoot the sun with sextants. Seamen scrubbed the deck with flat stones the size of prayer books, while others sat cross-legged with sails in their laps, mending tears with large needles. It looked endlessly complex and disorganised, but as she watched she began to see the orderly disorder of life at sea.

She looked towards the quarterdeck again and Captain Adney nodded to her and lifted his hat, indicating she should join him.

'Let me apologise for myself and all my fellow officers for neglecting you,' he said. 'Until Colonel Junot told us what was going on, we had no idea.'

Hopefully, he didn't tell you everything, Polly thought, even though she knew her secrets would always be safe with the Colonel. 'I am feeling much better,' she said.

'Excellent!' Captain Adney obviously had no desire to prod about in the workings of females, so there ended his commentary. He indicated the deck chair Colonel Junot had spoken of. Clasping his hands behind his back, he left her to it, resuming his perusal of the ocean.

Polly smiled to herself, amused by the workings of males. She looked at the chair, noting the chocks placed by the legs so the contraption would not suddenly slide across the quarterdeck. She tried not to hurl herself across the deck, wishing she understood how to ambulate on a slanted plane that would right itself and then slant the other way.

'Brandon, let me suggest that, when you stand, you put one foot behind the other and probably a bit farther apart than you are used to.'

She looked over her shoulder to see Colonel Junot on the steps to the quarterdeck. He came closer and demonstrated. She imitated him.

'Much better. When you walk, this is no time for mincing steps.' He smiled at her halting effort. 'It takes practice. Try out the chair.'

She let him hand her into it, and she couldn't help a sigh of pleasure. Amazing that canvas could feel so comfortable. *I could like this*, she thought, and smiled at the Colonel.

He smiled in turn, then went back down the steps to the main deck, where the Sergeant stood at attention now with his complement of Marines. A word from Colonel Junot and they relaxed, but not by much. In another minute the

Sergeant had dismissed them and he sat with Colonel Junot on a hatch.

Polly watched them both, impressed by their immaculate posture, which lent both men an ever-ready aspect, as though they could spring into action at a moment's notice. *I suppose you can*, she told herself, thinking through all of the Lieutenant Colonel's quick decisions last night. He had not hesitated once in caring for her, no matter how difficult it must have been. And he seemed to take it all in stride. 'You were my ever-present help in trouble,' she murmured.

She gave her attention to the Colonel again, after making sure the brim of her bonnet was turned down and they wouldn't know of her observation. While Colonel Junot was obviously a Scot, he did look French. She realised with a surprise that she wanted to know more about him.

Why? she asked herself. Knowing more about Lieutenant Colonel Hugh Junot would serve no useful purpose, beyond pointing her out as a flirt, something she knew she was not. 'Bother it,' she muttered softly.

She had convinced herself that the best thing she could do for the remainder of this voyage was to follow her original plan and have as little to do with the Marine as possible. Once he was busy with whatever it was that had taken him on this voyage, she would be ignored, which suited her down to the ground. She had never sought the centre of the stage.

Come to think of it, why was Colonel Junot on this voyage? *Bother it*, she told herself again. *I would like to ask him.*

She knew better. Through Nana, she knew these men sailed with specific orders that were certainly none of her business, no matter how great her curiosity. 'Bother it,' she muttered again, and closed her eyes.

She slept, thanks to the gentle swaying of the canvas seat, comforting after the peaks and troughs of last night's squall. When she woke, her glasses rested in her lap. Lieutenant Colonel Junot stood next to her chair, his eyes scanning the water. She was struck all over again with his elegance. Compared to naval officers in their plain dark undress coats, the Marines were gaudy tropical birds. He had not an ounce of superfluous flesh, which made him different from the men she noticed in Bath, who were comfortably padded in the custom of the age.

I am among the elite, she told herself, as she put on her spectacles, bending the wires around her ears again.

Her small motions must have caught Colonel Junot's eye because he looked her way and gave her a slight bow, then came closer.

'How are you feeling?' he asked.

'I am better today,' she said simply. 'Perhaps this means I will not have to seek Portuguese citizenship and remain on the Iberian Peninsula for ever.'

He laughed and looked around for something to sit on, which gratified her further. He didn't seem to mind her company. He found a keg and pulled that beside her chair.

He looked at her a moment before he spoke, perhaps wondering if he should. He cleared his throat. 'I suppose you will think me a case-hardened meddler, Brandon, but I have to know—how on earth did you receive permission to travel into a war zone?'

She was surprised that he was curious about her. She leaned towards him. 'Haven't you heard? I am to be a spy.'

'I had no idea, Brandon. I will tell only my dozen closest friends.'

It was her turn to smile and brush aside the crackbrained notion that the Colonel was flirting with her. Now it was his turn for disappointment, because she couldn't think of a witty reply. Better have with the truth.

'I don't know how I got permission, Colonel,' she told him. 'I wrote to my sister, Laura Brittle, whose husband, Philemon, is chief surgeon at a satellite hospital in Oporto.'

'I have heard of him. Who hasn't? That little hospital in Oporto has saved many a seaman and Marine in just the brief time it has been in operation.'

She blushed, this time with pleasure that he should speak so well of her brother-in-law. 'I wrote to Laura and told her I wanted to be of use.'

'I've also heard good things about Mrs Brittle.'

'She's incredible.'

'Aye. And your other sister?'

'Nana loves her husband and sends him back to sea without a tear…at least until he is out of sight,' she said frankly. There wasn't any point in being too coy around a man who, in the short space of twenty-four hours, knew her more intimately than any man alive.

He wasn't embarrassed by her comment. 'Then he is a lucky man.'

'He knows it, too.'

She realised their heads were close together like conspirators, so she drew back slightly. 'Colonel Junot, I thought I could help out in the hospital. Laura said they have many men who would like to have someone write letters for them, or read to them. I could never do what she does, but I could help.' She shook her head, realising how puny her possible contribution must sound. 'It isn't much, but...'

'...a letter means the world to someone wanting to communicate with his loved ones, Brandon. Don't sell yourself short,' he said, finishing her thought and adding his comment. 'Still, I don't understand how a surgeon and his wife could pull such strings. Are you all, by chance, related to King George himself?'

'Oh, no! I have a theory,' she said. 'Tell me what you think. I'll have to show you the letter from the Navy Board, addressed to Brandon Polly, which I received whilst I was visiting Nana. Do you think... Is it possible that Laura or Philemon transposed my name on purpose? Polly Brandon would never do, but Brandon Polly would cause not a stir.'

He thought a minute. 'What is more likely is at one point in the correspondence there may have been a comma between the two names. Orders or requests are often issued that way.'

He looked at her, and seemed to know what she was thinking. 'There now. You've answered *my* question, which surely must entitle you to one of your own. Go ahead and ask what everyone wants to know. How does someone who sounds like a Scot look like a Frenchman, and with a Froggy name, too?'

'I *am* curious,' she admitted.

'Simple. A long-ago Philippe Junot—he had a title, so I'm told—came to Scotland from France as part of the entourage of Mary of Scotland. No one precisely knows how it happened, but he managed to avoid the turmoil surrounding her and blended into the foggy, damp woodwork of Scotland near Dundrennan. He lost his title, but acquired considerable land near Kirkcudbright.'

'My goodness.'

'My goodness, indeed. The Junots are a prolific breed, and each generation traditionally rejoices in a Philippe. My father is still well and hearty, but some day I will head the family.'

'You chose to serve King and country?' Polly asked, fascinated.

'I did. Granted, Kirkcudbright is a pretty fishing village, but it is slow and I liked the uniform.' He held up his hand. 'Don't laugh, Brandon. People have been known to join for stranger reasons.'

'I cannot believe you!' she protested.

'Then don't,' he replied serenely. 'I love the sea, but I require land now and then, and an enemy to grapple with up close. That's my life.'

'What…what does your wife say to all this?' she asked. *That is hardly subtle*, she berated herself. *He will think I am an idiot or a flirt, when I am neither.*

'I wouldn't know, since I don't have one of

those luxuries. I ask you, Brandon—why would a sensible woman—someone like yourself— marry a Marine?'

He had neatly lofted the ball of confusion back in her court. 'I can't imagine, either,' she said without thinking, which made him laugh, then calmly bid her good day.

I've offended him, Polly thought with remorse. She watched him go, then reasonably asked herself why his good opinion mattered.

Captain Adney's steward kindly brought her bread and cheese for lunch. She went below later, and found that her trunk and other baggage had been returned to her cabin. The sentry had moved from the Lieutenant Colonel's door to her own, as though nothing had happened.

When she went topside again, the Captain told her the afternoon would be spent in gunnery practice, and that she might be more comfortable belowdeck in her own cabin, one of the few not dismantled, so the guns could be fired. 'It is your choice, but mind you, it's noisy up here,' he warned, then shrugged. 'Or down there, for that matter.'

She chose to remain on deck. The chair had been moved closer to the wheel—'Out of any stray missile range,' the captain told her.

He didn't exaggerate; the first blast nearly

lifted her out of the chair. She covered her ears
with her hands, wishing herself anywhere but at
sea, until her own curiosity—Miss Pym called
it an admirable trait, if not taken to extremes—
piqued her interest. Cringing in the chair, trying
to make herself small with each cannonade, she
watched as each man performed his task.

Someone tapped her shoulder. She looked
around to see Colonel Junot holding out some
cotton wadding and pointing to his ears. She
took the wadding from him and stuffed it in her
ears, observing that he seemed as usual, and not
in any way offended by her earlier comment.
Perhaps I make mountains out of molehills, she
told herself, as he returned to the main deck,
watching the crews there as she watched them
from the quarterdeck.

His eyes were on the Marines. Some of them
served the guns alongside the naval gunners,
and others lined the railing, muskets at the
ready, their Sergeant standing behind them,
walking up and down. A few Marines had ventured aloft to the crosstrees with their weapons.
Through it all, Colonel Junot observed, and took
occasional notes.

It was all a far cry from Bath, and she knew
how out of place she was. *I wonder if I really
can be useful in Oporto*, she thought. Nana had
wanted her to stay in Torquay. What had she

done of any value on this voyage yet, except make a cake of herself with seasickness? She wondered why Colonel Junot thought her worth the time of day.

It was still on her mind as she prepared for dinner that evening. Only three more days, she thought, as she reached around to button her last button.

When she ventured into the wardroom, Colonel Junot came up behind her and without a word, buttoned the one in the centre of her back she never could reach. The other men were already busy at dinner; no one had noticed. *I can't even dress myself*, she thought, flogging her already-battered esteem.

Polly had little to say over dinner. For all she paid attention, she could have been shovelling clinkers into her mouth, and washing them down with bathwater. All she could think of was how ill equipped she was to leave England. Probably she should never have even left Bath, uncomfortable as Miss Pym had made her, especially after she had turned down Pym's invitation to stay and teach the youngest class. At least at the Female Academy, she knew precisely where she stood, in the order of things.

Bless his heart, Colonel Junot tried to engage

her in conversation, but she murmured only monosyllables. Before the endless meal was over, even he had given up, directing his attention to war talk, and then ship talk. She was as out of place as a Quaker at a gaming table.

Polly had never felt quite this gauche before, almost as though her spectacles were ten times too large for her face, with every freckle—real and imagined—standing out in high relief. And there sat the Lieutenant Colonel next to her, an officer with handsome features, distinguished hair going grey. He was quite the best-looking man she had ever seen, and what had he seen of her except someone who needed to be cleaned up, held over a basin, or buttoned up the back? She burned at her own failings, compared to Colonel Junot's elegant worldliness, and longed to leave the table as soon as she could decently do so.

The dinner ended after a round of toasts to the ship, the men, and the King. She was free to go. She stood, and all the men stood out of deference, even though she knew in her heart of hearts that she was the weakest link at the table.

Polly was only two or three steps from her door, but there was the Colonel, bowing and offering his arm, as he suggested a turn around the deck. She didn't know how to say no, or even why she wanted to, so she took his arm.

The wind blew steadily from the west, making it the fair wind to Spain her brother-in-law Oliver had mentioned during his last visit to Torquay. Polly breathed deep, half-imagining she could smell the orange blossoms in Nana's garden, while she wished herself there.

Colonel Junot walked her around the deck, commenting on the workings of the ship, pointing out the phosphorescence in the water, which he didn't understand, but which intrigued him. She could tell how much he loved the sea, and she felt her shyness begin to recede. He still seemed to be taking care of her, as though someone had given him that role when he first saw her on deck in Plymouth. She knew no one had, which made her feel protected. It was not a feeling she was accustomed to; probably none of Lord Ratliffe's daughters was.

'This voyage has been a real trial for you, Miss Brandon,' he said finally.

She wished he had continued calling her simply Brandon. He steadied her as they went down the more narrow companionway, and into the wardroom again, which this time was full of Marines.

All twenty of the frigate's small complement of Marines had assembled, each carrying a flask. Private Leonard had borrowed a medium-sized pot from the galley, which he set by her door. He saluted the Lieutenant Colonel and stepped forwards, eyes ahead.

'Colonel Junot, if we may take the liberty...'

'By all means, Private.'

The Private looked at her then, flushed, and glanced away, addressing his remarks to someone imaginary over her shoulder. 'Miss Brandon, there's nothing pleasant about vinegar. We decided you should have an opportunity to wash your hair with fresh water. With the Lieutenant Colonel's permission, we decided to give you our daily ration, and we will not take no for an answer.'

He said it practically in one breath, then stepped back. As she watched, tears in her eyes, each Marine poured his drinking water for the day into the pot. When they finished, Colonel Junot went to his cabin and brought out his own flask, adding it to the water in the pot.

'You'll be thirsty,' she protested feebly, when everyone finished and stood at attention.

'Just for a day, ma'am,' the Sergeant of the guard said. 'We've been thirsty before.'

He turned around smartly on his heel, and with a command, the Marines marched back to their posts, or to their quarters between the officers' berths and the crew. Private Leonard remained at his post outside her door, eyes ahead again, every inch the professional.

'Open your door, Brandon, and we'll get the pot inside,' Colonel Junot said.

She did as he directed, standing back as Lieutenant Colonel and Private lifted in the pot, careful not to splash out a drop of the precious fresh water. She had never received a kinder gift from anyone in her life.

The Private went back to his post, but Colonel Junot stood in her room, a smile playing around his expressive lips.

'Colonel, I could have waited until we reached port. They didn't need to do that,' she said.

'It was entirely their idea, Brandon,' he replied, going to her door. 'They only asked that I distract you on deck long enough for them to assemble. Look at it this way: if you ever decide to take over the world, you have a squad of Marines who would follow you anywhere.'

'Why, Colonel?' she asked.

It was his turn to look nonplussed. He was silent a long moment, as if wondering what he should say to such a question. 'Possibly just because you are Brandon Polly, or Polly Brandon. Sometimes there is no reason.'

'No one ever did anything so nice for me before,' she said, wincing inwardly because she didn't want to sound pathetic. It was true, though.

'No? Not even your sisters?'

She could tell he was teasing her now, but there was still that air of protection about him, as though she had become his assignment for the voyage. 'My sisters are different,' she told him, feeling her face grow rosier. 'They are supposed to be kind.'

He laughed at that. 'So is mine,' he confided.

She didn't mean to look sceptical, but the Colonel seemed to be sensitive to her expression. 'Here's how I see it, Brandon—you've made a tedious voyage more than usually interesting.'

She couldn't imagine that tending a female through seasickness qualified as interesting, but she wasn't about to mention it. She knew she should just curtsy and wish him goodnight. She would have, if some imp hadn't leaped on to her shoulder, and prodded her. 'I…I…most particularly like it when you call me Brandon,' she said, her voice low. 'Some of the other students at Miss Pym's had nicknames. I never did.' She stopped in confusion. 'You must think I am an idiot.'

'Never crossed my mind, Brandon.'

She held her breath as he lightly touched her cheek.

'Goodnight, now,' he told her. 'If you need help with your hair tomorrow, I'm just across the wardroom.'

Chapter Four

Hugh couldn't say he had any power to encourage the wind and waves, but he considered it a boon from kind providence that Polly Brandon did need his help in the morning to kneel at the pot and wash her hair, while the deck slanted. They decided that his firm knee in her back would anchor her to the pot, and she had no objection when he lathered her hair, and rinsed it using a small pitcher.

The entire operation involved another pot and pitcher, which led him to comment that between pots and pitchers, women were a great lot of trouble. If she hadn't looked back at him then with such a glower, her hair wet and soapy, he could have withstood nearly anything. He had no idea a woman could look so endearing with soap in her hair. She wasn't wearing her spectacles, of course, which meant she held her eyes open wider than usual, perhaps seeking more depth and more clarity. The effect jolted him a little, because her nearsighted gaze was so intense, her eyes so blue. The shade reminded him of a spot of deep water near Crete where he had gazed long and hard when he was a younger man.

When not coated in vinegar, her auburn hair was glossy. Hugh was half-tempted to volunteer to comb the tangles from her hair, but he had the good sense to strangle that idea at birth. To his surprise, he was finding her uniquely attractive.

Even after two decades of war, he knew enough about women, having bedded them in all seaports when occasion permitted, no different from his navy brethren. By common wardroom consent after one memorable voyage through half the world, he and his fellows agreed that the most beautiful women lived on the Greek isles. He knew at least that *he* had never seen a flat-chested female there. So it went; he was a man of experience.

But here was Brandon—why on earth had he started calling her such a hooligan name?—who, even on her best day, could only stand in the shadow of the earth's loveliest ladies. It was all he could do to keep his hands off her, and he had seen her at her absolute worst. No woman could have been more hopeless than Polly Brandon of two days ago, but here he was, wanting to devise all manner of subterfuges to keep her talking to him. It was a mystery; he had no clue what had happened in so short a time.

He sat down at the wardroom table, hoping to keep her there with him while he thought of something clever to say. To his dismay, she went into her cabin, but came out a moment later with her comb. She was getting more surefooted by the hour, timing her stride to the roll of the ship, but she did plop unceremoniously on to the bench and laughed at herself.

She fixed him with that penetrating gaze he was coming to know. 'You have my permission to laugh when I am no more graceful at sea than a new puppy would be.'

'I daren't,' he said. 'Suppose some day you find me in desperate shape—say, for example, at Almack's? I would hope you would be charitable, so I will be the same.'

'Coward,' she teased. She unwound the towel, shook her head, and began to comb her hair. She seemed to be waiting for him to say something, but when he didn't, she took the initiative. 'Three days at sea and my manners have taken French leave, Colonel. Miss Pym always did say I was too nosy by half, but what are *you* doing here?'

Admiring you, he thought. That would never do; perhaps honesty deserved its moment in the sun. 'I shipped out to the Peninsula because I could not stand one more moment of conference meetings in Plymouth.'

'You're quizzing me,' she said with a laugh.

'Well, no, I am not,' he contradicted. 'I probably should have turned down my promotion from Major to Lieutenant Colonel, but one doesn't do that.'

'No harm in ambition,' she told him, trying to sound sage, and blithely unaware how charming was her naïveté.

'True,' he agreed. 'Trouble is, a step up means different duties at Division Three. Now I am chained to a desk and report for meetings, where I sit and draw little figures and yawn inside my mouth, so my tonsils won't be seen.'

She laughed and touched his sleeve. Just one quick touch, but it made him pleasantly warm. 'Colonel, I used to do the same thing in theology class, where God was so cruel as to make time stand still.'

'Exactly.' *Well, aren't you the charming rogue*, he thought. *No vicar for a husband for you, I should think*. 'As with most things, there is more to it than that. I went to Stonehouse Hos-

pital to visit the newest arrived Marines inva-
lided there. One of them died in my arms, after
wishing there was something more he and his
fellow Marines could do to end this stalemate
with Boney. I chose not to let his sacrifice be
for naught.'

Polly nodded, her face serious. He continued,
'I asked permission of the Colonel Commandant
to conduct impromptu visits to various ships off
the Peninsula, and in Lisbon where a Marine
brigade is based. I want to find out how the
men feel about what they do, and if, indeed, we
Marines could do more. Brandon, these are men
with vast experience, who surely have ideas! I
have *carte blanche* to stay as long as I wish, and
then compile a report. That is why I am here.'

She looked down at her hands, then up at him
over her spectacles. 'We are both running away,
aren't we, Colonel Junot? I could have stayed
in Bath and taught the younger pupils at my
school, or at least stayed in Torquay and helped
my sister Nana, who is increasing again.'

'But you want to see the wider world, even
such a tattered one as this is proving to be, with
its everlasting war?'

She frowned, and he could tell she had considered the matter. 'I think we know I don't
belong here. Maybe I should have stayed in
Torquay.'

Then I never would have met you, he realised. It was such a disquieting thought that he wanted to dismiss it. He chose a light tone, because that was all he could do, and even then, it was wrong to his ears. 'If it's any comfort, I felt the same way at my first deployment in service of King and country.'

'When was that? Where did you go?' she asked, her interest obvious.

What could he say but the truth, even though he knew it would age him enormously in her eyes. 'It was 1790 and I was bound for India.'

'Heavens. I had not even been born,' she told him, confirming his fear.

Get it over with, Hugh, he told himself sourly. 'I was fifteen and a mere Lieutenant.'

She surprised him then, as she had been surprising him for the three days he had known her. 'Heavens,' she said again, and he cringed inwardly. 'Colonel, I cannot imagine how fascinating India must have been. Did you see elephants? Tigers? Are the women as beautiful as pictures I have seen?'

She didn't say a word about his age, but calmly continued combing her hair, her mind only on India, as far as he could tell. He felt himself relax. 'Do you want to hear about India?'

'Oh, my, yes, I do,' she said, her eyes bright. 'Colonel, I have never been anywhere!'

'Very well,' he began, eager to keep her there. 'We landed in Bombay during the monsoon.'

'You were seasick,' she said.

'I told you I have never been seasick,' he replied, 'and I meant it.'

'Very well. Since I was not there, I shall have to believe you.' She put her comb down and clasped her hands together. 'Tell me everything you can remember.'

If some celestial scamp in the universe—an all-purpose genie would do—had suddenly whisked away all the clocks and banished time to outer darkness, Polly knew she would be content to listen for ever to Colonel Junot. While her hair dried, she and the sentry who joined them at the Colonel's suggestion heard of tiger hunts, an amphibious storming of a rajah's palace in Bombay, and of the rise of Lord Wellington, the 'Sepoy General'. India was followed by Ceylon and then Canada, as Colonel Junot took them through his Marine career.

It became quickly obvious to Polly that he loved what he did, because she heard it in his voice. She saw it in the way he leaned forwards until she felt like a co-conspirator in a grand undertaking. His storytelling had her almost feeling decks awash and seeing rank on rank of charging elephants and screaming Indians, as he told them so matter of factly about what he did to support himself. He was capability itself.

Through years of indoctrination, Miss Pym had pounded into her head how rude it was to stare at anyone, especially a man, but the Colonel was hard to resist. A natural-born storyteller, he became quite animated when he spoke of his adventures, which only brightened his brown eyes and gave more colour to his somewhat sallow cheeks—he had obviously spent too much time the past winter sitting at conference tables. She was having a hard time deciding if his finest feature was his magnificent posture and bearing, or his handsome lips, which had to be a throwback to his French ancestry.

Colonel Junot was different, she knew, if for no other reason than that he found her interesting. As she listened to him, injecting questions that he answered with good humor, Polly discovered she was already steeling herself against the time he would bow and say goodbye.

'And that is my career, Private Leonard,' Colonel Junot concluded, looking at them both. 'Private, as you were. Brandon, excuse me please.' He rose, bowed to her, and went his stately way up the companionway.

'I live such an ordinary life,' Polly murmured, watching him go.

* * *

She went on deck at the end of the forenoon watch, pleased to notice the chair she had sat in yesterday had been relocated to its original place, which probably meant there would be no gunnery practice today. She had brought a book topside with her, something improving that Miss Pym had recommended. She decided quickly that a treatise on self-control was a hard slog on a ship's deck where so much of interest was going on. She was happy enough to merely close it, when what she really wanted to do was toss it into the Atlantic. Maybe that wasn't such a shabby idea. Book in hand, she went to the ship's railing.

'Brandon, I hope you are not considering suicide.'

She looked around to see Colonel Junot. 'No, sir. This book is a dead bore and I am about to put it out of its misery.'

He took the book from her hand, opened it, rolled his eyes, then closed it. 'Allow me,' he said, and impulsively flung the thing far into the ocean. 'I hope you were serious.'

'Never more so,' she told him firmly. 'It was a gift from my aunt, who was headmistress at the female academy I attended in Bath, and—'

'I should apologise then for deep-sixing it,' he said, interrupting her.

'Oh, no. Don't you have any relatives who annoy you?'

He thought a moment, then he laughed. 'Who doesn't!'

Walking with more assurance back to her chair, she seated herself, giving the Colonel every opportunity to nod to her and continue on his way. To her delight, he pulled up yesterday's keg and sat beside her.

'Brandon, give me some advice.'

'Me?' she asked, amazed.

'Yes, you,' he replied patiently. 'Under ordinary circumstances, you appear quite sensible.'

'Thank you, sir,' she teased, and put a hand to her forehead like a seaman.

'I have told you what my aim is on my fact-finding mission.' He must have caught the look in her eye, because he wagged a finger at her. 'Don't you even presume to call it "taking French leave from the conference table".'

'I would never, sir,' she said solemnly, which made him look at her suspiciously.

'Seriously, Brandon, how can I approach Marines?'

She looked at him in surprise. 'Colonel, you would know far better than I!'

'I don't. On this ship, for example—which for our purposes we will call "Any Frigate in the Fleet"—I communicated my wishes to the

Sergeant, and he passed them to his men. Everyone is stiff and formal, and I can almost see their brains running, trying to work out what it is I *really* want to know.'

Polly thought about what he had said, but not for long, because it seemed so simple. 'Can you not just sit with them as you are sitting casually with me? Tell them what you told me about the dying Lieutenant, and what it is you wish to do. Look them in the eye, the way you look me in the eye—you know, kindly—and tell them you need their help. Why need you be formal?'

He watched her face closely, and she could only hope he had not noticed her odd little epiphany. 'You *are* kind, you know,' she said softly.

'Thank you, Brandon, but no one can get beyond my rank to just talk to me. There is a larger issue here, one I had not thought of: this may be the first time in the history of the Marines that an officer has actually asked an enlisted man what he *thinks*.'

'That is a sad reflection,' she said, after some consideration. 'Everyone has good ideas now and then.'

'We never ask.'

He was looking far too serious, as though his good idea in Plymouth was already on the rocks. She put her hand on his arm, and he glanced at her in surprise. *Just two days, and then you are gone*, she thought. 'I told you, you are kind. Don't give up yet. You'll find a way to talk to the men.' She took her hand away and looked down, shy again. 'When I was so desperate, you found a way to put me at ease.'

'That was simplicity itself. You needed help.'

'So did the Lieutenant who died in your arms, Colonel,' she told him, finding it strange that she had to explain his own character to him, wondering why people didn't see themselves as they were. 'Just be that kind man and you will find out everything you want to know.'

She stopped, acutely aware she was offering advice to a Lieutenant Colonel of Marines, who, under ordinary circumstances, would never have even looked at her. 'Well, that's what I think,' she concluded, feeling as awkward as a calf on ice.

He nodded and stood up, and Polly knew she had not helped at all. He put his hands behind his back, impeccable. 'I just go and sit on that hatch and call over the Marines and speak to them as I speak to you, Brandon?'

'You could take off that shiny plaque on your neck and unbutton your uniform jacket,' she suggested, then could not resist. 'Let them see you have on a checked shirt underneath.'

His smile was appreciative as he fingered the

gorget against his throat. 'I must remain in uniform, Brandon, and the gorget stays. I will try what you say.' He did not disguise the doubt in his voice.

She clasped her hands together, unwilling to let him go, even if it was only to the main deck. 'Colonel, you could practise right here. Ask me questions. I could do the same to you.'

'Why not?' He contemplated her for a moment, and she suddenly wished she was thinner, that her hair was not so wind-blown, and that her glasses would disappear. He was looking her right in the eyes, though, so maybe he didn't notice.

He flexed his fingers and cleared his throat. 'Private Brandon, as you were, please! Let me set you at ease. I'm here to ask questions of you that will never be repeated to your superior. I will not even name you in my report.' He looked at her, his eyes sceptical. 'What do you think so far?'

'You could smile,' she suggested.

'Too artificial,' he replied, shaking his head. 'That would terrify them because officers never smile.'

'I don't understand men,' Polly said suddenly.

'You weren't meant to,' he told her gently, which made her laugh. 'All right. All right. Private Brandon, tell me something about yourself.

Why did you join the Royal Marines? I'm curious.' He peered at her. 'Just tell me something about yourself, Brandon, something that I don't know.'

She thought a moment, and realised with a sudden jolt that she had reached that place where Nana had once told her she would one day arrive. '"Polly, dear, you must never deceive a man about your origins,"' Nana had told her only a week ago.

'My father was William Stokes, Lord Ratliffe of Admiralty House,' she said. 'I am one of his three illegitimate daughters, Colonel.'

To her relief, he did not seem repulsed. 'That accounts for all the years in boarding school in Bath, I suppose. Tell me more, Brandon. What do you like to do?'

'After that, you really want to know *more*?' she asked in surprise.

'Indeed, I do, Private Brandon,' he said simply. 'Remember—I'm supposed to extract answers from you and keep you at your ease. I am interested.'

'Our father tried to sell my older sisters to the highest bidder, to pay off his debts,' she went on.

'What a bad man,' the Colonel said. 'Is he the Admiralty official who died in a Spanish prison and is thought by some to be a hero?'

'He died in Plymouth, and, yes, some think him a hero,' she said, her voice barely audible.

He amazed her by putting his hand under her chin and raising it a little, so he could look her in the eyes. 'You managed to avoid all this? How?'

Don't you have eyes in your head? she wanted to retort. 'Come now, Colonel,' she said. 'I am no beauty. My father chose to ignore me.'

For some reason, her bald statement seemed to embarrass the Colonel, whose face turned red. 'Shallow, shallow man,' he murmured, when he had recovered himself. 'He never really took a good look at you, did he?'

Startled, she shook her head. 'He demanded miniatures of my sisters, but not of me.'

'Thank God, Brandon,' the Colonel whispered, his eyes still not leaving her face. He gazed at her for a long moment, and then seemed to recall what he was doing. He sat back and regarded her speculatively. 'I think I can do those interviews now,' he said. 'If I show a genuine interest in what these enlisted men are telling me, look them in the eyes and wait, I might have success. Is that it?'

'I think it is,' she replied, relieved that he had changed the subject, and a little surprised at how much information she had given him with so little encouragement. 'You're actually rather good at interviewing, I think.' Then she couldn't help herself. 'Only don't chuck them under the chin.'

He laughed and held up his hands in a surrender gesture. 'Too right, Brandon! Wait. You never told me what *you* like to do, only about your dreadful father. There's more to you than him.'

She had never thought of it that way before. 'I like to plant things. Before I left Torquay, I helped my brother-in-law's mother plant a row of Johnny Jump-Ups in pots. We...we were going to do snapdragons next, but the letter came and I went to Plymouth. It's not very interesting,' she said in apology.

'You'd like Kirkcudbright, the village where I grew up,' he said. 'Everyone has flowers in their front yard. It smells like heaven, around July. And it *is* interesting.'

The Colonel put his hand on her cheek then, as he had the other evening. 'Don't ever sell yourself short, Brandon,' he said quietly. 'Incidentally, I like to carve small boats.'

He bowed and left the quarterdeck for the waist of the frigate, where the guns were tied down fast. She watched as he spoke to the Sergeant of the guard, then sat down on the hatch.

'That's the way,' Polly murmured quietly, her

heart still beating too fast. 'Surely they won't remain standing if you are seated.'

Trying not to appear overly interested, she watched as the Marines not on duty approached Colonel Junot. He gestured to them, and in a few minutes, they were seated around him.

'Talk to him,' she whispered. 'Just talk to him. He's nothing but kind. All it takes is one of you to speak.'

One of the Privates squatting on the edge of the gathering raised his hand. Colonel Junot answered him, and everyone laughed, even the man who asked the question. Then others joined in, talking to the Colonel, to each other, and even calling over some sailors.

You just have to be yourself, she thought, imagining Colonel Junot's capable hands carving little boats for children. *Just be the man who was so kind to me.*

Chapter Five

Maybe it was the wistful way Polly Brandon had spoken of snapdragons. As Hugh had tried out his interviewing skills on a squad of obliging Marines, he'd found his mind wandering to the lady in the canvas chair.

He could be thankful he was aboard one of his Majesty's typical warships, which did not believe in mirrors on the bulkheads. He had enough trouble frowning into his shaving mirror the next morning and seeing nothing but grey hair starting to attack his temples. As he stared in total dissatisfaction, a brave better angel of his nature did attempt to remind him of his own words to Brandon a day ago, when he so sagely advised her not to sell herself short. The angel shrugged and gave up when he chose not to admit he was doing exactly the same thing to himself.

'I am too old,' he told his reflection in the shaving mirror as he scraped at his chin, which only made him wince—not because the razor was dull, but because none of those obstacles loomed any higher than the molehills they were to him. All he could think of was his August 9, 1775 birth date in the family Bible back home.

When his face was scraped sufficiently free of whiskers, he sat naked on the cold cannon in his cabin, glumly willing himself to be as practical as he ordinarily was. He reminded himself he was on duty, in the service of his King, headed into the war, and destined to be busy. Another day or two would pass and he would never see Polly Brandon again. For his peace of mind, it couldn't come too soon. Hugh did know one thing—what ailed him had a cure, and it was probably to continually remind himself that he was too old for the bewitching Polly Brandon.

Two days later, he could have made his resolve less problematic if he hadn't been pacing on deck in the early hours, dissatisfied with himself. If he had a brain in his head, he would skulk somewhere on the ship when it docked in

Oporto. Brandon would go ashore, and he would never see her again. He could go on to Lisbon.

That was his plan, anyway—a poor one, but serviceable enough. Trouble was, the view of Oporto took his breath away, and he was down the companionway in a matter of minutes, knocking on her door to tell her to step lively and come on deck for a look.

Why did you do that? he scolded himself, as he returned topside. His only hope was that she would look unappetising as she came on deck, maybe rubbing her eyes, or looking cross and out of sorts the way some women did, when yanked from slumber. If that was the case, he might have an easier time dismissing her. He could go about his business and forget this little wrinkle in his life's plan, if he even had a plan.

No luck. She came on deck quickly, a shawl draped over her arm. He smiled to see that she still couldn't quite reach that centre button in back. *I won't touch it,* he thought. Her face was rosy from slumber, her eyes bright and expectant. She merely glanced at him, then cast her whole attention on the beautiful harbour that was Oporto. She had wound her long hair into a ridiculous topknot and skewered it with what looked like a pencil. She looked entirely makeshift, but instead of disgusting him, he wanted to plant a whacking great kiss on her forehead and see where it led. *Lord, I am hopeless*, he thought in disgust.

She was too excited to even say good morning, but tugged on his arm. 'Where is the hospital?' she demanded.

He pointed to the southern bank. 'Over there, in that area called Vila Nova de Gaia. Turn round.'

She did as he demanded, and he buttoned up the centre button. 'You need longer arms,' he commented, but she was not paying attention to him.

'I have never seen anything so magnificent,' she said in awe. 'Perhaps it was worth all that seasickness. Have you been here before?'

'Years ago, Brandon. I think I was your age.' He chuckled. 'For what it's worth, my reaction was much like yours.' *There, Miss Brandon, that should remind you what a geriatric I am*, he thought grimly.

If she heard him, she didn't seem to mind. Brandon watched as a cutter swooped from the southern shore to the side of the *Perseverance* and backed its sails, then watched as the flag Lieutenant ran up a series of pennants. 'What's he doing?' she asked.

'Giving the cutter a message. Our surgeon told me the hospital sends out this cutter at every approach of the fleet, to enquire of the wounded. Ask the flag Lieutenant what message he is sending.'

Surefooted now, Polly hurried to the Lieutenant. 'He is signalling "Wounded man on board. Prompt attention." He said the cutter will take the message to the hospital wharf and there will be a surgeon's mate with a stretcher there when we dock,' she told him in one breath as she hurried back to his side.

'It appears that your brother-in-law doesn't miss a trick,' Hugh said. 'I'm impressed.'

Polly nodded, her eyes on the shore again. 'I asked the Lieutenant if he could also signal "Brandon on board", and he said he would.' She leaned against him for one brief moment, or maybe she just lost her footing. 'I have not seen Laura in nearly two years.'

The winds were fair into Oporto. As the harbour came nearer, she hurried below to finish dressing. When she came back, she was as neat as a pin. He stood close to her when they approached the mouth of the mighty river, knowing there would be a series of pitches and yaws that might discomfort her, as the Douro met the Atlantic. Besides, it gave him plenty of excuse to grip her around the waist to prevent her losing her footing. He couldn't deny he was touched by how completely she trusted him to hold her.

'I may never get used to the sea,' she confessed, as he braced her.

'It isn't given to everyone to relish going down to the sea in small boats, despite what the psalm says.'

'No argument there,' she agreed cheerfully. 'The less business I have in great waters, the better.'

It wouldn't hurt to ask. 'Of you three sisters, are you to be the only one who avoids the navy?' *What about Marines?* he wanted to ask.

She wasn't listening to him, but was back at the railing, intent on the shoreline, her mind and heart on her sister, he was certain. He tipped his hat to her and went belowdeck to find the letter Surgeon Brackett wanted him to deliver to Philemon Brittle. Better to just hand it to Brandon and let her do the honors. The voyage was over, after all.

He couldn't bring himself to hand it to her, not there at the railing, or after the gangplank came down on the wharf, and certainly not when Polly had thrown herself into the arms of a tall, beautiful woman with auburn hair.

It was a brief embrace. The woman—she must be Laura Brittle—quickly turned her attention to the foretopman on the stretcher, as her husband planted a quick kiss on Polly's cheek, shook hands with the *Perseverance*'s surgeon, and engaged him in conversation.

'Are you planning to stay in Oporto, Colonel Junot?' Captain Adney asked.

'Perhaps,' he temporised.

'We'll be at the navy wharf today and then sailing the day after, if winds and tide are willing.'

'Very well, sir. I'll sail with you.' He couldn't very well say anything else. He stood at the railing, uncertain, wanting to go down the gangplank and introduce himself, and suddenly shy. He looked at Polly for a clue, and she beckoned him.

That was easy. In another moment he was smiling inwardly at Polly's shy introduction, and bowing to Mrs Philemon Brittle, who truly was as beautiful as her younger sister had declared. Philemon Brittle held out his hand and he gave it a shake, impressed with the strength of the surgeon's grasp.

'Do join us for luncheon, Colonel, unless you have urgent business that takes you elsewhere,' Mrs Brittle said.

'Since the King of Portugal is probably taking his ease on a beach in Brazil, and Boney is on his way to Russia, if reports are accurate, I am at a momentary loss for luncheon engagements,'

he joked, which made her smile and show off
the dimple he recognised in Polly's cheek, too.

'Very well, sir. If Marshal Soult should show
his brazen face here again, we'll release you
before the sorbet. Come, Polly. Colonel?'

He walked up the hill from the wharf with a
sister on either side of him. He looked from one
to the other, which made Polly stop.

'Laura, this is droll! Colonel Junot is compar-
ing us!'

So much for my peace of mind, Hugh thought,
surprisingly unembarrassed, since he had made
an obvious discovery that was probably clear to
everyone except Polly herself. 'You have me,
Brandon. Anyone with two eyes can see that
you and Mrs Brittle are sisters.'

'I have told her that many times,' Mrs Brittle said. 'Perhaps she will choose to believe
me some day. Thank you, Colonel Junot!' She
paused then, and her eyes narrowed slightly.
'Brandon? Apparently you have either chosen
a nickname for Polly, or you are on to our own
effort to get my sister to Portugal.'

'You *were* right, Colonel!' Polly exclaimed.
'Laura, I don't know why he calls me that, but
we did wonder if perhaps some correspondence
came from Portugal requesting a Brandon Polly
for service.'

'It was the feeblest attempt,' Mrs Brittle

said as they resumed walking again. 'Philemon hoped some overworked clerk at the Navy
Board would apparently do what he did. Perhaps
I shall call you Brandon, too, my love. Welcome
to hard service in the navy.'

If Polly had a rejoinder ready, it went unno-
ticed when an orderly at the top of the hill called
for Mrs Brittle. Alert, Laura put her finger to
her lips and listened.

'Ward C, mum! Lively now!'

Without a word of explanation, Mrs Brittle
hiked up her skirts to reveal shapely legs and
ran up the hill, forgetting her company completely, it seemed. She stopped halfway up and
looked back, but Hugh just waved her on. He
took Polly's arm, content to walk the rest of the
way with her.

'I gather all the rumours are true, Brandon.
Wouldn't it be nice some day if your gifted sister could be recognised for what she is doing
here?'

'I doubt it would concern her,' Polly replied,
and he could hear the pride in her voice. 'She
would probably just laugh, and say the war is
harder on wives like Nana, who wait. It must be
so hard to be apart from one's love.'

Maybe I am about to find out, Hugh thought
to himself. *Or maybe I am just an idiot.*

They arrived at the convent and were greeted

immediately by a nun, who directed them to the dining room. The table was already set; from the looks of things, the Brittles had left their meal when the *Perseverance* docked. Hugh pulled out a chair for Polly, taking a deep breath of her sun-warmed hair as he did so, remembering how he had helped her wash it.

They were just beginning what looked like empanadas when Mrs Brittle came into the room, hand in hand with a youngster whose hair was the same shade as his mother and aunt's. She knelt gracefully and kissed his cheek. 'Danny, that's your aunt Polly Brandon.' She repeated it in Portuguese. 'His Portuguese is better than mine,' Mrs Brittle explained.

'Laura, he looks like you,' Polly said.

'The hair, anyway,' Laura said as she sat him down on a chair with a medical book as a booster. 'He has his father's eyes and general capable demeanour.'

'Does he run with the herd?' Hugh asked, gesturing towards the courtyard, which he saw through the open door. Other children about Danny's age played there.

'Indeed, he does, which frees me for hospital work,' Laura said.

Polly looked where he looked. 'Goodness, are you running an orphanage, too?'

'No, my love,' Mrs Brittle said. She hesitated,

glancing at Hugh, and he understood immediately whose children they were, considering Oporto's sad history with the French invaders.

She reached across her corner of the table and touched Polly's hand. 'When the French came here in '08, they brutalised the young women they did not murder. These children are one result of that misery.'

'Oh,' Polly said, her voice small. 'Where are their mothers?'

Hugh watched Polly's expressive face. *You are so young, so naïve*, he thought. *Let us hope this is the worst face of war you see.*

'Oporto is a sad town, my love,' Mrs Brittle said. She cupped her hand gently against her son's cheek as he ate his empanada. 'We have tried to make life as good as we can for these unfortunates.' She looked at Polly. 'Dearest, this is why we want you here.'

'I don't understand,' Polly said. 'I thought I was to help in the wards.'

'We want you to teach English to the young mothers—some are here—and to the nuns. I haven't time, and they would be so much more useful here. Perhaps, in time, they will find work with the English port merchants, when they return from Lisbon and London.'

'I can teach them,' Polly said. Her eyes on the

children, she rose and went to the door, where she could see the children playing. 'Seems a strange way to fight Boney.'

'Not at all,' Mrs Brittle said. She held a cup to Danny's lips and he drank in large gulps. 'Slow down, little one. You'll be back there soon enough.' She looked apologetically at Hugh. 'Colonel, you will find us a strange household. My husband sends his regrets, but ward walking always trumps food. Perhaps he'll wander through tonight for our evening meal, which I trust you will share with us.'

He didn't hesitate. 'With pleasure.'

'In fact, Colonel Junot, you may stay the night here, unless you prefer a smelly frigate.'

'I can do that, too,' he replied, glad for the invitation.

He looked at Polly, but her eyes were on the courtyard. As he watched her, she rose quietly and held out her hand to her nephew, who took it without hesitation and led her from the room in such a forthright manner that he smiled.

'Now there's a lad who has things under control.'

'I told you he was like his father,' Mrs Brittle said, her voice soft with love as she watched her sister and son.

He thought he should make his excuses and leave then. This was a busy woman. He made to rise, but she raised her hand to stop him, then poured him another glass of port. 'As onerous as work is here, we cannot fault the wine, Colonel.'

He drank, pleased to agree with her. His eyes went again to Polly, who was sitting on the grass now, with children around her. He watched as two women about her age came closer, hesitated, and moved closer. 'She's a bit of a magnet,' he murmured, more to himself than Mrs Brittle. 'I noticed that on the ship, too.' He chuckled, then stopped, because Mrs Brittle was giving him that thoughtful stare again.

'I think there were two Lieutenants who would have followed her to the ends of the earth,' he continued, speaking too fast. *Maybe one Lieutenant Colonel*, he thought, glad Mrs Brittle could not read his mind.

'She would only stare at you if you suggested such a thing.'

'I know, Mrs Brittle. She seems to think she is a duckling among swans.'

Mrs Brittle poured herself another glass. 'Thank you for being such a gallant escort, Colonel. I was hoping there would be someone mature like you on board, to shepherd her safely.'

Ouch, he thought, mentally counting every grey hair at his temples. 'You can always count on the Marines, Mrs Brittle.'

* * *

Lord, but that sounded feeble, he scolded himself as he said goodbye to Mrs Brittle and walked back to the dock down the well-travelled path, where he planned to retrieve a small duffel of his own and arrange for Polly's luggage to be sent up the hill. The Sergeant of Marines had released his men to shore, where he drilled them. Hugh watched in appreciation and some pride at their neat rank and file. 'We are so few in this war,' he murmured, and thought of Lieutenant Graves breathing his last in his arms. 'I have work to do.'

From the startled look on Laura's face, Polly knew she should have disguised her disappointment that Colonel Junot had left the hospital. 'I…I only wish he had said goodbye, but I suppose duty called,' she said. *And, oh, can I change a subject*, she thought. 'Laura, the young women are so shy. I declare they are like deer.'

Laura removed the medical book from Danny's chair and patted it. Polly sat down. 'You must treat them so gently. They have been through a terrible experience at the hands of the French.' She sighed. 'It is one I can appreciate more than most, perhaps. They were wretchedly ill used, and feel the world's censure.'

'You…you said some of the women returned to their villages and left their babies here?'

'They did, and I call it no foul. Everyone deals differently with violation of such a magnitude. I can assure you the mothers who remained love their little ones, who are surely not to blame for their entry into the world.' She took Polly's hand in hers. 'My dear, you and I know the inside of an orphanage. Only Nana had a home in her early years.' She looked Polly in the eye. 'Is it wrong of me to have thrust you into this?'

Polly shook her head. 'No, a thousand times, Laura. I trust this is one foundling home where the little ones are touched and loved.'

'You know it is,' her sister said firmly, then looked down as her cheeks flamed. 'Other than Nana's embrace when we met in Torquay, my beloved Philemon was the first person who ever hugged me, and I was twenty-seven.'

Polly moved her chair closer and they sat hand in hand until an orderly ran down the hall, calling for Mrs Brittle.

'Duty calls,' Laura said, but Polly heard no regret in her voice.

She stood up, but Polly did not release her hand. 'Tell me you don't mind all this hard work, sister,' she said, tugging on her hand, 'or the fact that you receive no recognition for it.'

Laura let go of Polly's hand gently. 'I only have to look into the eyes of the men I save, or into my husband's eyes, to receive all the reward I need, this side of heaven, my love. You'll understand some day.'

'That's what Nana says, too,' Polly grumbled. 'Some day. Some day.'

Laura laughed. 'Don't be so impatient to grow up! Go back to the courtyard and make some more friends.' She kissed the top of Polly's head. 'And if Danny gets stubborn and won't share, encourage him to do so. Mama says.'

She spent a pleasant afternoon in the courtyard, trying to imagine what Oporto must have been like when the French controlled it and the Portuguese suffered so greatly. She counted ten little ones, all about two years of age, like her nephew. Two of them decided to nap on cots in the shade of a mimosa tree, and three young women watched over them all.

One of the women, Paola, could speak some English, but Polly found herself mostly smiling and wishing she knew more of the language. She did learn a handclapping game in Portuguese, where even Danny corrected her pronunciation. She decided the whole afternoon was a lesson in humility for Miss Pym's star pupil and spent her time more profitably, sitting cross-legged in the grass and folding bits of paper into hopping frogs, a skill she had learned from Nana.

The whole time, Paola sat close to her in the grass, with several children in her lap. 'I am determined to learn Portuguese,' Polly told her, and smiled back when the young girl smiled at her.

The smile left Paola's face when she heard footsteps and looked over her shoulder. Polly watched her freeze and seem to shrink inside her own skin.

She looked around, wondering what could be the trouble. Colonel Junot stood in the open doorway to the courtyard, watching them, a smile on his face. Polly carefully put her arm around Paola, who had moved her legs to the side as though she wanted to leap to her feet. 'No, no,' Polly whispered. 'He is a friend. *Amigo?*'

Paola froze where she was, scarcely breathing. Imagine that much fear, Polly thought. She tightened her grip on the young girl. 'Colonel Junot, if you don't mind, you're frightening this girl,' she said softly.

He stared at her in disbelief at first, and then he sighed and turned away. She heard his footsteps recede down the corridor. *Please don't leave before you say goodbye*, she thought in sudden anguish.

Chapter Six

To Polly's infinite relief, Colonel Junot joined them for dinner. 'I was afraid you had come to the courtyard to say goodbye to me,' she told him.

'Oh, no, Brandon,' he assured her. 'Your sister kindly invited me to eat here and then stay the night. I have been quartered in a chaste cell formerly inhabited by someone—perhaps her name was Sister Quite Prudent—who obviously had God's ear. It can only do me good.'

I'm going to miss your wit, she thought suddenly. *What a short acquaintance this has been.*

Dinner was sheer delight, with young Daniel Brittle sitting on the medical books again, and Philemon actually free to join them. 'What do you think of our society?'

'I like it, Surgeon Brittle,' Hugh said. 'You run a shipshape operation with good results.' He lowered his voice. 'I'm afraid I frightened one of the young women in the courtyard this afternoon. I suppose one uniform is pretty much the same as another to them.'

'Alas, yes,' Laura chimed in. 'No one wears a uniform here, and our Marine sentries don't go in the courtyard.'

While the Brittles listened, Hugh explained his purpose in coming to Portugal. 'Surgeon Brittle, I would consider it a special favour if you or your excellent wife would show me around the hospital tomorrow. I'd like to reassure myself that your protection is adequate.'

'We can do that.' Philemon leaned back in his chair and glanced at Laura. 'Danny appears to be drooping, Laura. Colonel Junot and I can entertain ourselves with Oporto's major export, if you and Polly want to see him to bed.'

The little boy went with no protest, happy enough for his mother to tuck him in bed, sing a lullaby in Portuguese, and watch until he slept, his arm around a doll made of surgical towels.

'You look a little weary yourself, sister,' Laura said. 'I can't think of a lullaby for your age, but you can tell me about the voyage, and how our sister does.'

Polly decided bliss was a flannel nightgown,

two pillows behind her head, and sharing family stories with her sister, a luxury of such magnitude she never could have imagined it only three years ago. She described Rachel at three, and Nana's quiet competence, as counterpoint to the tremendous strain she lived under, and the next expectation, due in September.

Laura listened, adding her own commentary. During a lull, she cleared her throat, then sat up a little higher in the bed. 'Polly, I don't want to pry… Oh, yes, I do! It seems to me that Colonel Junot—heavens, he sounds more Scottish than Macbeth—is your champion.'

Polly stared at her, eyes wide. 'Champion?' she repeated. 'I can't imagine.'

Laura levelled her with a glance, probably one she practised on Danny. 'Confess,' she said.

There obviously wasn't any point in trying to keep the events of the voyage a secret. 'Several centuries back, his ancestors came to Scotland from France with Mary of Scotland. That's why he is "Junnit" now, and—' Polly stopped, and looked at Laura for reassurance. 'As for champion—sister, I don't think I would have survived the voyage without him.'

As Laura listened, only interjecting a faint 'Oh, my', or 'Gracious', as the tale became more fraught, Polly described the whole voyage, leaving nothing out. 'When…when I was feeling better, I honestly tried to avoid him, so he wouldn't have to be reminded of the embarrassing circumstances I had placed him under, but he was just so matter of fact! You would have thought he had done nothing more than… than pull a splinter out of my finger. I tried to be mortified, but he never let me.'

Even Laura, who had probably seen everything by now, stared at her. 'Polly, Colonel Junot may be as rare a man as I have ever heard of! We all owe him a debt.' She thought a moment, choosing her words like ripe strawberries in a summer market. 'That is all you owe him, though.'

Polly watched her sister, unable to overlook the worry in her eyes. She decided to put her at ease. 'Sister, he is much too grand and important to pay me any attention, beyond that which I have described to you.'

She did not expect to feel any pain at that bald announcement, but she did. 'He's a man of some distinction, Laura. Men like that don't…' She couldn't say it. 'Well, they don't.'

'You don't think he's too old for you?'

Surprised, Polly sat up. 'I…I never thought of him that way.' She swallowed, suddenly wanting this conversation to end, because she felt unwanted tears teasing her eyelids. 'Age never entered in. Heavens, sister, he is a Colonel of

Marines! I doubt he will even remember my name next week.'

'Are you so certain?' Laura asked. Suddenly the air hung heavy between them.

It was as if they both decided to change the subject at the same time, and spoke next of inconsequentials. Gradually Laura said less and less. Soon her head drooped on Polly's shoulder and she slept. Polly made herself comfortable, knowing that Philemon would eventually come in search of his wife. Finally, she heard Colonel Junot's firm footsteps receding down the long corridor. Philemon knocked softly on the door, then opened it.

Polly put a finger to her lips, and he smiled to see his wife asleep. Walking quietly to the bed, he picked her up, winked at Polly, and mouthed 'goodnight'. He looked down at his sleeping wife, then at Polly. 'You're just what this doctor ordered,' he whispered, then grinned. 'And you brought along your own Marine for protection.'

'He's not *my* Marine,' she whispered back. Philemon left the room as quietly as he had entered it. Polly frowned at the ceiling. 'What is wrong with my relatives?' she asked out loud.

Hugh's peers back in Plymouth would never believe him if he told them he spent the night in a nun's bed. He woke early, as usual, but felt disinclined to move. Miracle of miracles he hadn't roused earlier, considering the amount of port he had drunk last night, which also accounted for the slight buzz in his brain.

Part of the pleasure Hugh felt was his convivial evening with Philemon Brittle, a remarkable man, if ever there was one. He had handed over the letter from their mutual friend, Owen Brackett, which Brittle read right then, after apologies to his guest.

In the manner of men engaged in years of warfare, they had spent the next half-hour refighting naval battles, discovered they had both served at the Battle of the Nile and Trafalgar, and had decided—Brittle, anyway—each was deserving of confidences.

'Polly's a sight for Laura's sore eyes,' Brittle had said, as they finished one bottle and popped the cork on another. 'She works so hard, and misses her sisters so much.' He poured another measure. 'I hope it is not a felony to bamboozle the Navy Board, but we thought it worth a try to get Brandon Polly here.'

'I've been calling her Brandon,' Hugh confessed. 'I suppose that is rag manners, but it was one way to take her mind off as wicked a case of the pukes as I have ever seen.' He laughed. 'She told me she was determined to take up residence in Portugal and never attempt the ocean again.'

They had sailed into more prosaic conversational waters then, concluding only when the surgeon stoppered the bottle of port, telling Hugh it was time he went in search of his wife.

He had found her in Polly's room. Hugh had continued down the hall, but stood in the shadows and watched as, a few moments later, Brittle came out carrying his sleeping wife. He knew he was a voyeur, but Hugh had not looked away when she woke and her arms went around Brittle's neck and she kissed him.

Well, Surgeon Brittle, I shall have to report to Owen Brackett that you are enjoying a better war than most, Hugh had thought, as he went into his virginal cell and closed the door quietly. His dreams had been livelier than usual that night.

Preparing for the day was no more bare bones than usual. His only misgiving came as he dressed, wearing the black-and-white checked shirt that Polly seemed to have taken a shine to. He tucked the long tails into his navy blue trousers, and stood there a long minute, holding the gorget he had worn around his neck for years. Habit prevailed. He hooked it around his neck, but tucked it inside his shirt because he was out of uniform. Feeling decidedly naked without his uniform coat, he settled for a nondescript waistcoat he usually kept in his duffle as an antidote to cold mornings. *I must look like a brigand*, he thought, then reminded himself that vanity in a Lieutenant Colonel of Marines was out of place.

He retraced his steps to the dining room, hoping to see Polly Brandon. He was disappointed; Laura Brittle sat alone at the table, sipping tea. He hesitated to enter, but she had heard his footsteps.

'Do join me, Colonel Junot,' she called. When he came in the room, she indicated the food on the sideboard. 'Philemon is already ward walking, Danny is in the courtyard, with my sister.'

Porridge, cream, and yesterday's empanadas seemed to be the menu. He filled his plate and joined her as she poured him tea. He wasn't inclined to converse much over meals—maybe this was a consequence of the urgent nature of his wartime life—and she seemed to sense that. When he finished, he sat back. Something slightly militant in her eyes told him she did not suffer fools gladly, or, apparently, Colonels.

'Colonel, as much as you would probably rather not mention it, I must thank you for your unparalleled kindness to my sister on the voyage. She told me how you helped her.'

'It truly was nothing,' he assured her. *That is safe enough*, he thought, daring to relax. 'I only feel sorry it was necessary for a young lady to have to pawn her dignity so completely.' He laughed softly. 'She ain't much of a sailor, but she is a trooper.'

They laughed together. He watched Mrs Brittle's expressive face, seeing so much of Polly in her that it surprised him. Physically they were different—Laura tall and slim, and Polly shorter and probably destined to a life of decisions between one cream bun or two—but he could not overlook the matching dimples and lovely hair.

Then it came; he could see it in her eyes and the way she set her lips in a firm line. He braced himself.

'What do you know of us sisters?' she asked.

He shrugged, not sure of himself, but too stubborn to roll over and play dead. 'I have heard things,' he said simply. 'In fact, she told me about her father.'

He had startled her, but she recovered quickly. 'It's true. We have all decided never to gild a lily, Colonel. Still, I have to wonder why she said so much.'

Hugh said nothing, unwilling to pave her way. He poured himself more tea, then gave Mrs Brittle his full attention. He wondered for only a short moment what her game was, because he realised how transparent he must be to an observant woman who was a great protector of her sisters. 'Say on, madam,' he murmured, bracing himself.

'Nana was able to get away to safety in Plymouth with her grandmother. I had no one's support, so my first marriage lined our father's pockets and fair ruined me. Polly was never a victim because our father never could see past her spectacles. For that, Nana and I are profoundly grateful. Polly sees it differently, I think.'

Chastened, Hugh allowed his gaze to wander. *I was one of those shallow ones, at first, but you'll never hear that from me*, he thought.

What she was telling him became clear. He knew superior intellect had no role in his sudden wisdom because he knew himself well enough. 'Which is worse, Mrs Brittle—to be in peril because of beauty, or ignored because of perceived lack of it?'

'*Touché*, Colonel,' she said, impressed. 'Polly feels like a wren among birds of paradise, although nothing could be further from the truth. But *you* have noticed.'

He looked at her, his heart sinking because he knew she had taken his measure, no matter how well he had thought to hide it. 'You have me, Mrs Brittle. I'll admit that I have become an admirer of your sister. It only took a short voyage.'

'I thought as much,' she replied, her tone in no way calculated to embarrass. 'I have to ask—

are you even aware that you have a proprietary air around her?'

It was his turn for surprise. 'No!'

'You do,' she said, giving considerable weight to two words.

He thought a long moment before he spoke, knowing that what he said would end any further connection. 'I'm certain she has no notion of my regard, beyond any consideration of a gentleman towards a female travelling alone. I helped her. That was enough, as far as she is concerned. How could I possibly mean anything to her on such short notice, and in such a circumstance?'

'I trust you are right,' Laura said.

He could hear the finality in her voice. 'I am right, madam. I...I have no plans to pursue the matter, so rest assured.' He made himself smile. 'Nothing like a good war to put the screws on an actual life, eh?'

He should never have said that, because it broke his heart, even as he knew he had ample cause to dislike Laura Brittle.

Not willing just then to stay another moment in Mrs Brittle's company, he stood up. 'Enough said,' he told her, with what he thought was an admirable bit of forbearance. 'I'll only be here the rest of the day, then off to Lisbon on tomorrow's tide.'

It pleased him a little to see her suddenly unsure, as though she regretted her interference in Polly Brandon's life. Maybe she could tolerate his plain speaking, since she was so eager to dish out her own. He took a deep breath. 'You and Mrs Worthy still see Brandon as a child, don't you?'

'She is,' was Laura Brittle's firm reply.

'Take another look,' he said quietly, then bowed and left the room.

Philemon had told Hugh last night where the principal ward was located. He reminded himself that his sole purpose in Oporto was to further his interviews with the Marines serving in small detachments. He would have got off scot-free if he hadn't glanced into the courtyard as he strode so purposefully away, ready to chew nails.

He slowed down; he stopped, making sure he was in the shadow of a colonnade. There she sat on the grass, cross-legged but decorous—Brandon Polly on the Navy Boards rolls, and Brandon for ever in his heart. He knew it now; Laura Brittle had succeeded in convincing him of the matter, even as she pulled the rug out from under him.

Brandon was dressed in something light and her hair was again atop her head in that silly

way she had of twisting it there with a pencil or
skewer. She had already attracted her nephew
to one leg, and a darker-skinned youngster of
roughly the same age—some Frenchman's
memento—was ready to plop himself down on
the other. Her arms were full and her face so
pretty in that way of women with children.

How bitter this was. Polly Brandon was precisely the woman he wanted to mother his own
children, children destined never to be born
because the timing was off, and Napoleon, that
bastard, insisted on hogging everyone's attention and effort. *Brandon, you are the wife I
will never have*, he thought. *At least there is no
crime in remembering you.*

He moved quietly from the shadow and continued his way down the corridor to the convent's chapel, which had been appropriated as
the major ward. Philemon had told him that
since the French has desecrated it, the Catholic
hierarchy in Portugal had been willing enough,
and marvellously patriotic, to turn over the use
of major portions of the convent to the Royal
Navy as a satellite hospital.

He walked into the ward, looking for
Philemon Brittle, and found him in a former
lady chapel, seated at a desk, poring over a sheaf
of papers.

Brittle smiled to see him and indicated a

chair. 'Feel free to talk to my Marine guards,' he said. 'I have them posted in here, as you can see, and by my apothecary, and at each entrance.'

It seemed so few to Hugh. 'Do you feel secure enough which such a small detail?'

The surgeon shrugged. 'I confess I do not think about the matter over much. We're close to the navy wharf for safety—you were there yesterday—and this side of the Douro River is under control. We never cross the river to Oporto proper without an escort, though, mainly because none of your Marines has any faith in the British army's ability to keep the Frogs away.'

They both laughed, as only a navy surgeon and a Marine could who were well acquainted with service jealousies. 'I suppose we're a pack of fools, Colonel,' Philemon admitted. 'There's been no indication of French in the vicinity, but it's lively enough this summer, with Beau Wellesley on the prowl east of us, and Soult and Marmont playing their cat-and-mouse games.'

'And here all is peaceful.'

'For now. My own sources suggest battle soon, although the fleet itself seems quiet.' Philemon leaned back in his chair. 'You'd be amazed how this chapel can fill up with army wounded. They've taken to shipping us their worst cases, even though this was never in-

tended as an army hospital. The advantage is
we can get them off the Peninsula sooner, so
it works out. I leave it to the Admiralty and
Horse Guards to squabble, and let us alone to
heal whom we can.'

Philomen peered closer at Hugh. 'But you are
not concerned about that, are you?' He paused,
but only briefly. 'Did my wife give you what-for
over Polly?'

'She said my proprietary air was too obvious, and perhaps I should turn my attention elsewhere, since Polly is so young,' Hugh admitted,
miserable and hoping it did not show. 'I assured
her I would be gone soon enough and not likely
to return. I admit I was not as nice to Mrs Brittle
as I should have been. She still sees Brandon as
a child.'

Out of the corner of his eye, Hugh could see a
nun standing in the doorway. Philemon nodded
to the woman, then rose. 'Duty calls. Don't look
so glum, Colonel Junot! If it's any consolation,
Laura and I don't see eye to eye on some matters. Oliver Worthy and I can both testify to
the value of persistence, where the daughters of
the late and unlamented Lord Ratliffe are concerned. Good day, now. Feel free to roam the
place and question whomsoever you will.'

Hugh did, visiting first two Marines in hospital, and then making his rounds of the build-

ing, explaining himself and then questioning. The result was more food for thought, and the satisfaction of knowing he was improving in his offhand interrogations. His pleasure in whatever good he might be doing gave way to a gnawing feeling that he wanted to at least glimpse Polly Brandon again, before he made his way back to the navy wharf and his duty.

He passed through the corridor again, and this time was rewarded. There she was now, her hair more decorous, and her admirers grown to include more children and young mothers, some of whom looked no older than his nieces living so peacefully in Scotland on his land. He had heard stories of the French in Oporto, and the terrible prices exacted so often by conquerors.

He hoped he would not frighten anyone, but he had to say goodbye to Polly Brandon. There were a few startled glances in his direction as he crossed the courtyard, but no one scarpered away. To his gratification, Polly rose to meet him, a smile on her face.

They met in the centre of the courtyard, and the sun was warm on his back. The scent of orange blossoms was all around, and the peppery odour of roses, fragrances he knew he would always associate with Polly Brandon, even if he never saw her again, which seemed likely, considering her sister's vigilance.

'I approve the shirt,' she told him with no preliminaries.

'I'll pass your encomium on to the Navy Board's chief commissary, who is probably some poor overworked functionary behind a tall desk,' he teased back.

How could he have ever though her plain? Were all men, when faced with spectacles, as stupid as he was? If anything, the spectacles gave her an impish look, especially since they always seemed to be perched a little low on her nose.

He couldn't help himself. He pushed up her glasses. 'You could probably tighten the little screws in the corner.'

Her cheeks grew quite pink then, and he liked the overall effect almost well enough to kiss her, except it had been ages since he had kissed a woman, and he probably wasn't all that good any more, if he ever had been.

Why couldn't he just say goodbye? Just a word and bow and off he would go, back to war. All he could do was stand there, filled with so much regret he wanted to drop to his knees in utter misery.

'You're leaving,' she said quietly.

'Time and tide, Brandon,' he told her. 'I want to talk to the Marines at the wharf, and get on board the *Perseverance*.' Unable to look into her eyes, he looked at the young women watching them. 'You are making friends. Are they to be your pupils?'

'They are,' she said, 'and any of the sisters who care to join us.' She frowned. 'It isn't much of a way to fight Boney, though, is it? Not like my sisters.'

'Be your own person, Brandon,' he said, not meaning to sound like a Colonel of Marines, but unable to help himself. 'I mean… No, that's what I mean.'

'Grow up?' she asked him, her eyes on his. 'And make up my mind about things?'

As he said his goodbye, it occurred to him that maybe, just maybe, he meant something to her. Too bad he had so much to do. Too bad armies were on the march. Too bad Laura Brittle stood in the doorway, watching them.

He wanted to clasp Polly Brandon in his arms. He had watched over her on the *Perseverance* and he was uneasy about leaving her without his protection. *Yes, I am proprietary*, he wanted to shout to Laura Brittle. *Why is it your business?*

He did nothing of the sort. 'Stay off the water, Brandon, and you should be all right,' he said gruffly, then turned on his heel as smartly as any Marine on parade, and left her standing alone in the courtyard.

Chapter Seven

Life at the Convent of the Sacred Name answered every wish of Polly's heart. She was busy; she was with a beloved sister; she was doing worthwhile work. In the month since Colonel Junot left her so alone in the courtyard, she was everything but happy.

A sensible woman, she assured herself that the pain of his departure would go away. Even her sheltered life in a female academy had taught her that people come and go, exerting their influence for a brief time. She remembered one dance instructor—an Italian *émigré*—whom all the students had swooned over. He left, after a six-weeks' course of instruction. By the end of the following week, all she could remember about him was his last name and his brown eyes.

Colonel Junot was proving to be more difficult to forget. True, he was handsome by anyone's standards, made even more beguiling by the unexpected brogue when he spoke. She, who had endured too many years of constant reminder about posture—head up and chin back—could only envy his elegant way of carrying himself. Beyond the superficial, Colonel Junot was stalwart, capable, and kind, and she had never met anyone like him.

That he orbited far out of her sphere was a given, and should have made it easier to forget him. She couldn't, though. She thought she knew why, but there was no one she could talk to, not even Laura, who had seemed relieved when Colonel Junot was but a distant figure in a scarlet coat, far below at the navy wharf.

I should set Laura's mind at ease, Polly thought, as the days passed. *I'm being foolish to even think Colonel Junot has spared a single thought for me since he said goodbye.* Trouble was, she didn't know what to say, so said nothing, choosing instead to throw herself into the work ordained for her in the convent, trusting to time to smooth away any sharp edges. As the days passed, it did; given another year or two, she knew she could forget Colonel Junot.

The Convent of the Sacred Name had been a large community, before the French desecrated its holiest places, and violated and murdered so many of its gentle inhabitants. Most of the surviving nuns had retreated to the safety of their motherhouse in Lisbon. The few who returned were resolute beings, which made them superbly useful in establishing and maintaining smooth order in Philemon's satellite hospital.

Essentially, these were women not afraid of anything. Philemon explained it to Polly one afternoon when he had a moment to sit in the courtyard with his little son in his arms. 'It's a fine line, my dear. People who endure the worst are either broken by it or strengthened.' He ruffled his son's auburn hair. 'I refer you to your own sisters.'

Polly was not slow to understand. 'These young girls I am to teach—they seem to always move in the shadows. Where do they fall in the spectrum of what you are saying?'

Philemon passed his hand in front of his eyes, as if trying to brush away terrible visions. 'So many women were treated so cruelly by the French. Many took their own lives. Others were turned off by their families, who could not manage such shame, in the middle of other misery. Mind you, loss of what they call "honour" is a terrible thing to citizens of this peninsula. Bless their hearts, most of these girls still love their little ones, even conceived in such a way. I own that I admire women, and these brave souls in particular.'

Polly leaned against her brother-in-law. 'I should be more than a teacher, Philemon?'

'Aye, much more,' he replied firmly. 'Be a friend.'

That was her mandate, she decided, after another night of tossing and turning in her narrow bed. When she rose with the dawn, she decided that was her last sleepless night; there was work to be done. Everyone around her had been affected by war, which made her concerns puny, indeed. War meant sacrifice; it was no respecter of persons. She could understand that. Obviously Colonel Junot did. When he had left her so alone, he had not looked back.

Before she began, she needed an ally. She found her sister sitting quietly on a bench, obviously enjoying a moment of rare leisure. 'You have a look of enquiry, dearest,' she said to Polly, and patted the bench.

Polly sat down. 'I need an ally—someone who speaks English at least a little, so I can communicate.' She leaned close to Laura. 'What do you call these young girls?'

'I've been calling them "little mothers" in Portuguese—*pouco mães*—because they have been helping me so materially with Danny. I remind them I could never do my work without their help.' She sighed. 'They just don't quite believe they have any value. Learning English would be a start.'

'Who can help me?'

Laura sat back, her eyes thoughtful. 'There is only one woman, Sister Maria Madelena. She is a dragon, but she speaks English and Spanish.'

'A dragon?'

'Indeed. I would say she is more Pym than Pym, without the hypocrisy.'

The sisters looked at each other and burst into laughter. 'Where might I find this paragon?' Polly asked.

'Try the old chapel.'

So Polly made her way to the small chapel, which had existed since the Middle Ages. It was dark and redolent of centuries of incense, but there was a small nun, ferociously clicking the beads on her rosary, impatience evident in every contour of her compact body. She must have heard Polly enter, but Sister Maria Madelena did not turn around.

More interested than frightened now, Polly sat down quietly on one of the few benches near the entrance. She looked around her at the simple stations on the cross and wondered how many prayers had risen through the incense-darkened ceiling, low and decidedly pre-Gothic. *What did they pray about then?* Polly asked herself. *The Black Death? Moors at the gates?*

Finally the click of Sister Maria Madelena's beads ended with a finality that made Polly smile, in spite of her fears at approaching Laura's dragon. Polly jumped when the nun slapped the flat of her hand against the stone floor, as if impatient for God to smile down on the Portuguese, who had been getting the short end of some cosmic stick for so many years now. She turned around quickly and Polly swallowed. She opened her mouth to speak, but Sister Maria Madelena spoke first.

'I need your help, Miss Brandon.'

Surprised, Polly stared at her for a moment. 'Actually, I…I…was going to say the same thing to you, Sister,' she managed to blurt out, unnerved by the jagged scar that ran from under her wimple by her ear, across her face under her nose, cut through the corner of her mouth, and wound up on her neck, where it vanished from sight under her habit.

She would have been almost pretty, but for the scar. *Don't stare*, Polly tried to tell herself, but it was too late. All she could do was stare, and wish for the first time that she could telescope herself back through the weeks and into Miss Pym's classroom again, where no one saw such sights.

'I'm sorry,' she said finally. 'I should not stare. Please forgive me.'

If she expected the dragon to suddenly hiss fire at her, she was mistaken. The woman smiled, or at least, it would have been a smile, except that the corner of her mouth drooped, rendered her more sad than terrifying.

'Considering Our Lord, these are burdens easily borne,' she said, the voice of practicality. 'We have not met, but I have heard your name from the *pouco mães*. Sit, sit.'

Her English was excellent, and she wasted not a moment. 'My dear, what is it you want of me?'

Polly had to laugh then. She needed to make up for her rudeness, and Sister Maria Madelena did not seem to be one to bamboozle. 'You asked first, Sister,' she said, seeing nothing but kindness in the nun's eyes, belying the fearsome scar.

'I did, but you are the guest here in our convent,' she replied graciously. 'Very well, then. It is not a small thing. Would you be willing to help me at night, when the little mothers cry in their nightmares?'

Polly could not help the shudder that ran through her body. 'What could I possibly do?' she asked, when she could speak.

'Hold their hands. Sit with them until the terror passes. I cannot be everywhere.'

It was simply said, as if she had asked Polly to water the flowers in the courtyard. 'I will help you,' Polly said, thinking how Colonel Junot had helped her without a complaint in her worst moments; surely she could do no less. 'Of course I will help. When do I start?'

'Tonight.' Sister Madelena rose quickly. 'Now I have much to do.' She nodded at Polly and starting walking briskly to the low door, where she ducked and paused. 'What was it you came to see me about, *senhorita*?'

It seemed so unimportant. 'I wanted your help in teaching the little mothers English.' Polly stood up.

'Of course I will help,' Sister Maria Madelena said. 'When you have their hearts, my dear, by watching over them at night, you will easily engage their minds.'

It sounded so true that Polly could only nod. 'Your English is excellent, Sister,' she said. 'Where did you learn it?'

Sister Madelena looked at her, as if wondering how much truth to tell. 'I haven't always been a nun, and I am well named, Senhorita Brandon. I used to be mistress to an Englishman who managed Sandeman's vineyards.

He thought if he talked English loud and slow enough, I would learn.'

'How is your hearing?' Polly asked, laughing.

'My English is better. I will come for you tonight after Compline.'

Polly changed her mind several times before Compline, but when there was a soft tap on her door, she rose at once.

'Follow me,' Sister Maria Madelena said, returning with her to the older part of the convent, the section far away from the satellite hospital. 'At first, Surgeon Brittle thought the little mothers would prefer to be together, so we housed them in the old refectory,' the nun said. 'They kept waking each other with tears and shrieks, so we decided on the old cells.'

Polly rubbed her arms, feeling the hairs rise on them. It was the middle of summer, but she shivered. 'Their children?'

'They sleep with their little ones, those who have children.'

Even though every fibre in her body screamed out to stop, Polly let herself be led down the corridor to its intersection, where a padded chair had been placed, looking out of place amid the austerity of a much earlier age.

'Make yourself comfortable here,' Sister Maria Madelena said, as she fluffed up a pillow.

'I will be at the other end of the corridor. If you hear someone cry out, just go to the chamber.'

'And do what?' Polly asked, utterly unprepared.

'What your heart tells you to do.' She left Polly alone.

Polly sat, deeply aware of her utter inadequacy. She leaned back carefully, afraid to make the smallest sound and waken anyone from already uneasy slumber. *You could have stayed with Nana*, she reminded herself. It sounded so cowardly to even think such a thing that she felt ashamed. She thought of Colonel Junot then, and the kindness in his brown eyes when he had told her not to sell herself short. She yearned to see him again so she could tell him she was trying, even as she hoped this would be the night when no one cried out.

She did not get her wish. The smell of incense was cloying but comforting, and there was just the hint of orange blossoms and gardenia from a courtyard they had passed. She drew her legs up under her and rested her cheek on her hand.

Polly sat up, straining her ears. The lowest keening seemed to come up from the very stones on the floor, causing her to clutch at her arms in fear. The sound stopped; she was prepared to swear she had never heard it. When it started again, it was louder, and she knew right where to go, provided she wasn't too afraid to get up from the chair.

Shame on you. Suppose Colonel Junot had chosen to ignore you? Polly told herself. She rose, drew a deep breath, and walked down the corridor, pausing at one door, then moved to the next, until she found the right one. She opened it.

The window was tiny, but the moon shone in bravely, casting its light on an empty bed. Alarmed, Polly closed the door behind her, then let out her own cry of terror as someone grabbed her by the wrist.

The young girl had been hiding behind the door, pressed against the wall. She barely came up to Polly's shoulder, making her wonder what age the French soldiers considered too young to violate. With a great gulp, she swallowed her fear and put her hand on the girl's hand, not trying to pry off her cold fingers, but just to let her know she had a friend. Whether any of that would be conveyed by her almost-involuntary gesture, Polly had no idea, but it was the only tool in her skimpy arsenal.

Since her Portuguese was non-existent, Polly thought of Sister Maria Madelena's well-meaning British lover and spoke as softly as she could. 'You've had a fright, haven't you? You must be tired. Let me help you back to bed.'

She moved, expecting resistance, but found none. Polly wondered if the girl had been sleep-walking. She led her back to bed, tucked her in, and then looked around for a baby. There was no crib. This must be one of the girls without babies that Sister Maria had mentioned. She found a doll made of surgical towels like the one her nephew adored, and tucked it in the crook of the girl's arm. With a sigh of relief, the girl—scarcely more than a child, herself—rested her cheek against it and closed her eyes as she caressed the towel doll. Polly sat with her until her breathing was slow and steady.

Shaken, Polly returned to her chair in the hall. She sat for only a moment, then hurried to another room, where a shriek was followed by a young child's startled cry. Polly ran to the room to find a young woman huddled on her pillow, her eyes wide and staring. She had wakened her child, who sat up in his smaller bed, crying. Polly went to the child first, soothing the little boy until he returned to sleep.

Polly sat on the bed, her mind a complete blank. In desperation, she started to hum a lullaby she had heard Laura sing to Danny. To her relief, the girl's eyes began to close and her head drooped forwards. She resisted Polly's first effort to induce her to lie down. After two more choruses of the simple tune, she did not object to sliding between her sheets again and closing her eyes. She did not release Polly's hand until she was deep in slumber.

'I understand you,' Polly whispered. 'Colonel Junot held my hand when I could have sworn the ship was sinking. Can I do any less for you?'

So it went all night. She went from room to room down her side of the intersecting corridor while Sister Maria Madelena did the same in the other hall. Some rooms she went to twice to console young girls too soon old. One girl could not be consoled until Polly took her in her arms and held her as a mother holds a child. Her horror at such terrible treatment at the hands of French soldiers turned to rage that anyone would harrow up the innocent. When dawn came, Polly knew she would never be the same again, not if she lived another fifty years.

Exhausted in body, one part of her brain wanted to sleep until the war was over. The other part told her she must return every night, until the last victim in the world had been consoled. She wanted to tell Sister Maria Madelena everything she had learned, but she was too tired to do more than nod, when the nun came to her and said it was time to leave.

They walked in silence. Soon Polly was back in the part of the convent familiar to her. She smiled to hear Philemon and her sister in the dining room, laughing over something, ready to begin their own hard days as she had just ended hers. She turned to the nun.

'How can you do that, night after night?'

'I cannot sleep at night.' The nun looked away, as if wondering what to say. 'I know what it is like.'

Polly didn't even try to hide her shock. 'Oh, Sister,' she said, her voice breaking. 'I...I... Oh, I didn't know.'

'When the French came, Mr Wilson brought me here, thinking it would be safe. We retreated to the kitchen when the...the *crapaud* came. She told me not to, but I tried to defend the Mother Abbess with one of the cook's knives. They took it from me, and then all of them held me down for their own amusement...' She couldn't go on.

'I didn't know,' Polly said again, appalled.

'When I thought they were done, they used my own knife against me. I was determined not to die, though all around me were dead.' She shrugged. 'Who else would bury them?'

Polly gasped. 'Surely you did not...?'

'I had help. Not all of the community were murdered. We made our way down the coast to Lisbon and safety. Mr Wilson was killed here in Porto, defending casks of port—imagine how unimportant that is, Polly. I decided to join the order.'

Polly could not detect an ounce of self-pity in Sister Maria Madelena's voice. 'And you are here again.'

'There is work to be done,' the nun said, her voice brusque again. 'Go to sleep now, if you can. Compline will come too soon, I fear.' She peered at Polly. 'You will join me again tonight?'

'Certainly.'

'Excellent!' Sister Maria Madelena nodded and turned towards the sound of children in the courtyard. 'Your nephew Danny and João have turned into such ringleaders! I had better go administer some discipline, or we will be accused of raising wolves in Porto.'

'João?' she asked, remembering the dark-haired child who played most often with Danny.

'Yes, my dear. He is *my* son.'

Chapter Eight

Polly knew she would not sleep, so she did not try. She sat at the desk in her room, took out a sheet of paper, and began a letter she would never send.

She wrote 'Dear Colonel Junot', then paused, because the word 'dear' loomed up at her like a vulgar word, even though thousands of letters began that way, even those from prosaic counting houses. She drew a line through it anyway, then crumpled the page. She reminded herself that the letter was going nowhere, and wrote 'Dearest Hugh' on another sheet.

Freed of that constraint, she said whatever she wanted. She described the long night of comforting sorrow of such a magnitude she scarcely could grasp it. The words poured on to the page, and another like it and another, as she wrote of the young girl who spent her entire night patting the bedclothes and searching the room for her little one, a half-French infant strangled at birth by a midwife in a remote Portuguese hamlet.

She faltered a moment, then wrote of the girls whose troubled minds compelled them to act out their rapes over and over. Maybe even more frightening were the young girls who lay perfectly still in as small a space as they could contort their figures, eyes wide and staring in the dark.

Exhausted and weary with tears, Polly wrote it all to Hugh Junot, her friend, so he would know what a pathetically tiny bit of good she was doing at Sacred Name. 'Knowing you'—she put down the pen, unable to continue for a moment. She picked it up, reminding herself calmly that she did know the man, and knew what he wanted to hear from her. 'Here is what I have learned: it is possible to survive, when all hope has perished.'

She didn't need to reread anything, because the experience of that night would never leave her mind, no matter how many years passed. Polly picked up the pencil again, rubbing it against the end of the wooden desk to get one more sentence from the lead, one more line no one would ever see. 'I wish you were here, Hugh. I would feel more brave.'

'I miss you,' she said out loud as she folded the letter. 'Your loving Brandon.'

Hugh kept himself supremely busy in Lisbon, which was not a hard thing to do, considering the confusion, intrigue, and bustle in the old seaport. Over excellent port, which only served to remind him of the town he had just left, Hugh listened as the Major in charge of the Marine detachment told him of the summer campaigns underway throughout Spain.

'Where are the armies?' Hugh asked.

'Sir, we believe Wellington is drawing out a fight near Salamanca. After that, if he wins, the road is open to Madrid,' the Major said. He tipped the last of the wine into Hugh's glass. 'Could this be our last summer in this wretched country? Shall we drink to that?'

They did. The major invited Hugh to join him at his favourite brothel, but Hugh shook his head, returning some vague regret about reports to write.

Hours later, restless and tangling his sheets into ropes, Hugh wished he had accepted the Major's invitation. He knew how badly he needed the comfort of a woman's body. Trouble was, he only wanted one body, and its owner was far away, unaware of his admiration.

His thoughts were not chaste. He had never wanted a woman more than he wanted Polly Brandon. He got up and went to the window. *How does anyone explain this feeling?* he asked himself as he watched the Marine sentries below, taking their prescribed steps, about faces, and returns. *I never expected this. How is it I have lived on the earth this long, and never felt this way before?* It was just as well he had not accompanied Major Buttram to the brothel; he would only have disappointed whomever he paid to service him.

He was disgusted with himself. In her polite way, Laura Brittle had made it plain he was not to reappear at the convent in Vila Nova de Gaia. She was a sister watching out for her own, and he obviously did not meet her standards. In misery, he knew that if he paraded his rank before Laura Brittle, the family wealth, and a handsome estate in a charmed corner of Scotland, it would make no difference. Laura Brittle thought him too old, and he was not good enough.

He paced the floor, angry at the unfairness of it all. He tried to remind himself of the misery around him in this tragic country, which had sacrificed so much, but it didn't work this time. He could only think of his sacrifices, and how this war had cost him wife and children. There was no one he could make love with whenever the mood grabbed them; no bright eyes looking into his as they shared the same pillow; no smile to greet him across the breakfast table, telling him prosaically of bills and schooling; no one to sit with in a pew on Sunday morning; no one to tease him when he stepped on her foot during a waltz, as he invariably would have; no one to turn the page for him when he played the piano; no one. It chilled him to the bone and gave him grief beyond parallel.

He sat at his desk. Laura Brittle be damned; he would write to Polly Brandon, even though it was an ill-mannered thing to do. 'My dearest love' came from his pen. He shared his whole heart to her, page after page, leaving nothing unsaid of an intimate nature. He had never been one to gild a lily, either, and he was too mature to begin now. When he finished, he signed it 'Love from all my heart, Hugh', then immediately ripped it into tatters.

'That's out of your system, you randy goat,' he murmured, and took out another sheet. He began this one 'Greetings, Brandon, from someone with rag manners. I suppose I deserve a slap across the face for being so bold as to write to you, but I am wondering how you are.'

This letter was as easy to write as the first

one. He described Lisbon, that dirty, charming city so full of intrigue. He wrote of the Marines he had chatted to, his conversations with the great and the lowly. He told her he wasn't satisfied he had learned enough to write a report yet, but that autumn would probably see him back in Plymouth, doing precisely that, and chained to a conference table again. 'What, no sympathy from you, Brandon? You don't like a whiner? Take care of yourself. Hugh Junot.'

He read it through and found nothing objectionable. Because he had the liveliest confidence the Brittles would make sure Polly never received it, should he be so bold as to send it, he added a postscript on the other side: 'Damn me, if I don't miss you, Brandon.'

He addressed it to 'Brandon Polly, Convent of the Sacred Name, Vila Nova de Gaia', knowing full well he would never send it. Still, it looked good on his desk, almost as though these were normal times and he was writing to a beloved wife far away. There was no reason he couldn't just leave it there and return to bed.

When he woke hours later, he saw that the letter was gone, along with yesterday's towel and last night's slop jar. After his initial jolt, he found himself surprised that Portuguese servants were so efficient. He relied on the Brittles to intercept his bit of nonsense.

Polly knew she would never get accustomed to the misery of her nightly duty at Sacred Name, but as July wore on, she learned to adjust to it. Sister Maria Madelena was right—because of her tender sympathy during night-time ordeals, the little mothers had no hesitation in sitting with her in the courtyard during the afternoons and learning what little English she had time to teach. It went well; so well, in fact, that she started taking out the letter to Colonel Junot she was never going to post and adding on to it, describing the mothers and children and their efforts to learn English. 'You were right, Colonel,' she wrote. 'I am useful here.'

Her usefulness continued in a way she had not anticipated. She was not even certain she liked the next change—travelling upriver with Sister Maria Madelena to shepherd other young girls to the sanctuary of the Sacred Name.

'How do you learn of them?' Polly asked, as they sat with the children in the afternoon sun.

Sister Maria kissed her son, then sent him back to play. 'There is a network of interested folk who hear things. We take a *barco rabelo* upriver to the village of São Jobim, where we

find the young girls waiting for us, some Portuguese, some Spanish.'

'It's not dangerous?'

The nun shrugged. 'Who is safe anywhere
in Portugal? There has been no trouble in more
than a year, although we always travel with a
small detachment of Marines. You will be safe.
Ask your sister.'

Polly did. 'I think that is an excellent idea,'
Laura told her. 'Sister Maria tells me you already have a wonderful rapport with the young
mothers. Perhaps it is because you are so young,
yourself.'

'Laura, I am not so young, not compared to
some of them. I'll be nineteen this autumn.'

Laura seemed almost surprised. 'Why, yes,
I suppose you will,' she murmured. 'I was reminded recently that I am at fault in thinking
you younger than you are. You may go upriver.'

Her only regret in the journey was the mode
of transportation, one of the flat-bottomed sailing craft used to transport kegs of port wine
downriver from wineries farther up the Douro.
The war had disrupted the thriving business upriver and the *barcos* were used now to transport
people across the Douro to Oporto proper, and
to move what wine was available closer to Vila

Nova and the ships anchored at the mouth of the mighty river.

'Ships are the bane of my existence,' Polly muttered the next morning to the nun as she allowed a Marine to help her into the craft as it bobbed at the wharf. 'I will claim a spot near the gunwale and try not to make a total fool of myself.'

The wind blew inshore, so the *barco* sailed along against the current, expertly guided by a Portuguese sailor at the long pole in the stern. She and Sister Maria Madelena watched the river narrow and its sides steepen as they travelled through the canyon cut by the Douro. Throughout the morning, Polly watched other *barcos rabelos* coming downstream flying British ensigns. There were wounded men on the deck, with surgeons bending over them. Last week, news had reached the convent of a battle in north central Spain in the Arapiles hills near Salamanca, and Philemon had told Laura over the breakfast table to prepare for casualties.

'My sister tells me even the army sends the worst of the worst to Philemon's hospital,' she couldn't help saying proudly to Sister Maria. 'It was only supposed to be a satellite naval hospital.' She looked closer. 'Oh, Sister, excuse me. I didn't realise you were praying.'

* * *

It was dusk by the time they reached the village of São Jobim. 'Ordinarily, we try to leave earlier in the morning, so we can make the trip in one day,' Sister Maria Madelena said, as they approached the wharf.

There were few people about. Polly couldn't see any men at all. She looked at Sister Maria Madelena, a question in her eyes.

'The men have gone with the army or the partisans,' the nun explained. 'So it is, in every village in Portugal.'

What happened once the *barco* docked was a marvel of efficiency, testament to how many times Sister Maria Madelena had made this voyage of rescue. From the Marines to the Portuguese mariners, everyone worked quickly. Escorted by the Marines, they were helped ashore and into the church across the square in a matter of minutes.

'I thought you said we were in no danger?' Polly asked.

'That is correct,' the nun replied, as she nodded to the priest approaching them. 'We are merely careful. Good evening, Pai Belo. Do you have someone for me?'

He did, pointing to a young woman huddled on a bench and shivering, despite the warmth of a late July sun only just now setting west across the Douro. Polly glanced at Sister Maria, as her eyes caught the motion of the priest passing a note to her. It was done so quickly she might have mistaken it. Well, never mind, Polly thought, going to the girl and sitting beside her. She knew enough Portuguese to murmur, 'You are safe now', not touching her, but sitting close.

Sister Maria joined her. 'Pai says she is from across the border, where other young girls have come lately.'

'It's so far,' Polly said, resting her hand gently on the girl's shoulder.

'Not so far,' Sister Maria contradicted. 'I come from beyond the border myself. I have a brother—' She stopped, as if to remember him. 'I have a brother there. It is not so far.'

They spent the night in the church, sharing a frugal meal of bread and cheese, while the Marines ate their own rations and stood sentry duty. Sister Maria and the priest conversed in low tones, with occasional glances at Polly and the young woman—her name was Dolores—who rested, silent and fearful, her eyes wide.

Before the rising sun cleared the canyons of the Douro, they were on the water again, relying this time on the strong current to carry them west to Oporto. After resigning herself to her by now obligatory offering to Neptune or

Poseidon, or whatever mischievous god governed the waves that so discomfited her, Polly turned her face to the sun and held Dolores's hand for most of the rapid trip downriver to the sea.

They arrived by noon on the speedier return trip, docking at the navy wharf and sharing a cart to the convent with Laura and other wounded from upriver. Swallowing her fears in the face of her sister's single-minded duty, she let Laura press her into duty, washing dirty limbs and cutting away bloodsoaked clothing. 'If I didn't need you so badly…' Laura began, and then her words trailed off as Philemon—his arm red to the elbow—directed her to another crisis.

After a night of unending work, Polly fell into bed, not bothering to remove her clothes, now as stained and reeking as those of the wounded she had helped. Her head crunched on paper, but she only touched it and closed her eyes.

The warmth of the afternoon sun woke her, coupled with her own hunger and the twine tickling her nose. She brushed at her face and opened her eyes so see a letter bound in heavy paper and tied in a bow. She thought she recognised the casual handwriting, and 'Brandon

Polly' confirmed it. Colonel Junot had written to her.

Polly took her time opening the letter, savouring every second. As she opened it, she wondered if Laura knew she had received a letter from Colonel Junot. Maybe in the press of yesterday's activity, someone else had put the message on her bed.

She took a deep breath and began to read. *Greetings, Brandon, from someone with rag manners*, she read. *I suppose I deserve a slap across the face for being so bold as to write to you...* She read the letter, full of news of Lisbon and his work there, ran her finger slowly across his name, caressing it, and read it again. *I have been on your mind*, she thought, so pleased that she hugged herself, then laughed out loud.

It was out of the question that she should be so presumptuous as to answer his letter, and she knew it. She glanced at the letter again, wishing she dared to write back.

If only. The letter contained nothing lover-like or anything that she couldn't show to Laura or Philemon. So she would have thought, if she hadn't turned over the final sheet and seen the postscript. 'Damn me, if I don't miss you, Brandon.'

A pleasant warmth descended on her then. The sole human being on earth who had seen her at her noxious worst missed her. She gently ran her finger across the words. He missed her.

She hid the letter next to the intemperate one she had written to him and never sent. Laura never questioned her about the letter, so Polly knew she had neither seen nor delivered it. Polly gave herself a mental shake and went back to work.

Chapter Nine

Hugh knew Polly Brandon would never answer his letter, if she even received it. He felt a little foolish as he listened every day for the drum rolls in the Marine barracks indicating mail call. He was a Lieutenant Colonel; any correspondence intended for him would have been taken to him. Still, he listened for the drum roll.

He had made the mistake of accepting Major Buttram's invitation to the brothel and spent an hour with a languid lass who otherwise would have pleased him greatly, if he hadn't been thinking of Polly. Too soon he found himself wishing that it was Polly's heels digging into his kidneys as he rode her, and Polly's breath warming his cheek, and Polly's head turning from side to side as he satisfied her, or at least, when she pretended so. Something told him Polly would never pretend, not if he was at the helm.

July turned into August and then early September, as he took one short hop to the Mediterranean on a sloop of war and visited the Marines on Malta, always a charming city to visit. He tried to drink himself silly one night, but that was an even greater failure than the prostitute in Lisbon. He had no real liking for any spirits other than grog, which had always been a source of amusement to his brother officers, who generally assumed he was, at the very least, a Madeira man. All he had to show for an evening in his cups was a head as big as all outdoors and Brandon's inability to maintain stuff in the gut where it belonged.

If women and liquor couldn't assuage him, he had more success writing his report back in Lisbon, busying himself with facts and figures. That lasted about three days, until he found himself staring at the wall and seeing Polly Brandon in the stucco. 'All right, lassie,' he said one afternoon to his wall, 'did ye or did ye not even receive my letter? If ye did, congratulations on having superior manners and not responding. If ye didna, well then, I'm nowhere different than I was when I started speculating. Lord, what a chowderhead. Listen to your sister and stay away from Marines.'

And that was that. Or it would have been, if he hadn't decided to take the next frigate north to Ferrol Station for a look around. His only interesting official correspondence had come encrypted from Plymouth. When the translated message reached his desk, he read of Admiral Sir Home Popham's campaign into the Bay of Biscay, with Santander as the hard-won prize. 'Major Buttram, I want to watch our Johnnies in action,' he said the next morning as he packed. 'Is something heading north at least to Ferrol Station?'

Something was—a sloop of war captained by a young Lieutenant. Considering all of his years rubbing shoulders with the navy, Hugh should have known they could not slide by Oporto without stopping, considering the drinking habits of the Royal Navy's officers. The sloop's skipper had a heavy purse from thirsty men who wanted to turn gold into port, alchemy common in the navy.

'We'll be here a day at least, I fear, sir,' the Lieutenant said. 'I've promised port to ever so many ships. Um, if you're bored, I hear there are excellent cafés in Oporto, and the women are the…um…easiest in Portugal,' he concluded in a rush, his face red.

The women are not easy in Oporto, Hugh thought sourly. 'I'll remain on board,' he said, and turned on his heel.

By early September, Polly had made four trips upriver with Sister Maria Madelena. Typically, they left before sunrise, to ensure a quick return that day. There were no more lighters descending the Douro, bearing wounded, because the season of campaigning was winding down. Dispatches had reached Oporto that Beau Wellesley and his army had marched in triumph to Madrid, and that several French armies in the region were in motion, as well, some moving towards the capital city and others scattering. No one knew what to believe.

'And still there are those who need our help,' Sister Maria Madelena said, as they came in sight of São Jobim.

Polly knew the routine now. She hurried ashore and followed the sentries into the church, where the heavy door swung shut and was barred. There were two girls this time, one with a baby. Both of them, Spanish sisters, shrank from the sight of the Marines, even though Sister Maria Madelena said '*Ingleses*' over and over.

Polly wished she felt less uneasy about this run. Lately, she had been watching Sister Maria

Madelena and the priest more closely. They almost always stepped aside where no one could hear, to talk in low whispers, and sometimes exchange notes. They seemed to be arguing this time. The priest shook his head and there was no note.

'We would be a happier country without *any* soldiers,' Sister Maria said as they prepared to leave.

Polly wondered if she should speak. *What could it hurt?* she thought at last, and cleared her throat.

'Sister, did you feel that someone was watching us this time?' Said out loud, it sounded foolish; she regretted her words at once. Sister Maria Madelena would think her a coward. She never asked about the notes; the one time she had, the nun had ignored her.

'What's this?' the nun asked gently. 'Did you feel a prickling of your neck hairs? Fingers along your spine?'

'I am being foolish, I know,' she apologised.

'No, you're not. I felt it, too. I look around, then I remind myself that we are on God's errand.' She shrugged. 'The feeling always passes.'

Maybe for you, Polly thought.

Despite her misgivings, which Polly knew better than to voice again, the trip downriver was as calm as the other ones. She cautiously complimented herself on keeping down that morning's meal, and almost enjoyed the race down to the sea, propelled by a splendid current as the Douro rushed out of the mountains and gradually changed character into a dignified, formidable river that widened with each mile closer to the Atlantic.

They reached Vila Nova as the sun was low in the sky. The slower swells of the turning tide made the bobbing of the small vessel an instrument of torture to her sorely tried equilibrium.

Small, but bristling with guns, a sloop of war was tied to the dock. She glanced at it, then stared, because Colonel Junot stood there, gazing towards the convent. *It cannot be*, she thought first, mainly because she did not want him to see her looking so green under her unladylike tan, and getting ready to lean over the side of the *barco*. Then, *Perhaps he will not notice me*, she told herself, as she vomited into the river.

If the Spanish girl's baby had not started to cry, maybe he would not have looked around in surprise. When he saw her, he flashed as broad a smile as she had ever seen.

He doffed his hat to her, and bowed.

'I am mortified,' Polly whispered to Sister

Maria. 'He probably thinks I get seasick in my bathtub.'

'That is Colonel…how do you say…Junnit? He is the one who…'

Polly nodded. 'I did not really think I would see him again. Perhaps he will not come on shore.'

She couldn't look, but Sister Maria Madelena had no qualms about the matter. 'He appears to be heading to the gangplank, Polly,' she whispered back.

Faster than she would have credited, he was standing beside the *barco*, ready to give her a hand. He helped her over the gunwale and on to the dock, beamed at her, then held out his hand to the young woman with the baby, who hesitated.

'Almira, he is my friend,' Polly murmured in her sketchy Spanish, which changed the girl's worry to relief. Shyly, she handed her baby up to Polly, then took Colonel Junot's hand and let him help her on to the dock.

Suddenly too shy to say anything, Polly stood there with the baby. The Colonel was not smiling now, which caused her to look at him more closely, and then quickly hand the baby over to his mother.

'Colonel?' Something had happened, and she hadn't the slightest idea what it was.

'What were you doing upriver?' he asked, his tone chilly.

She felt like a child under his question. 'We… we retrieve young women from the interior of Portugal who have been…' She hesitated.

'…raped by the French,' he concluded bluntly, as she felt her face flame. He took her arm, a grasp more urgent than angry. 'Brandon, what harsh duty is yours at this convent?'

He took her to a bench and sat her down, then sat down beside her. He seemed to know he was taxing her; she watched him take a deep breath and visibly calm himself. He did not release her arm, but his grip loosened.

She almost wished now she had sent the letter in the bottom of her trunk. It would be easier than explaining to a man what she did. She took a breath of her own. 'Oh, Colonel, it *is* harsh, but not for me. The *pouco mães* wake up at night with terrible dreams. I go from room to room, trying to comfort them.'

His frown only deepened. 'That is not a job for one so young. Is there no one else who can do it?'

She winced, because he had touched a vulnerable place, one that had begun to trouble Laura. 'Colonel, they respond to me, and I certainly have their trust. I sleep in the mornings, and by afternoon, teach a little English here and there, although I must admit I seem to be learning more Portuguese. Some Spanish, too.'

She said that to hopefully make him smile a little, but he did not. What he said surprised her.

He released her arm then and sighed, leaning back against the railing of the wharf, something she doubted he did very often, considering his military bearing. 'Don't go upriver again, Brandon,' he said finally.

'It's safe, Colonel,' she reminded him. 'Everyone says so.'

'Nothing is safe in the Peninsula,' he replied, and she could not overlook the concern in his voice. 'Armies are marching, and whenever armies march, all kinds of people are put in motion.'

'We don't go so far upriver. Just to São Jobim: six hours up, four hours back, or less.'

'It's too far,' he said flatly. 'Don't do it, Brandon.'

Suddenly, she wanted to agree with him, tell him about her misgivings, and never leave the shelter of the convent again. She might have, if she hadn't looked at Sister Maria Madelena just then, as the nun helped the two sisters with the baby into the back of the ox-led wagon that met every vessel.

She stood up. 'I have to go now,' she told him. 'Sister Maria needs me.'

* * *

Hugh had seldom felt helpless in his maritime career. He felt helpless now, because he had no *force majeure* to work on Polly Brandon, nothing a husband would have. He had no tie, no commitment, nothing beyond his feeble effort to get a good woman with charity on her mind to listen to his worries that, for all he knew, were totally unfounded. It was a position he did not like.

Still, he could tell that she left his side reluctantly. For the tiniest moment, he wondered what she would do if he told her he loved her and would she please listen to him? He was being absurd, of course—too bad for her, too bad for him.

Since she seemed disinclined to leave him there, even as the wagon began its slow trip to the top of the bluff, he walked beside her. He noted that her hair was twisted in its funny knot, with a skewer through it. Without thinking, he suddenly pulled out the wooden wand, and smiled when she laughed and hit his arm.

'Laura calls me a ragbag,' she said cheerfully, as she took the skewer from him and wound up her topknot again. 'Nana would scold me and ask how I ever planned to find a husband.'

Just look at me seriously, he thought. *You'd have your answer.* 'It's a good question, Brandon,' he said, thinking how stupid it was the moment he said it.

'Gentlemen never look past my spectacles, Colonel, so it doesn't matter. Philemon tells me to forge my own way, precisely as my sisters have done. Everyone has advice,' she grumbled.

She peered at him then in her kindly way that made him understand, no matter how grudgingly, what Sister Maria and the pitiful female dregs of war already knew: Polly Brandon was good and loyal and not afraid, no matter what she might say about herself to the contrary. They probably did need her. Too bad the thought gave him no comfort.

'Come to dinner this evening,' Polly asked him. 'Colonel? Colonel? When I used to wool-gather like you are doing, Miss Pym would rap my knuckles.'

Wordlessly he held out his hand, palm down, and she laughed, even as she blushed. Delightful.

'I must say no,' he replied, as they continued their slow walk to the convent. 'I have already promised myself to the Lieutenant of Marines at the dock.'

She stopped. So did he. A fine frown line appeared between her eyes and she pursed her lips ever so slightly, just enough to make his back break out in sweat. 'Are you avoiding me?' she asked.

'No, ma'am, I am not,' he lied, 'even though dinner with Lieutenant Stephens means the mess hall. It is another opportunity to speak to the men I am interested in hearing from, to complete my report. I have a purpose here, too, you know.'

It came out more sharply than he intended, and Polly had nothing more to say as they walked to the top of the hill. He had shut her down, the last thing he wanted to do, especially when he was so worried.

'Perhaps I could stop by at two bells into the dog watch. That's seven o'clock, Brandon. You need to learn these things,' he added, although why that would be necessary, he couldn't say.

She grinned at him, then hurried ahead to catch up to the cart. He watched her go, admiring her purposeful stride that made her muslin gown sway so nicely, then did an about face and went down the hill.

Hugh hoped he would not see Laura Brittle when he returned to the convent at two bells, full of excellent Portuguese sausage and just enough grog to render him optimistic.

He barely saw Polly. She was lying in the grassy courtyard, dim now with twilight, a child sitting on her stomach and leaning against her upraised knees. The two were silently observing each other, until Polly suddenly darted her fingers into the soft places under his arms and he chortled. Hugh squatted on his heels beside her. The little boy observed him with solemn brown eyes, but did not seem intimidated.

'This is João,' she said. 'João, this is Colonel Junot.'

'You should teach him what my grandmama taught me,' he said. With his forefinger, he began to describe a wide but narrowing circle targeting the child's stomach. '"There was an old bee who lived in a barn, he carried his bagpipe under his arm, and the only tune that he could play was bzzz!"' He aimed his finger at the little boy's navel and zeroed in, to the child's delight.

'Say that again,' Polly demanded, as she raised her hand to do as he had done.

He repeated the little rhyme that every child in Scotland probably knew, as Polly's finger spiralled down, ending in the soft stomach of her totally willing target, who laughed again and made his own buzzing sound, as he tugged at her finger.

'The tough part now is to convince the child he doesn't want to do it any more,' Hugh teased. 'Good luck.'

She smiled at him, which made his heart leap, then continued the finger play. When another child tossed a ball in his direction, João finally moved off. Polly stayed where she was in the grass. 'I didn't think I would see you again,' she said.

'It was a surprise to me, as well,' he told her, as he plucked handfuls of grass and tossed them on her, enjoying her laugh as she let him. 'We are heading to Ferrol Station, where I hope to catch a coastal lighter to Santander. Apparently Admiral Popham has been using his Marines to good effect in taking the town.'

'Is it dangerous?'

He shrugged. 'No more than anything else during a war. When I finish, I will take a frigate to Plymouth.'

She was silent for a long time. He stopped scattering grass on her and turned his attention to the children at play, obviously getting the last bit of fun out of whatever remained of daylight. He noticed Laura Brittle observing him from the shadows of the colonnade and nodded to her. When he looked back at Polly, she was asleep.

When on earth do you really sleep? he thought, wanting to pick her up and deposit her in a bed of his choosing. *I'm a fool*, he told himself, as he got to his feet, brushed the grass off his hands, and left the courtyard and the sleeping woman who meant more to him than anyone he had ever met.

Philemon sat farther away in the colonnade, holding his son. 'Do that bee thing for me,' he said.

Hugh laughed and did it again. 'It's probably a more popular export than Knox's spare Presbyterianism and oatmeal porridge. Certainly better than haggis, but what isn't?' He sat beside the surgeon.

'You have not been cured of my sister-in-law,' Philemon said, with utterly no preamble.

'No,' Hugh said, amazed at the surgeon's direct approach, but not entirely surprised by it. He had discovered years ago that people with no time to spare seldom wasted words.

'Then you can understand Sister Maria Madelena's need of her. Polly has such a calming effect on those broken reeds she ministers to.' Philemon kissed his son. 'Polly is so self-effacing that she has no idea of her effect on people. Maybe on you, too?'

'You know.'

'Of course I know,' Philemon replied, with all the complacency of a happily married man, damn his eyes. 'I am married to her sister, who has that same effect. I know Laura Brittle better than any human alive, and I tell you these three daughters of a terrible man are rare and special.'

'Do you want me gone, too?' Hugh said bluntly.

'I don't think so. Don't be discouraged.' Philemon looked at Hugh, as though measuring him. 'I don't know what will happen with you and Polly; wartime is not so amenable to courtship. But things happen.'

'Maybe not right now, though,' Hugh said.

'Maybe not,' Philemon agreed, his voice as kind as one could wish. He nodded to his wife, who was approaching them, her arms held out for her son. 'Laura, take this rascal and put him to bed. I'll see the Colonel to the door.'

He was being dismissed. It was not late, but the Brittles probably wanted Polly to sleep as much as she could, before the midnight hours came when the young women were restless in their dreams.

Philemon was in no hurry to usher him out. They took their time getting to the massive door, with its Marine sentry. Hugh tried one more time.

'I wish Miss Brandon would not go upriver.' He stopped, not mistaking the wary look on the surgeon's face. 'I know, I know! You all think I am being overly proprietary. If the interior of Spain were not in such turmoil this past month, I would say nothing.'

'She's going again tomorrow,' Philemon said.

'No! Don't allow it.'

'We got word at dinner. There was one more girl who made it late to São Jobim. There was some sense of urgency in the communication from the priest.'

'Then insist on more of an escort,' Hugh said.

'Perhaps I can. It's going to be another day trip, that is all.'

'Brandon—Miss Brandon—doesn't have to go, does she?'

'I doubt she sees it your way, Colonel.' The surgeon looked him in the eyes. 'By the way, all mail is delivered to my desk. If Laura had seen the letter you so brazenly sent to her sister, she would have chased you out of the convent with a capital knife.'

'It was cheeky of me,' Hugh admitted. 'Did you deliver it?'

'Guilty as charged, Colonel Junot. You're not such a bad man,' Philemon said generously.

The surgeon's teasing gave him heart. 'Thank you! Now, if you could use your almighty powers of persuasion to convince your sister-in-law to stop those river trips, this Marine could embark for Ferrol Station and then Plymouth with an easier conscience.'

He could tell the surgeon was wavering, but he looked at his timepiece.

'I have to go, Colonel Junot,' he said. 'I'll think about what you suggest.'

Hugh sighed and walked slowly down the hill to the wharf, knowing he would toss and turn all night and probably get even less sleep than Polly Brandon.

Polly had managed to snatch a few moments of sleep in the corridor that night. Before dawn, after a quick kiss on Laura's cheek, she hurried to the wharf. The *barco*, still wreathed in shadows, was the only vessel showing signs of activity. She waited as the three Marines filed on board and sat down near the curved bow. Polly sat near the mast, wrapped her cloak tighter and closed her eyes.

'Goodbye, Brandon. I hope you have a wonderful life, wherever it takes you.'

Startled, she strained her eyes to see Colonel Junot standing on the dock, looking down at her. 'Why, thank you,' she said, wishing she didn't sound so furry with sleep.

He doffed his hat to her and she waved, then closed her eyes again, wishing he had not shown up last night, but determined not to be miserable. As the Portuguese sailor cast off the lines, she felt a sudden thump and a sway. To her utter amazement, she opened her eyes to see Colonel Junot pick his way carefully to the bow. He sat down with the sentries, who looked as startled as she did. He glanced over his shoulder at her.

'I just changed my mind,' he said. His expression suggested to her that he was as surprised as she was to find himself on the *barco*. 'The sloop of war won't get underway until night. You promise me we'll be back here by late afternoon?'

'Certainly. But why…?'

'I have a sudden hankering to see São Jobim, Brandon.'

Chapter Ten

Polly could have told him São Jobim wasn't much of a village. In a peaceful world, one where Englishmen with nothing better to do liked to take the Grand Tour, even the old church was not one of the Seven Wonders.

She couldn't overlook her growing discomfort that he had come along because he was worried about another trip upriver so soon after the last one. She knew he had better things to do, and she doubted he had ever done anything as lowly as escort duty in many years. Still, she had to admit there was some gratification in knowing someone was so concerned about her welfare.

To her relief, she kept down breakfast, which gave her some hope that she could outgrow her tendency to seasickness. *Anything is possible,*

Brandon, she told herself, as she leaned against one of the wine kegs lashed to the deck. *Perhaps you can outgrow a certain fondness for the man who was so kind to you. Anything is possible, but it might be easier if he had not been so impulsive.*

She watched the Colonel as he sat with the sentries, impressed, as always, by his military bearing. She watched him gesture to the Private beside him, using what she knew were his considerable skills in getting the sentries to talk to him, man to man, and not as Private to Colonel. In his letter to her, he had told her what questions he asked, and how he was becoming more proficient in the art of interview. *At least I think I am,* he had written. *Perhaps I will show you my list of questions and you can tell me if I have forgotten anything.* Polly smiled to herself, wondering if she had memorised his entire letter.

He couldn't have picked a better assignment for himself, she decided, as she watched all three sentries unbend enough to talk and then laugh. The Colonel had a pad of paper resting on his thigh, and he wrote on it with a pencil, not even looking down, doing nothing to call attention to his actions. She knew it was more than mere command that compelled the sentries to relax enough to talk to Colonel Junot. 'If he says he is interested in what you do, he most certainly means it,' she whispered to herself. 'I could tell you that.'

Lulled by the monotony of motion, she closed her eyes again, relieved for no particular reason that Colonel Junot had decided so impulsively to come along. There was no reason she should feel any safer; unlike the sentries, he carried no weapon. In her brief acquaintance with so august a character, Polly knew he was steadfast. That was enough to send her peacefully back to sleep.

When she woke, he was sitting beside her, gazing out at the shoreline. They had entered one of the gorges where the river narrowed and the current grew stronger. The *barco* had begun to pitch and yaw as the two-man crew accommodated themselves to the new forces at play on their flat-bottomed boat. She sat up, well aware that this was the one place in the river's journey where she felt supremely entitled to her queasiness.

'It looks like a rough go here, Brandon,' was all Colonel Junot said.

She nodded, gratified and not a little touched that he had recognised the fact and come back to sit with her through the canyon. 'You're certain you are never seasick?' she asked.

He smiled and shook his head. 'Brandon, I

have been bobbing about in small boats since I was not a lot older than your nephew. Do you want me to tell you about it?'

She did, even as she recognised what he was doing to keep her mind off the tumbling water as the *barco* pushed against the current. 'Indeed, I do, Colonel. Talk away, and distract me from all the waves and toothy things probably swimming around right under the water's surface.'

'You are a silly nod,' he told her, matter of fact. 'I am from a stretch of choppy water near Kirkcudbright, in the western part of Scotland. No one in our current generation has much of a clue how our French ancestor managed to end up in such an obscure place, but we're glad he did, cold knees and oatmeal notwithstanding.'

Her mind partly on the rough passage, but increasingly more on him, she listened as he told her of a childhood she could scarcely imagine: the oldest of three children, and the one always inclined to more adventure than his bookish little brother—now a barrister in Edinburgh— and his sister, who had his same love for tumult but the misfortune of her sex. 'Jeannie should be the Colonel Commandant of the Third Division,' Colonel Junot told her. 'As it is, she and her husband run the estate west of Kirkie, since our da decided to indulge in a life of leisure in

his old age. The estate will be mine some day—
hopefully, not too soon.'

'Do you miss it?' she asked, wanting to reach
out for him because she knew the upcoming
stretch of water was a personal trial.

Maybe she made an involuntary gesture.
Maybe he just knew almost as much about
water as her brother-in-law Oliver. He took her
arm and tucked it next to his side, forcing her
to move closer to him, which bothered her not
a bit.

'Aye, I miss it,' he told her, his lips close to
her ear as the crew manoeuvred the *barco* expertly past the rocks and into a calmer place.
'More lately than usual. Maybe I'd like to drop
a line in a trout stream I know about, and sleep
in my own bed.'

It was too much. She ducked her head into his
shoulder and he pulled her close with his other
hand, speaking louder. 'Ah, now, Brandon. Do
I have to do the buzzy bee to distract you?'

She tried to laugh, even as she swallowed the
gorge rising from her sorely tried stomach. 'No,'
she said, wishing she meant it. 'Let go!'

He did instantly, but put his hand inside the
collar of her dress, gripping her, as she leaned
over the gunwale. 'Brandon, it's a good thing
you weren't married to one of Noah's sons.
Imagine forty days and nights of this.'

'Don't,' she said as she sat back and he released her. 'I don't even like *reading* that stretch of Genesis.'

He laughed and wiped her mouth with her own skirt. 'I think…this is just my opinion, but perhaps Sister Maria Madelena will let you stay at Sacred Name in the future, and avoid this watery purgatory.'

'Perhaps. I am inclined to agree.'

After one more visit to the gunwale, Polly sat back for the smooth portion of the ride, where the Douro widened out slightly, and the canyon was breathtaking in its wild beauty. It pleased her that Colonel Junot seemed to enjoy the view, too. When she returned to his side, he took hold of her again. Although she knew they had traversed the last gorge before São Jobim and she did not need his protective hold on her, she remained where she was in the security of his arms.

'Beautiful, isn't it?' she asked.

'Mostly I am noticing what an advantage anyone with a mind for mischief would have, sniping from canyon walls,' he told her. 'Then I notice the beauty of things next, Brandon. It's what I do. How many times have you made this trip?'

Polly decided he could change the subject

faster than most people could think. 'This is the fourth or fifth. Why?'

'In that case, then I am impressed with your own toughness, considering how you feel about the water, and knowing these watery traps are here to ensnare you.'

'I like to make myself useful,' she said.

'I understand,' he replied, after some thought. 'Still, this is a war zone—yes, even peaceful São Jobim—and I worry. There's something about this place… Oh, well, I cannot put my finger on it. Brandon, doesn't a quiet life at home sound appealing to you?'

'I've never actually had a home,' she told him, 'but, yes, it sounds agreeable. It sounded agreeable after my first night in the English Channel.'

She wished Colonel Junot would not look at her with such sympathy. Perhaps he was thinking of his own childhood. Since she had never enjoyed a childhood like his, it was hard to miss it, she reasoned. 'I spent my earliest years in an orphanage, and then I went to Miss Pym's Female Academy in Bath.'

That should remind you of everything you need to know about my parentage, in case you have forgotten, she thought grimly. She looked for some disgust, but Colonel Junot seemed unperturbed by her words.

'Take my word for it then, Brandon. Staying at home is a good thing, and I recommend it.'

'You didn't,' she pointed out.

'Of course not. I am a man and I know my duty, even if I do work for the English and my pay chit comes from London.'

Trust you to joke and be serious in the same sentence, she thought. *And to distract me.* He had graciously handed back her serenity, which she accepted without comment. In another minute she disentangled herself from his grip, simply because it was time she remembered.

Polly looked around as the *barco* approached São Jobim. Sister Maria Madelena sat by herself as she always did, her eyes on the rosary in her lap as she fingered it. Their heads together, the sentries were talking as usual, unmindful of the *barco*'s approach to the dock because the duty of snubbing the rope on the cleat belonged to the crew.

What happened next happened fast, so fast she could never have put a sequence to events, even if a jury had demanded it. She looked at the wharf and then the cobbled street where people were usually passing by, especially at noonday. Bells began to sound in her brain, loud and all at once. There were no fishing boats, no vendors, no children at play in doorsteps, no one. São Jobim looked as deserted as villages Laura had described to her in earlier letters, when the French still rampaged in Portugal.

Startled, she turned to Colonel Junot, then tugged his arm. 'Something is…'

'…wrong,' he finished, rising and gesturing to the Marines at the same time, moving fast but not fast enough.

He never got out another word before the shore erupted in flame and smoke. Sister Maria Madelena screamed as the helmsman, a bullet hole drilled through his brain, dropped to the deck. More popping sounds came immediately after each other and two Marines slumped sideways.

Polly took a deep breath, willing herself not to move, even though she wanted to leap up and run somewhere, anywhere. At the same time, Colonel Junot threw her sideways against the gunwale and covered her with his body. She struggled, but he clamped a hand on her head and forced her down into the damp, where river water always puddles. Colonel Junot moulded his body to hers and pulled her in close to him, his hands on her head and belly.

Completely beyond words and thrust into a land of terror she had never known, Polly felt herself start to shake. She stopped when she felt a slight concussion as a rifle ball thudded into Colonel Junot. He let his breath out with a quiet huff that ended in a sigh, but did not loosen his grip on her.

'Colonel?' she managed to ask. She struggled to turn around to look at him, but he was too heavy.

'Hold still, Brandon. My God, don't move.'

Her cheek jammed against the deck, she had no choice but to do what he said. Terrified, she strained to hear his even breathing, knowing he must have been hit, and wondering at his own calmness in the face of calamity.

She thought she heard the remaining Marine returning fire, but then there was silence on the deck. To her frightened reckoning, a century or two must have rolled around before she felt the boat sway as men clambered on to the *barco*, shouting in French. She opened her eyes, which she must have screwed shut, and saw with terror that the damp under her cheek had turned pink.

The soldiers were dressed in green tunics, with reinforced trousers and copper helmets with fur lining that reminded her of pictures of Roman legionnaires. Their boots extended above their knees. 'What? Who?' she managed to gasp.

'Dragoons,' Hugh whispered in her ear. 'How's your French?'

'Adequate,' she told him, amazed that she

could even get out another word, much less one that made sense.

'Don't move until I tell you. Oh, God!'

Please, please, don't let them shoot him again, she thought. She listened then, hearing what must have torn the words from him, as Sister Maria began to scream and then plead. More men jumped on the *barco* and then the footsteps came closer. Colonel Junot groaned as someone kicked him, and his hands, so tight around her body, went slack.

Turn and face them, she ordered herself as she struggled loose from the Colonel's limp grasp.

'Don't shoot him,' she said in French in as firm a voice as she could muster. She twisted around and slowly rose to her knees for her first look at the deck, which ran with blood now. So many green-coated soldiers had leaped on the *barco* that the deck canted away from the dock and towards the river, causing the blood from the dead Marines and crew members to pour in her direction as they came closer. How much of it was Colonel Junot's blood, she didn't dare speculate. He was unconscious, with the beginning of an ugly welt on his temple.

Polly knew she would never forget the sight before her. Her wimple torn away, Sister Maria Madelena knelt before her captors, who jabbed at her with their muskets, lifting her black skirt.

'Don't do that,' Polly said, her voice louder.

The soldiers wheeled around in surprise to look at Polly. Her own knees turned to jelly as their expressions went from surprise to speculation, much as a cat cornering a mouse. As two of the soldiers swaggered towards her, one already unbuckling his sword belt, she sat down, mainly because her knees had stopped holding her up. Her eyes on the soldiers, she yanked Colonel Junot into her lap and wrapped her arms around him.

The effort must have roused him. He shook his head slightly, uttering another quiet sigh. 'Brandon, we're in a pickle,' he whispered.

She watched the soldiers out of the corner of her eye, too frightened to look at what was happening to Sister Maria Madelena, but unable to look away. One of the Dragoons jerked her to her feet while another slapped her hard, then slapped her again.

Colonel Junot didn't want her to look, either. 'Keep your eyes on me,' he ordered. His voice tightened as he tried to move his arm, the one that must have been hit. 'And if you can think of something... My head...'

Only one feeble idea came to mind, one so puny that on an ordinary day, it would never have seen the light of day. She kissed Colonel Junot on his cheek and then his ear, all the while tightening her grip, looking at the approaching soldiers, who had stopped to watch, wary but interested. 'This is my husband, Lieutenant Colonel Hugh Junot of the Royal Marines. Please do not kill him.'

At nearly the same time she spoke, Colonel Junot did, too, also in French that sounded much better than hers. 'Don't touch my wife,' he said, his voice weak, but with as much determination as she had ever heard from any soul living. 'We are worth more to you alive.'

His eyes so serious, Colonel Junot kissed her cheek. He turned around again and made himself comfortable, his head against her breasts in a gesture both familiar and possessive. The French soldiers squatted on the deck, uncertain and coming no closer.

'Where were you hit?' she asked him softly in English. Then, 'We're married. I couldn't think of anything else.'

'The back of my arm. Nothing much. You can treat it with a strip of petticoat, my love,' he told her. 'As for being married, I couldn't think of anything else, either. I recommend it right now, even though our courtship was amazingly swift.' He took one of her hands that crossed his chest, and slid it inside his uniform jacket in an intimate move.

He sat so calmly that Polly felt herself begin

to breathe normally again. 'I don't remember saying yes.' It was the feeblest of jokes in the most dire of situations, but she had to concentrate on him.

'You didn't say yes,' he assured her, settling back more comfortably. 'I told you it was swift. Brandon, we might keep each other alive. I can't think of a better way.' He took her hand out of his uniform front and kissed it. 'Apparently you couldn't, either.'

Sister Maria Madelena shrieked as the soldiers carried her off the *barco*, set her on her feet and stripped off her habit in one wrench, leaving her standing on the dock in her chemise. She dropped to her knees, crouching there with her arms wrapped around her, and looking around wildly.

'We have to do something,' Polly urged, even as the Colonel turned her face gently towards his chest and pressed it there with his hand, shielding her from the terrible sight before them.

'We won't do anything until I see someone above the rating of Private, Brandon. Just hold me. Look at me now. Not at the dock.'

She did as he said, even as she heard Sister Maria Madelena's terrified screams. Her breath must have been coming faster and faster, because the Colonel told her calmly to breathe in and out more slowly.

'We can't help her right now. If we try anything, you will be next,' he said. 'My God, Brandon. What can have happened?'

She shook her head, then looked up when she heard a new voice shouting at the dock. Another soldier ran from the church and was flailing about his own men with his sword, beating them back from Sister Maria Madelena. Polly looked down again, in tears now at the sight of the nun kneeling on the cobblestones, her arms pinned back, her head down.

'It's a Sergeant,' Colonel Junot said, and there was no mistaking the relief in his voice. 'Brandon, help me to my feet.'

Not even sure she could stand on her own, Polly surprised herself by doing exactly what he asked. She hauled him upright, and then braced herself against the gunwale as he sagged against her, then slowly straightened up.

'Don't let go of me,' Colonel Junot ordered. 'Put your hand through my belt. I'll hold you as tight as I can.'

She did as he said, clutching him in a firm grasp. The Colonel leaned against one of the kegs lashed to the deck as ballast. Polly gasped and turned her face into his uniform jacket when one of the soldiers on the dock grabbed Sister Maria Madelena by her arms, slung her over his shoulder and walked towards the church, even as she shrieked and begged for mercy,

'Deep breaths, Brandon,' Colonel Junot said. 'Perhaps I should call you Polly now.'

He stayed where he was, but he stood taller, almost willing himself into his usual impeccable posture and bearing, even though the welt on his face was turning a mottled colour and blood seeped from his sleeve. Polly released him long enough to hand him his hat, then twined her hand through his belt and clutched it.

'Sergeant, I am Lieutenant Colonel Hugh Junot of the Third Royal Marine Division of his Majesty's British maritime forces. I implore your protection for my wife, Polly.'

He spoke calmly, but his voice carried across the bloody deck, where the bodies of the Marines lay sprawled and the *barco* crew was silent in death. Polly held her breath as the French NCO scowled at them. Decades seemed to pass before he gestured them forwards.

'One foot in front of the other, dear wife,' Colonel Junot said. 'That's how any journey begins.'

Chapter Eleven

Colonel Junot staggered, but Polly held him up, her arm tight around him. She draped his arm over her shoulder and they stumbled across the deck. When they reached the opposite gunwale, the Sergeant nodded to one of his Privates, who held out his hands and helped them to the dock.

'We did not expect to see a Colonel,' the Sergeant said in French. He gestured towards the dead Marines. 'We have been watching, too, for several days. Is the war going so ill for England that Lieutenant Colonels come on patrol? I cannot think you were much help.'

Polly felt Colonel Junot stiffen. 'No, I was not, was I? We are your prisoners, Sergeant.' With some effort, he unbuckled his sword without releasing her and handed it to the NCO, who grinned at the sight. 'I surrender to you and implore your protection for my wife.'

'Not you?' the Sergeant asked, a slight smile on his face, as he accepted the sword, then casually tossed it to a Private, who looked at it and threw it in the river.

'Damn! That was a gift from my father,' Hugh said in English.

The Sergeant laughed at the look on Junot's face. 'Why would anyone want your stupid sword?' he asked in French. 'Why do we even want you, Colonel? Your delicious wife? Now that is another matter.'

'Sergeant, I implore your protection for her,' Hugh said again, his voice softer this time, more pleading. Polly could hardly bear to watch him pawn his dignity, but there was the Sergeant, running the blade of his sword across her breasts now.

The Sergeant apparently had no intention of making anything easy. He walked around them, patting the back of Polly's dress with his sword, then ran the blade slowly down her hips and legs. Hugh set his lips more firmly in a tight line.

The Sergeant continued his leisurely circuit, this time standing too close to Polly and flicking her hair with the point of his sword. 'Here we thought only to bag partisan scum passing information, and what do I find but a Colonel? *Mon dieu*, war is strange.'

She flinched, scarcely breathing. When his words finally settled in on her terrified brain, she wondered if she had heard him correctly. 'Information?' she asked, hoping she sounded much braver than she felt.

Obviously enjoying himself at their expense, the Sergeant smiled broadly as he flicked the blade across the front of her dress, slicing off a cloth rosette. 'And you did not know? Answer this one carefully, *s'il vous plaît.*'

'There was nothing to know,' she replied, trying to slow her breathing so her breasts would not rise and fall so rapidly. 'What can you mean? Sister Maria Madelena and I come to São Jobim to take young women who have been—' She stopped, wondering at the wisdom of saying more about the girls violated by French troops. 'We come here to take young women to a safer place, in time of war.'

The Sergeant was practically standing on her toes now, his eyes on hers. Polly glanced at Hugh, who was breathing shallowly, too. The Sergeant took the pommel of his sword and put it under her chin, raising her face to meet his scrutiny. 'Why is this man along? Your husband, you say?'

'My husband is here because he has been in

Lisbon for a month, is headed out on another assignment, and wanted to see me in between. I am certain you understand.'

The Sergeant stared at her. She gazed back, not even blinking. He took the sword from her chin. 'You must be a challenge for him,' he said, stepping back. He looked at Colonel Junot. 'How do you manage her?'

'Very gently,' Colonel Junot said, his voice firm.

'With a whip? How is she to ride?'

Polly felt the blood drain from her face, as Hugh stepped close to the Sergeant this time. 'Sergeant, I resent your foul comments about my lady,' he said, biting off each word, as if he spoke to troublesome Marine Privates, and not the man holding all the cards. 'Do not tell me Napoleon makes war on officers' wives now. I would not have believed him capable of that.'

The men stared at each other. Polly held her breath, waiting for the Sergeant to run the Colonel through with his sabre. At the same time, she felt a spark of pride at Colonel Junot's defence of her, and both of them so powerless.

Hugh spoke first, and his tone was conciliatory now, although by no means subservient. 'Sergeant, has a mistake been made here? This nun only seeks to rescue those who often get trampled upon in time of war.'

'No mistake,' the Sergeant said crisply. 'None at all.' He shook his sword at Polly. 'We have been watching you.'

'In the greater scheme of things, I can't imagine why,' Polly murmured.

'Oh, you cannot? Let me enlighten you. This way, please, you two. Do you need some help, Colonel?'

'You're so kind to ask,' Junot said. 'My wife will help me.'

Escorted by Dragoons looking hugely interested, they followed the Sergeant across the small square. Polly stopped once when she heard a series of splashes, and looked back to see other Dragoons throwing the dead Marines and crew of the *barco* overboard. 'Sergeant, can they not have decent burials?' she asked, horrified.

'The British? Why, *madame*?' was all he said, sounding supremely bored.

'Don't worry, Polly,' Colonel Junot whispered. 'This is better. The bodies may get snagged on limbs and rocks on the way downriver, but perhaps one of them will reach Vila Nova de Gaia.' He sighed. 'It's puny, but all we have, my dear.'

She was silent then, as the full force of their capture slammed itself home. The village appeared deserted. Who knew what terrors the French had promised to the townspeople if anyone so much as made a peep to the allies down-river? Uneasy, Polly looked up at the Colonel, and was comforted to see him looking at her.

'We haven't had any chance to get our stories straight,' he whispered in English. 'What say we've been married since June?'

'Where?'

'Vila Nova, where your brother-in-law gave you away.'

Thinking of Laura and Philemon brought tears to her eyes and she looked away. In answer, the Colonel tightened his grip on her shoulder and kissed the top of her head. 'We'll stick together like glue, Brandon,' he assured her. 'I'm not leaving your side.'

They reached the closed door of the church, thick doors that she already knew could muffle any sounds, because she had been inside several times and enjoyed the ecclesiastical quiet within. It was different this time. Shivers travelled up and down her spine as she heard Sister Maria Madelena screaming. Unnerved, Polly stopped, but was prodded from behind. In response, Colonel Junot pulled her in front of him, protecting her with his body.

The Sergeant bowed elaborately and opened the smaller man-gate. 'Do come in, Colonel and *madame*,' he said, gesturing as though he welcomed them to a farmhouse in Gascony.

'Think of this as a wayside shrine on the way to perdition.'

Even at mid-day, the squat building's interior was shrouded in shadow. This was no church of the Renaissance, but a shabby little relic of the Middle Ages, charming in its own way, but not now, and probably never again.

Clad in her chemise, Sister Maria Madelena crouched below the altar, her screams tinged with madness. Before she could react, Colonel Junot turned Polly's face into his tunic. 'Oh, God, don't look!' he said, his voice suddenly filled with horror. She felt his fingers shaking as he forced her against him.

Other hands pulled his fingers away, compelling her to stare at the altar and then up to the large crucifix, where the French soldiers, those students of the Revolution, had crucified São Jobim's parish priest. Naked, pitiful, he hung on the cross, his arms bent at weird angles, his head down as though contemplating the ruin of his pudgy body. In his own death agonies he had moved his bowels.

Polly couldn't help herself. Her knees sagged and it was the Colonel's turn to hold her up. He stepped in front of her, blocking the view, but she knew she would never forget the sight before her. She wanted to close her eyes and keep them shut until the whole nightmare went away and she was back on the *barco*, with nothing more on her mind than negotiating the next stretch of white water. How puny that seasickness had been her biggest fear, how trivial.

Instead, she opened her eyes and looked into the Colonel's concerned face, so close to her own. 'I'll be all right,' she whispered to him. 'The poor man. What did he do to deserve this?'

Colonel Junot shook his head. 'There is a deep game going on here, Polly. I don't think we know even half of it.'

With his help, she stood upright again and turned away resolutely, to find herself looking at Sister Maria Madelena, kneeling and sobbing. Shaken, Polly turned her attention to the Sergeant, who seemed so sure of himself, almost swaggering in his command of this sorry situation. This was probably no more than a typical day for him. 'How can you permit your men to…to…?' She stopped, unable to think of a word to adequately cover what was happening, considering her own genteel Bath French.

The Sergeant mocked her expression, bowed elaborately, and held out a note. 'Perhaps you might consider what she has been doing to *us*!' he declared, triumph in every line of his body.

As she watched, aghast, he stalked over to Sister Maria Madelena and shook her by the hair. Colonel Junot tightened his grip on her when she started towards the nun. 'Don't move,' he whispered. 'These men are wolves.'

'But he's—'

'Stand still.'

She did as the Colonel said, even when the Sergeant tightened his grip on Sister Maria's hair and pulled her head up. 'Tell this Colonel's wife how you have been taking notes from the priest to the Navy docks in Vila Nova,' the Sergeant roared, shaking her head like a terrier with a mouse.

'Sister Maria, you don't have to tell me anything,' Polly said in English, as the Colonel tightened his arms around her.

'Tell her!' the Sergeant demanded of the nun, shaking her again and again until Polly wanted to scream. He looked up at the dead man and let go of Sister Maria Madelena. 'We...persuaded the priest to admit he gave her communiqués to pass on from the interior. Tell her, you whore!'

Polly couldn't stop shaking, not even with Colonel Junot holding her so tight. She leaned back against him, trying to keep the crucified priest and nun out of her sight. 'Sister Maria?' she asked softly, her voice quavering.

The Sergeant released the nun and she struggled into a sitting position, trying to cover herself with her arms. As Polly watched, horrified, she willed herself into a state of calm and then slowly raised her bruised head and held her hands out, palms up, in supplication.

But it wasn't supplication. Polly jumped when Sister Maria Madelena suddenly clenched her hands into fists. Her tired eyes flashed, and the scar across her face stood out in raw, red relief against her paleness.

'Viva Portugal e viva España!' she declared in a loud voice.

'There's your answer, Polly,' Colonel Junot murmured in her ear. 'She *was* a messenger. Is she even a nun?'

'I…I…I didn't know,' Polly whispered. 'I did wonder once…. I thought I saw a note.' She turned her face into Colonel Junot's tunic. 'I do know she was a victim, too, like the young women we cared for.'

'Madame Junot,' the Sergeant said. He was closer to her now, stepping over the nun, who had slid back on to the stones, exhausted and drained. 'Madame Junot?'

'Polly,' Colonel Junot said in English, 'he is talking to you. Polly, pay attention and remember who you are.'

It was her turn to get a firm grasp on her emotions, to dig down deep inside herself where she had never gone before, and pull out more courage than she knew she possessed. Perhaps the Sergeant would not know how terrified she was. He was addressing her as Madame Junot; she would have to remember that and respond.

'Yes, Sergeant?' she said, as she rubbed her cheek gently against the Colonel's tunic as his hand went up to caress her hair.

'Did you know of this deception? Do answer carefully.'

I am no liar, she thought. She continued to rest her head against Colonel Junot, as she realised it was time to think of him as Hugh, the dearest person in her universe. She chose her French with precision. 'Sergeant, on the last trip, the one yesterday, I thought I saw her take something from Pai Belo. It was the merest glimpse. It could have been anything.'

The Sergeant grunted and took the folded scrap from his tunic again. 'This is what he gave me today, just before we hoisted him on high.'

Polly shuddered as she looked at the bloodstained sheet. To her horror, it was covered with numbers, and she recognised the Portuguese words for 'regiment' and the names of Spanish towns.

'We have other messages,' the Sergeant told her, folding the note. 'How many trips have you made to São Jobim?'

'I hope you are not planning to implicate my wife in any of this,' Hugh said.

She wondered at his ability to sound so protective, when he was as much a prisoner as she. 'Hush, my love,' Polly said. 'This is my fifth trip, Sergeant. That is all. I have only been in Vila Nova for eight or nine weeks, visiting my sister.'

'And not your husband?'

She realised her mistake, and fought down panic. *I am no actress, either*, she thought. 'Sergeant, surely that goes without saying. We were only married in June, and this war keeps getting in our way.'

To her relief, he seemed to find her statement funny and laughed. 'Oh, you British!' he exclaimed, his tone almost fond in a way that Polly found more repulsive than a curse. 'What am I to do with you?'

'What will you do with *her*?' Colonel Junot asked, looked at Sister Maria Madelena.

The Sergeant glanced around almost carelessly, as though she was already someone in his distant past. He shrugged. 'I will turn her over to my soldiers. They will make sure she is dead when they are done. You can watch. In fact, I will insist.'

Unable to help herself, Polly sobbed out loud. 'Shh, shh, my love,' the Colonel crooned, his hand gentle on her hair again. 'I have no say in this, Sergeant, but I wish you would just kill her outright. If she must die—if she is a spy, you have your rights, I acknowledge—then kill her cleanly.'

The Sergeant smiled and squatted on the floor by Sister Maria. He lifted her head by the hair. 'Do you hear that? This Englishman harbours a soft spot for guerillas like you.'

'Viva Portugal,' she murmured.

Her heart in her throat, Polly watched the Frenchman as he squatted there, engaged in thought. He rose then, and inclined his head towards them. 'Very well, Colonel. Since you are so concerned, you kill her.'

Hugh made that same huffing sound that had escaped him on the *barco* when he was shot. He took an involuntary step back and Polly had to steady him as he threatened to topple them both.

'Please, Colonel,' Sister Maria whispered from the floor. 'Please.'

Polly reached both arms around the Colonel and held him as close as she could, her hands splayed across his broad back. He buried his face in her hair, and she just held him.

The Sergeant came closer until Polly smelled all his dirt and perspiration. 'In fact, Colonel, I insist. If you do not kill this spy, I will see that your little wife suffers the fate I originally intended for her, and you can watch that.'

'I will do it,' Hugh said immediately. 'Certainly I will. Hand me a pistol.'

The Sergeant laughed as he gestured to one of his men. 'Don't you wish you had not come upriver today, Colonel?'

While the Sergeant took Hugh aside and handed him the pistol to load, Polly gathered up more courage from a hitherto unknown source. Ignoring the soldiers, she walked to the nun, knelt on the floor and wiped Sister Maria's battered face with the altar cloth. She draped the cloth around the woman's bare shoulders.

'I never meant you to be involved,' the nun whispered.

'I wish you had not invited me upriver,' Polly replied, dabbing carefully around the woman's ears. 'How could you put us in such danger?'

She hadn't meant to be harsh, not with a woman about to die, but she could not help herself. *I can repent later*, Polly told herself resolutely, as she dabbed away. *If there is a later.*

'I love my country more,' Sister Maria said. She grasped Polly's arm with fingers surprisingly strong. 'Watch over João for me.'

Polly nodded, ashamed of herself. 'We will treat him as our own son.' She glanced at Colonel Junot, surprised at herself. *He is not my husband, but that came out so naturally*, she thought.

Sister Maria Madelena nodded, her face calm now. 'Come closer,' she whispered.

Polly crept closer on her knees, as though to arrange the woman's hair.

'I never was a nun. Hear me out! My brother is El Cuchillo, a guerilla of León. He said he would always watch out for me…' Her voice trailed off and she looked up at the dead priest above them. 'Perhaps one of his men is watching now. Be ready for anything.'

'Don't give me false hope,' Polly whispered. 'You have done enough.'

There was more she wanted to say, but she knew it would not make her feel any better. Then the moment was gone, when one of the soldiers grabbed her by both elbows and lifted her off the floor. She shrieked, unable to struggle.

'Polly, my love, steady as you go,' Hugh said, as the soldier pinioned her arms behind her back and led her away from Sister Maria Madelena, who crouched and clutched the altar cover, her face calm.

'Madam Junot, you must not struggle so!' the Sergeant admonished. 'I am handing your husband a pistol now. You are my guarantee that he will not turn it on me.' He shrugged elaborately. 'Call me cautious. I have not lived from Jena and Austerlitz by being overly trusting. You understand?'

'I understand,' Polly replied, her voice soft. 'I'm sorry, Hugh.'

His face pale, his eyes so serious, the Colonel looked at her for a long moment, as though willing her to understand that what was about to happen was not his choice. No matter—she knew that, and tried to communicate her emotions with a return gaze as compassionate as his own.

He squared his shoulders and took a deep breath. 'I will do this my own way, Sergeant, and in my own time. Don't interfere with me or my wife.'

He stood a moment in silence, head bowed, then walked to the altar, where Sister Maria Madelena knelt. He squatted beside her and carefully draped her hair over her shoulder, away from the back of her neck.

'What is your name, my dear?' he asked, his voice conversational.

'Maria Ponce, from León,' she replied in English, 'although my family is originally from Portugal. Your wife will tell you of my brother.'

He squeezed her shoulder gently, stood up, and cocked the pistol. 'God forgive me,' he said.

'He already has,' Maria Ponce said.

Polly tried to look away, but the Sergeant put the blade of his sword against her neck and gently forced her to watch.

'If there is any foolishness, Colonel,' the Sergeant called, 'I will violate your wife myself.'

'I know that,' Hugh said with a certain weary patience, as though he dealt with a child. 'There will be no foolishness. You have my word as an officer and a gentleman, if that holds any merit with a soldier of La Belle France.'

'It's quaint, but I like it,' the Sergeant said. 'An officer, a gentleman, a murderer. Hurry up.'

Hugh pointed the pistol towards the nape of Maria Ponce's neck, then lowered it. 'No. Not this way,' he said, speaking to the Sergeant. 'I don't want my wife to see this.'

'Poor you,' said the Sergeant, when he finished laughing.

'I mean it,' Hugh said. Polly watched as he seemed to stand taller. 'Sergeant, do you have a wife?'

The Dragoon took the blade of his sword away from Polly's neck. She held her breath. 'I do. She is no concern of yours.'

'What is her name?' Hugh asked calmly, with all the force of his rank and age behind the question, to Polly's ears. *You are so audacious*, she thought. *You are trying to bend this man to your will and you have no power whatsoever.*

'Her name is Lalage,' the Sergeant said, speaking as though addressed by a French officer, and not a British captive. Polly could hardly believe her ears.

'Lalage is a beautiful name,' Hugh said. 'Madame Junot is *my* Lalage. She is my love and my life. Would you want *your* Lalage to witness what I must do here? I cannot imagine a loving husband would do such a thing in France.'

Polly reminded herself to breathe as the two men stared at each other. The Sergeant looked away first. He sheathed his sabre and took Polly by the arm, shoving her towards one of his Dragoons.

'Take her outside. Sit with her on the steps.'

'*Merci*, Sergeant,' Hugh said. 'I would ask all of you to leave. Let this be between me and Sister Maria Madelena.'

'I can't do that!' the Sergeant protested, but his voice had lost its edge.

'You can, Sergeant,' Hugh said. 'If this woman kneeling before you is not dead when I come out of the church, you may shoot me next, after I have killed my own Lalage.'

Again the two men stared at each other. Again the Sergeant yielded. He gestured to his troopers, who followed him into the sun. Polly felt as though she stood on blocks of wood instead of her feet. With a look at Colonel Junot, one that tried to convey every emotion she was feeling, she forced herself into motion and left the chapel of São Jobim.

The sun was hot on her face. She welcomed the warmth, even as she shivered and knew she would never be warm again. The Sergeant sat her down on the top step, then pulled her up gently and took her down several more steps. He sat down beside her, not looking at her.

Polly steeled herself against the sound of the pistol, but when it went off, she still jumped and cried out. The Sergeant gripped her shoulder, but it was not the grip of a captor. He did not release her until she heard Hugh's steps behind them.

He came towards them slowly, going down each step as though he weighed a thousand pounds. Polly knew if she lived to one hundred, she would never be able to entirely erase from her mind his expression. She couldn't interpret it. She had thought to see revulsion at the terrible act he had been forced to perform. There was something thoughtful in his look, instead. If she hadn't known it was impossible, she would have called it relief.

He sat down heavily beside her and gathered her close to him, his grip as tender as the Sergeant's had been.

'Where is the pistol?' the Sergeant demanded.

Hugh shook his head and gestured behind

him. 'You can get it. I'm not going back in there.' He looked across Polly at the Sergeant, wonder in his voice now. 'I pointed the barrel right at the nape of her neck. Before I could fire, she grabbed the gun and killed herself.' He began to weep.

It was Polly's turn to gather him close, uttering sounds of comfort that had no language, as he sobbed into his hands. To her surprise, the Sergeant and the Dragoons left them there on the church steps as they went inside again.

'Oh, Colonel,' she whispered into his neck, at a total loss for words.

'From now on, I am "Hugh, love" to you,' he said, after a long moment. 'Never forget it. Our lives depend on it, Polly, dear wife.'

They held hands and sat as close together as they could while the Dragoons finished up whatever business they had in the church. When they came out, the Sergeant gestured for them to stand up.

'What do you intend to do with us, Sergeant, now that Sister Maria has done our dirty work?' Hugh asked.

'Dirty work it is, Colonel,' the Sergeant said. 'Do you know who the whore's brother is?'

'El Cuchillo,' Polly said. 'Sister Maria told me before she died.'

The Sergeant's smile broadened. 'Poor you,

indeed, my Colonel! He is a guerilla leader of León, where we are heading.' He sheathed his sword. 'I have always been amazed how word gets around. El Cuchillo will probably assume you killed his sister. You might as well paint a bull's-eye on your back.'

'Perhaps you should just kill me now,' Hugh said, pulling Polly closer.

The Sergeant laughed and shook his head. 'And miss the fun? Never. They say he likes best to kill with a long needle through the eye.'

'Well, into every life some rain must fall, I suppose,' Hugh replied, with just a touch of amusement.

'You're a cool one,' the Sergeant said.

'No, I am not. Actually, let me suggest a very good reason why you should keep me and my wife alive.'

The Sergeant looked down on them from the step above, perfectly at ease again and in charge, looking for all the world like a cat with cornered mice. 'Colonel, will you never cease to entertain me?'

'Probably not,' Hugh said, his tone equally affable. 'In a word, Sergeant, money. This knowledge is for you alone. You have no idea how rich Madame Junot is.'

Chapter Twelve

❦

'So that is why you married her,' the Sergeant said.

Polly flinched, which made Hugh's heart sink even lower. *Bastard!* he thought. *Damn the man.* But this was no time to argue, so he merely shrugged. 'Think what you will. I am speaking of money. *Dinero, dinheiro, denaro, geld.* Think of all the words for money you have learned as you have tramped through Europe! Imagine that in your pockets.'

He had no idea how this would play. If today was his unlucky day—so far, there was nothing to dispute the notion it could be the unluckiest day of his life—then he had just attempted to bribe one of the few incorruptible men in anyone's army. He stood up, pulled Polly to her feet, and started walking away from the church. One step, two steps, another. The Sergeant did not stop him, but walked at his side. Was it possible even a battle-hardened veteran of Napoleon's campaigns didn't care so much for what had just happened? One could hope; Hugh did. But then,

'A bribe? You want to bribe *me*, Colonel?' the Sergeant asked, putting out his hand to stop them.

I found the only honest man in Napoleon's army, Hugh thought with regret. *Well, then, we have nothing to lose.* 'I suppose I do,' he said frankly. 'One doesn't make Colonel without exercising some initiative. Not in the Royal Marines, at least.'

He knew how that sounded in English. In French, Hugh thought it had a certain Gallic panache. At least the Sergeant hadn't motioned for one of his men to run him through with a sword.

In fact, the Sergeant was smiling—a little smile, to be sure, but a smile. After a long pause, the Sergeant even chuckled. *In for a penny*, Hugh thought. 'It's not for me, especially,' he said. He turned to Polly and gave her a kiss on the temple and a little shake to get her attention. 'And it's not even just for my wife.' He nudged Polly again. 'Shall I tell him, darling?'

He looked her in the eyes and she gazed back

through those spectacles that magnified her eyes a little. *Follow me with this*, he thought, trying to communicate through nothing more than a look, something he knew his parents, married years and years, had been quite good at. To his infinite relief, she inclined her head towards him as though the conversation was a delicate one.

'It's this, Sergeant: my wife is in the family way. I especially want her to survive this experience and at least give my estate an heir.'

To her credit, Polly didn't even flinch. He knew she understood his French, because her lips came together in a firm line and she concentrated on her shoes.

'If you can help us, it is worth a great deal to me, Sergeant,' he concluded simply.

They were in the square now. Hugh concentrated all his attention on the Sergeant, even as his skin crawled at the sound of women and children screaming in some of the buildings. The Sergeant seemed almost reflective, as though he stood in a glade in southern France filled with carnations. *My God, these are hard men*, Hugh thought. He almost hated to interrupt the thought process of a man who obviously had the power to end his life in the next second, but time was passing.

'I know you have a wife, Sergeant,' he said. 'Do you and Lalage have children?' Maybe it wasn't such an unlucky day. While not appearing to stare, Hugh watched the Sergeant's face, and at least thought he saw a slight thawing. He breathed more regularly when the Sergeant gestured with his hand towards a bench and spoke to Polly.

'Madame Junot, let us sit here. You look done for.'

It was probably the understatement of the ages, considering what had just happened in the chapel. Polly nodded, her pale face tinged with pink now, as though she were shy about sharing her *faux* husband's phony admission with a complete stranger, much less the enemy.

Hugh kissed Polly's temple again and whispered in her ear as he sat her carefully down on the bench, 'You're a game goer, Brandon.'

In response, she burrowed in closer to him, shivering in the warmth of the afternoon sun. In a more familiar gesture, Hugh put his hand on her waist and pulled her as near as he could. She responded by resting her hand on his thigh. *Bravo, Brandon*, he thought, enjoying the act.

'Can I get you some wine, *madame*?' the Sergeant asked.

Polly nodded, and the Sergeant gestured to one of his men and made his request. The Corporal shook his head and indicated there was none. The Sergeant merely nodded philosophically. 'We travel light, *madame*. Perhaps he can find something in this pathetic village.'

'Water will do,' she said.

The Sergeant was silent until the Corporal returned with water in an earthen jar. Polly tried to take it from him, but her hand shook so badly that Hugh took it instead and held the jar to her lips until she sipped. A frown on his face, the Sergeant observed her terror.

He spoke at last. 'We have two sons on a farm near Angoulême. It is a small farm.'

Hugh nodded. 'If you will see to my wife's safety, I can promise you your wife will receive whatever sum you consider appropriate.'

The Sergeant nodded, and gazed across the small square of São Jobim, where his men were methodically going through the buildings. He rubbed his unshaven jaw, looking unconcerned as flames suddenly roared skywards from a home. It was just another day in Portugal.

'Of course, I cannot promise anything until we—or she—is restored to Allied lines, but you can trust us to deliver what you wish, and where,' Hugh added, keeping his voice soft, hoping not to distract from whatever the Sergeant might be thinking.

'Because you are an officer and a gentleman?' the Sergeant said suddenly, and his voice was harsh again.

'No. Because I want to be a father,' Hugh said. 'You understand.'

The Sergeant stood up suddenly and slapped his worn gauntlets on his thigh. Hugh had always been a praying man, much to the amusement of his fellow Marines, and he prayed now, as the Frenchman weighed the offer on a scale of delicate balance.

Polly tipped it, to Hugh's everlasting relief. 'Sergeant, what are your son's names? And who are you?'

The Sergeant looked down at her, and Hugh thought he saw pity in the man's eyes, as brown as his own, and something more: a father's love. 'Emile and Antoine,' he said. 'I am Jean Baptiste Cadotte. Colonel, I will help you if I can.'

'I am in your debt,' Hugh replied simply.

'I can promise you nothing.'

'I know that.'

Most of São Jobim was blazing when the Dragoons mounted the horses that had been stabled inside the town hall. Two of the lighter men doubled up and the Sergeant directed Hugh to mount the other horse. He tied Hugh's hands together, then tied Polly's, only not so tight. To Hugh's amusement, Cadotte directed a man to hand her up carefully to sit in front of him. She tried to sit sideways at first, as though she rode a sidesaddle, but gave that up quickly and threw her leg over the saddle, which raised her skirts to her knees. To her credit, Polly scarcely seemed to mind. Directing her to lean forwards, Hugh raised his roped arms and lowered them over her body, resting them against her stomach. The Corporal took the reins and led the horse behind his own.

Polly was still shaking and there was nothing he could do about that. After what seemed like an hour of travel on what was a little-used track, he felt her shoulders lower as her jangled nerves attempted to relax. She said nothing, though, which suited him well enough, since he couldn't think of any words to comfort her. Just as well. Unaccustomed to riding horseback, Hugh felt his inner thighs begin to burn and his buttocks go numb.

After several hours of steady climbing, Sergeant Cadotte raised his hand and the Dragoons stopped. Everyone knew what to do. In another moment, all the men were urinating into the road.

'My blushes,' Polly said, the first words she had spoken since leaving São Jobim.

Hugh chuckled. 'Boys will be boys,' he told her. 'I hope Cadotte will take a little pity on us, too.'

He did. When the men were standing by their mounts again and eating what looked like hardtack, Sergeant Cadotte sent a trooper to help Polly off the horse. He untied her hands and helped her down, then indicated that Hugh should throw his leg over the saddle and slide off.

'I can't,' Hugh said, looking at Cadotte. 'Sergeant, you'll have to appreciate that I am a Royal Marine and not a horseman of any kind. Undo my hands, please, and I will struggle off and probably fall on my face, to your total amusement.'

Cadotte laughed and told the Private to untie his hands, but was kind enough to steady Hugh as he dismounted. He sank immediately to his knees. All the men in the troop laughed, but Hugh only shrugged and staggered to his feet.

'You meant what you said,' Cadotte murmured. 'Take your wife and go relieve yourselves.'

'Merci,' Hugh said with a grimace. 'Just let me stand here a moment and see if there is any blood in my pathetic body willing to circulate to my ass again.'

'But he is never seasick,' Polly said suddenly in French, which made the men laugh again.

In good humour, Cadotte gestured to the stand of trees. 'Have a little privacy, Colonel.

That ought to be worth the price of a few cows at my farm by Angoulême.'

'A whole herd,' Hugh said as he took Polly by the hand. 'Come, my love, and let us find a tree.'

To his relief, the Dragoons turned away and squatted on the far side of their horses, some smoking and others conversing. Wincing at every step, Hugh led Polly into the stand of trees. 'Well, my dear, turn your head and give me a moment.'

Her face bright red, she did as he said. When he finished and buttoned his trousers, he pointed towards a fallen log. 'It's the best we can do, Brandon,' he said, and turned around to face the Dragoons on the road while she took care of her own business.

'You needn't stand so close,' she scolded, when she had finished and joined him.

'*Au contraire, ma chérie*, I'm going to stick to you like a medicinal plaster. If you have any inhibitions about that, I suggest you abandon them right here.'

He watched her expressive face, still red, as she considered his words, then nodded. 'Consider them abandoned, Colonel—'

'No. No. "Hugh, my love",' he teased.

'Hugh, my love, you're trying me,' she shot back, which made him smile and took the lump of fear out of his stomach for the first time.

He draped his arm across her shoulder and gave her a squeeze. 'Adventures never are as much fun as bad novels make them out to be, Polly.'

'I can see that,' she said, as she tucked her fingers in his swordless belt. 'Just don't think for a minute you are going to take advantage of me!'

He kissed her temple and whispered in her ear, 'I already did, Polly. You're going to be a mother, remember?'

'How could I forget such an immaculate conception? I defy even the Pope to be more surprised than I.'

They laughed together, which made Sergeant Cadotte turn around in surprise. With a scowl, he motioned them closer to retie their hands and continue the journey.

They travelled off the beaten track until they came to a deserted village just at sunset. The casual way the Dragoons rode into the abandoned town told Hugh volumes. 'I think this must be where they bivouacked on the journey to São Jobim,' he whispered to Polly. 'Look how familiar they are with it. They knew it was deserted.'

He could feel Polly sigh against his chest. 'We might have been travelling on the moon,' she whispered back. 'This poor country. Does no one live in the interior any more?'

'Precious few, I gather. Only think how many armies have picked it clean, like a flock of vultures dining on one thin rabbit.'

Hugh put his head closer to hers to keep his voice low, but also because he could not deny the comfort he derived from her presence. 'I can't help but think this patrol of Dragoons was a forlorn hope.'

'I don't understand.'

He could see Sergeant Cadotte watching them. 'I'll tell you later.'

With help, they dismounted for the first time since the afternoon, with the same results. In agony, he leaned against Polly, who held him up, then kissed his cheek. 'You Marines are pretty worthless on horseback,' she chided.

'Aye, aye, wife. Just wait until you're back on a ship.'

He wanted her to laugh, but tears came to her eyes. 'Hugh, it couldn't be a moment too soon, even if I vomit from Oporto to Plymouth,' she whispered, her face turned into his chest. All he could do was hold her and silently agree, with all the longing of his deepwater heart.

Expertly, the Dragoons took their mounts into the half-burned church while Hugh and Polly stood in the square, then gradually edged over to a bench, where he spent a long moment trying to decide if sitting down again was worse than standing. He sat down gingerly, grateful at least that the bench wasn't going anywhere.

The evening meal—eaten in a barren interior courtyard—continued to confirm his suspicions about the nature of the French army in Portugal. He knew how fond Napoleon was of exhorting his soldiers to live off the land, but the Peninsula was frail and bare. Dinner was a stew of French hardtack soaked in a broth of wild onions and nothing more, washed down, at least, with excellent port someone must have pilfered from farther downriver. The men were already on starvation rations.

They sat close together in the cool evening air that was beginning to feel like autumn. Rains would come soon enough, spreading enough discomfort around to last a lifetime, if they were still prisoners on the trail. *Or we could be dead, my lady and me*, he reminded himself. It was better not to borrow trouble from tomorrow.

His thoughts were unprofitable, so it was with some relief they were interrupted by Sergeant Cadotte, who motioned for them to rise. He felt the hairs prick on the back of his neck. Was this the end, then? Was the Sergeant going to shoot him and turn Polly over to his soldiers? Hugh forced himself to subdue his rising panic.

He could have sobbed with relief when the Sergeant untied their hands, handed him a dusty blanket, and gestured towards a beehive-shaped stone cairn. 'You two will stay in the granary tonight,' Cadotte said.

He had to go on his knees to get into the granary and Polly bent double. The Sergeant put in a bucket. 'For your needs,' he said gruffly, and to Hugh's ears, almost with an undertone of compassion. 'I have no candle or lantern. And do not worry about mice, Madame Junot. It's been picked clean. See you in the morning.' He closed the door behind him and threw the bolt. They were in total darkness.

Hugh stood up, gratified that the ceiling was just tall enough to accommodate him. He put his arm on Polly's shoulder again, and walked with her around the granary, touching the wall, feeling for any weakness. There was none. From what little he knew of Portuguese history, the villagers' ancestors had built the granary to resist Huns and Visigoths and Moors. *They have come and gone and now we are here*, he thought, as the weight of the whole débâcle clamped down on his shoulders like mortar.

With a groan, he sat down and tugged Polly down beside him. Without a word, he sat cross-legged, when he could force his legs to move, and pulled her on to his lap.

It was all the invitation she needed to do what she had been holding back all day. She put her arms around his neck and sobbed into his tunic, as he knew she would. And somehow, he knew she wouldn't be startled if he joined in. They cried together, and soon, to his own sorely tried heart, she was crooning and rubbing her hand on his back.

'I'm sorry you had to be Sister Maria's witness, Hugh.'

Her soft words, whispered through her own tears, comforted him as nothing else could have. He almost believed her.

'I have dealt out my share of death and destruction, thanks to Boney, but I have never been jolted like that before,' he confessed, hardly able to get out the words.

She sat up in his lap and found his face in the dark, pressing her hands against his temples. 'He shouldn't have made you a party to that!'

Her voice was fierce, and he was glad he could not see her face in the darkness. He was a professional Marine engaged in a long war, and that was his life. Either she was the world's greatest actress, surpassed only by Siddons herself, or this young woman sitting on him in the dark didn't want him to suffer for the shocking death he had been forced to deal out. She seemed to care less for her own safety, than that he not suffer. It touched him.

When her tears stopped, she sniffed a few times, then managed a watery chuckle. 'I'm about to commit such a social solecism,' she said. She leaned sideways and he could feel her tugging at her skirt. In another moment she was blowing her nose on the fabric.

'Uh, I do have a handkerchief in my tunic,' he said. 'You should have asked.'

She leaned back against him again, warming his heart. 'Save it. We might really need it later,' she told him. Her voice faltered. 'At least, I hope there is a "later".'

'So do I, Brandon, so do I,' he said.

'That's "Polly, dear",' she reminded him, and he smiled.

'There is something I should do,' she told him. He heard a rip of fabric. 'Hugh, take off your tunic and shirt and let me bandage your arm.'

He had to think a moment like a village idiot, because his wound seemed to have happened years ago. 'It's not bleeding now,' he said.

'Look you here,' she demanded. 'I ripped off this strip and I intend to use it. Do what I said.'

'You're a taskmaster,' he teased, as he un-buttoned his tunic and removed it after she got off his lap. He unbuttoned his shirt and winced when he pulled his arm out of the sleeve. 'Learn that from Laura Brittle?'

'No. From my dear Nana, when she scolds her three-year-old,' Polly retorted.

She felt along his arm, which made him smile in the dark, then rested her finger lightly on the track of the ball that had slammed into him on the *barco rabelo*. 'We will pretend I am spreading on some of the salve that Philemon formulates,' she told him. 'At least it appears to have merely grazed your arm. Are you bulletproof?'

'Nearly so. Ah, that should do it, wife. You're a handy little wench.'

She laughed softly. 'You are a rascal! There is no one you need to impress in this wretched granary. There now. Put on your coat again.'

Polly made no objection when he pulled her on to his lap again. She was silent for a long time, but he knew she wasn't asleep. When she spoke, her voice was timid. 'I should be braver in the dark, but I am not, Colonel.'

'That's Hugh,' he pointed out prosaically. '"Hugh, darling", to be exact. You keep forgetting.'

Her voice turned apologetic. 'I should beg your pardon for saying we were married, but I couldn't think of anything else on short notice that might help us both.'

'It was the only thing I could think of, too, on short notice.'

'And now you have got me with child, Hugh…'

'…darling,' he finished.

He felt her laugh more than heard it. '"Hugh, darling", then! We will be in trouble if the French keep us for too many months. Even *they* can count!'

He joined in her laughter, but sobered quickly. 'Setting aside our fictitious fertility, we're in murky water, Brandon.'

She nodded and sighed, and he kissed the top of her head before he realised there wasn't any need in the pitch-black granary to fool any Frenchman. 'I fear these French, but we have reason to be wary of how desperate is their own plight.'

'Desperate?' she asked.

'Yes. I learned a great deal in Lisbon about insurgents. They call themselves *guerrilleros*, and they do not play fair. I am reminded of my Commandant's disgust of Americans in that late unpleasantness in the United States. The rebels shot from behind trees, and dropped logs across roads, robbed supply trains, and engaged in vastly ungentlemanlike behaviour.'

'I thought that was the point of war.'

'Well put, Brandon, you practical chit. You

don't think armies should just line up carefully and shoot at each other?'

'Seems a little stupid,' she replied, and he was glad to hear her voice getting drowsy. He didn't plan to ever sleep again, but it would be good if she could.

'Apparently those shadowy armies of Spain and Portugal would agree with you. It could very well be that this squad of Dragoons is in considerable danger from guerrillas. Besides that, I think they are a forlorn hope.'

'You did mention that. I don't understand.'

'This may have been almost a suicide mission,' he explained. 'From what I learned in Lisbon, Admiral Popham's landing north of us at Santander is finally threatening French power in León. I think Sergeant Cadotte's commanding officer is desperate to shut off any trafficking in information, because his position is none too secure. Just a suspicion, mind.'

She digested that thought, then stated calmly, 'It's a good thing you have on a red coat, isn't it?'

'And I intend to keep it on, and you close by me at all times.' He kissed her head again and tightened his arms around her. 'It's this way, Brandon—we truly have to think of ourselves as married. We must trust each other completely and look out for each other. I meant what I said about never letting you out of my sight. I intend to watch over you, as I did on the ship.'

'You are the kindest man I have ever met, but you are probably regretting you jumped into the *barco* so impulsively. Was that only this morning?'

He pulled her back against him and rested his chin on her head. '*Au contraire*, wife. That is the one thing about this day that I do *not* regret,' he declared, his voice firm. 'If I had not been along, there is no telling what would have happened to you at São Jobim.'

'Yes, there is,' she replied quietly. 'We know what would have happened to me.'

'Then it was for the best.'

He didn't think his heart could have felt any fuller just then, except that it did when she found his hand, and kissed the back of it like a supplicant. 'I am for ever in your debt,' she told him, then pulled his hand across her body to her shoulder until she was completely entwined in his arms.

There was no reason for him to feel even the slightest optimism, but something about holding Brandon in his arms lightened his mood. 'You know, Sergeant Cadotte was entirely wrong,' he told her.

'Not about Sister Maria Madelena, he wasn't,' Polly said.

'No, he wasn't.' He compromised, found her hand, raised it to his lips, and kissed it. 'I certainly didn't marry you for your money.'

She was silent for a minute, and then started to laugh. There was nothing of hysteria in her laugh, so he found himself smiling in the dark, and then laughing, too.

'You are more of a rogue than I suspected,' she declared, when she could speak.

'But not a mercenary one,' he added, which sent her into another peal of laughter.

It was easier to settle down then, his arms still tight around her. She sighed, laughed low once more, and then slept. He stared ahead into the darkness, knowing that it would be ages before he would not see Sister Maria Madelena pointing the pistol at her own throat.

'God forgive her,' he whispered into the gloom. 'God protect us.'

Chapter Thirteen

Polly panicked when she woke and could not feel her spectacles on her face. Terrified, she patted the ground beside her, trying not to wake up the Colonel as she searched. She stopped only when he gently took her hand and touched it to his uniform front, where she felt the outline of the glass.

'I took them off you at some point last night. What I cannot understand, Polly, dear, is why these pesky things didn't break yesterday. Do you want 'um now?'

She shook her head. 'No. There's nothing to see. Do you think it's morning?'

'It must be,' he told her. He cleared his throat. 'You'll have to excuse my vast indelicacy, but I need to get you off my lap and edge gracefully around this granary for private purposes. You might hum loudly to drown out the symphony, or marvel at the simplicity of male anatomy.'

'That *is* indelicate,' she agreed, then laughed. 'Just do your business! We're not standing much on ceremony, are we?'

'No, indeed. We cannot.'

She helped the Colonel to his feet when he found he could not stand, after all those hours of holding her on his lap. It took him a moment to stand up straight.

'Good God, Brandon. I will announce to you right now that I am feeling every single year this morning! I am also never going to joke again about men on horseback. How do they do it? I am still in pain from gripping that damned beast. My kingdom for an ocean.'

He stood another moment in silence. She was too shy to ask him if he needed assistance in walking across the granary. After copious cursing under his breath that she chose to ignore, he got himself in motion. In another moment, she heard the homely sound of water against the wall.

When he returned to her side, it was her turn, moving slowly in the other direction until she found the bucket. When she finished, she groped along the wall, following the sound of the Colonel's voice until she ran into him again. When she sat by his side this time, his arm seemed to go around her automatically.

He yawned. 'I think I could eat a whole pig, but something tells me we're not going to be well fed on this journey.'

'I must be philosophical,' she told him. 'I told myself when I came to Portugal that this would be a good time to get rid of what Miss Pym called my baby fat.'

'Miss Pym be damned,' he replied mildly, 'and spare me skinny females. I might remind you that you're supposed to be eating for two.'

'Wretch!' she said with feeling. 'Perhaps to while away the hours, we should play a game of "It Could Be Worse".' The words weren't out of her mouth before she saw Sister Maria Madelena, kneeling in the church. 'No. No. Not that.'

'No,' the Colonel agreed. 'We know it could be worse.' He touched her head with his. 'Tell me something about yourself that I don't know already, Brandon.'

She thought a moment, remembering what he already knew about her that she had divulged on the trip across the Channel. 'You already know I am the illegitimate daughter of a scoundrel whom you have resurrected and made into a wealthy man, for Sergeant Cadotte's benefit, if I am taken care of. That was a nice touch, husband.'

'Why, thank you,' he said modestly. 'If raising the dead to provide money in desperate situations doesn't paint me as a Scot, I don't know what would, considering my own French ancestry.'

She laughed. 'Hugh, darling, I would say your ancestors were quick studies.'

'They were, indeed, Polly, dear,' he teased, unruffled. 'There's nothing like political intrigue, plus menace from Queen Elizabeth and her Privy Council, to sharpen the mind, apparently. The original Philippe d'Anvers Junot obviously knew when to fold his tent and steal away. Evidently he also discovered he preferred oats and Calvinism to truffles and popes. What a resourceful man.'

Her laughter bounced back at her from the opposite wall. 'Your French is so good. Does the ghost of Philippe Junot the First linger in your family's schoolroom?'

The Colonel pulled her on to his lap again, and she couldn't think of a single reason to object. 'Our estate is too new to be haunted, Brandon! Your brain is overactive. We "Junnits" have always learned to speak French. It's a family tradition. I was luckier than most—I have no particular ear for language, but in 1803 before that laughable Peace of Amiens, I spent six months cooling my heels in a French prison. What a tutorial.'

Polly squinted into the darkness, trying to see some evidence of dawn. 'I hope you had more light than in here.'

'Light and then some, Polly, dear. That southern coast of France is devilish hot.'

He didn't say anything else, but she suddenly found herself longing for him to keep talking, to distract her from the granary, her hunger and the itch between her shoulder blades, and the fear that seemed to overlay every rational part of her brain.

'I'm afraid,' she said finally, speaking low, maybe not even wanting him to hear her. 'Please keep talking.'

He did, to her relief, telling her about his childhood in Kirkcudbrightshire, where it rained six days out of seven; the gardens of madly blooming roses in everyone's front garden; the hours he spent in small boats in the Firth of Solway; the year he chafed away at the University of Edinburgh until he convinced his father to see him into the Royal Marines; and his years in deepwater service, doing exactly what he loved.

As she listened to his musical accent and soothing voice, she realised how little her life was, in relation to his, how modest and unexceptionable. She knew that most women lived quiet lives at home. Her beloved sister Nana waited, agonised, and bore up magnificently under the strain of loving a man too often gone. Her equally well-loved sister Laura had chosen a different path, but it still revolved around her husband and her son, even as she used her own medical skills quietly in the shadow.

'Women don't amount to much,' she said, when the Colonel finished.

'What brought that on?' he asking, laughing.

'I was just thinking about how little I do, compared to you. We women wait, mostly.' She smiled in the dark, casting away whatever of her reserve that remained of the intimate situation in which she now found herself. 'We have husbands and babies, real *or* imagined, and that is all.'

'"That is all", eh? I doubt even Nana Worthy realizes how much her Captain yearns for her. I suspect she is his centre of calm in a world gone mad. He probably even calls her his True North. I would, and I don't even know your sister.'

Leaning back against the Colonel, Polly digested what he had said. Her first reaction was embarrassment, because this man she admired had no compunction about speaking his mind in such a frank way. She was struck also by her own words. 'We women' had seldom entered her mind before, let alone her vocabulary. Maybe her years as a student, and then the cushion, three years ago, of discovering her own protective sisters, had helped to keep her young. Maybe it was the casual way she now sat on the Colonel's lap and how suddenly she was so aware of his arms around her. Something stirred inside her, and it wasn't hunger or fear.

Maybe it had even stirred yesterday on the *barco*, when she dragged the partially conscious Colonel Junot on to her lap to protect him. Protect him from *what*, when women were so easily thrown aside and trampled on? *I thought I could save him*, she told herself in the gloom of the granary. *I felt stronger than lions, just then.*

'Maybe you'll understand better when you fall in love some day, Polly, dear,' the Colonel said in her ear.

She had to think of something to lighten her mood, which was troubling her almost more than the total darkness and the potential brevity of her life. 'You sound like someone who knows,' she told him.

'Aye, Polly, dear, I know what it is to love someone,' he said after a lengthy pause.

I am put in my place, Polly thought, embarrassed. Of course Colonel Junot had a lover somewhere. Why would he not? Who could there possibly be in the universe who did not think him attractive and worth more than gold?

She couldn't think of another thing to say, but it didn't matter, because the bolt was thrown on the granary's small door, and it swung open to reveal bright morning outside. She squinted in the light, then glanced at the Colonel, who was doing the same thing. She also knew she should get off his lap, but his arms tightened around her.

'I wish I knew what was coming, Polly, dear,' he murmured. He loosened his grip. 'Up you get, but I'm going out first.'

She willingly let him, not eager to have a soldier on the outside grab her hand. With a groan that made the soldiers outside laugh, the Colonel crawled through the entrance. Captured by the irrational terror that someone would slam the door now and leave her there in eternal darkness, Polly wanted to race after him. In another moment, Colonel Junot's hand reached for her. She grasped it for a second, then crouched her way out of the granary.

Polly took his hand again and they stood shoulder to shoulder, watching the enemy, looking this morning like most men campaigning in any army: dirty, smelly, and barely awake. She thought of her brother-in-law Philemon glowering at the breakfast table until Laura brought him tea.

It was obvious there wouldn't be any tea, and

not even anything beyond yesterday's hardtack, doled out in a smaller amount. When Hugh asked Cadotte if he could fetch water for all of them from the well in the square, the NCO only shrugged.

'You would not wish it, Junnit,' he replied. 'The well is full of either Portuguese corpses or French ones. I didn't look too closely.'

Polly shuddered and moved closer to the Colonel. Cadotte unbent enough to nod to her. 'Madame Junnit, I do wish we had something more to offer you than hardtack. I truly do.'

It stung her to think the Sergeant was worried about her non-existent unborn child. All she could do was blush and avert her gaze from his, which—all things considered—was probably the correct attitude. Coupled with her lie, the knowledge of her hypocrisy only stung her more.

'You are too kind, Sergeant,' she murmured.

It was Cadotte's turn to appear uneasy. He frowned and looked away, growling at some fictitious misdemeanor perpetrated by one or another of his hardened Dragoons to alleviate his embarrassment. Or so she thought, as she watched. 'I must keep reminding myself that he is some woman's husband,' she whispered to the Colonel.

'That will render the Sergeant less odious?' Hugh asked, amused.

'Certainly,' she replied crisply. 'Hugh, darling,' she added, which made him chuckle.

Because there was no food, there was little preparation before the Sergeant gave the order for his men to mount. Lips twitching, he watched Colonel Junot heave himself into the saddle with a sigh and a grimace. Without a word, Cadotte tied his hands together again, then tied Polly's together before lifting her gently into the saddle in front of the Colonel.

'I wish you would trust me enough to leave my hands untied,' Hugh grumbled as he lifted his arms and encircled Polly again.

'Trust you enough? I don't trust you at all,' the Sergeant said frankly, as he mounted his own horse. 'We are riding north and east now, covering rough terrain and staying off the roads. If we see partisans, we will hide, because we are a small squad that probably never should have survived our mission to São Jobim, so close to the British lines.'

'I thought as much,' Hugh murmured. 'You were some Lieutenant's forlorn hope, weren't you?'

Cadotte looked down his long nose at them until Hugh was silent. 'That is hardly your business, Colonel. If we encounter partisans and you do anything to attract them, I will shoot you and turn Madame Junnit over to my troopers. Am I perfectly clear?'

'As crystal,' Hugh snapped.

The two men glared at each other. Cadotte handed the reins of Hugh's horse to his Corporal and spurred his horse to the head of the line. The squad began to move at a moderate gait, leaving the deserted village behind and turning away from the Douro.

Polly looked ahead at the mountains and shook her head. 'We're to cross *those*?' she asked.

'It would seem so,' Hugh replied. 'Our Sergeant knows he is in dangerous territory. I'm a little surprised he didn't make me take off my red tunic.' He sighed. 'Of course, any remaining mountain people—*montagnards*—are probably no more fond of the British than they are the French. Portugal is a carcass picked clean.'

'Do you wonder why he didn't just shoot us back there?' Polly asked.

'Polly, dear, I'm actually surprised he let us out of the granary,' the Colonel replied, and tightened his arms around her at her sudden intake of breath. Glancing at the Sergeant, who was watching them, he nuzzled her cheek. 'I don't think he believes I will give him any money for his farm. Men at war tend to be cynical, and who can blame them?'

'Then why are we alive?'

'Polly, dear, I wish I knew his game.'

It was no game, she decided, after three days of weary riding through narrow mountain passes that made her close her eyes and turn her face into Hugh's tunic. Her jaws ached from gritting her teeth as the horses—the big-boned animals that French cavalry used—sidled along nearly imaginary trails far above boiling mountain streams.

She knew the heights bothered Hugh, although he did not admit as much. Once when their horse stumbled, sending rocks plunging down into the gorge, he came close to admitting his own fear. 'Polly, dear, I would trade about five and a half years off my life this moment if we were suddenly transported to the deck of a frigate.'

You must be sorely tried, to admit as much, Polly thought, as she screwed her eyes shut against that awful moment when they would plunge off the mountain face. 'Hugh, darling, you must have mice in your pockets,' she managed to squeak out, when she could talk. 'You know how *I* feel about life on the rolling wave.'

He was silent for a long moment, then all he

said was, 'Bless your heart, Brandon, you're a rare one.'

She didn't feel like a rare one. She was grimy, smelly, and hungry, with filmy teeth and a constantly growling stomach. The blood from the noisome floor of the church at São Jobim had stained her light blue muslin dress, which was also torn now, and muddy from a night spent shivering in the Colonel's arms as they were tied to a tree. Still, she decided the tree was better than the claustrophobia of the granary, if only she weren't so cold.

Somewhere, far below in the lovely coastal valleys of the Rio Douro, it was late summer. Here in the *tras o montes* region, autumn had begun, and with it a light mist that fogged the upper valleys and brought relief only to the Dragoons. Now the troopers travelled with caution, but visible relief, because the mist obscured their presence from watchful partisans. They stopped for nothing after the second day, when even the hardtack gave out.

'Tell me, Hugh, darling, are the French so poor they cannot even feed their soldiers?' she asked the Colonel after one noon stop when the only refreshment was cold water from a stream.

'It's not that they cannot, but that they choose not,' Hugh said, as they walked shoulder to shoulder along the bank. 'Napoleon believes that his *Grand Armée* should feed itself in the field.'

'I don't think much of that,' she retorted.

Hugh laughed softly. 'You should demand that Sergeant Cadotte take you to Napoleon so you can give him a piece of your mind.'

Polly glared at him. 'I know you're hungry. Don't try to tell me you're not.'

'I'm hungry,' he agreed, 'but I've been hungrier. Brandon, as long as we get drinking water, we'll be all right. You'll be amazed how long we can last without food.'

'Mostly I'm tired,' she admitted, and stopped walking. 'What can I do about that?'

'Get something to eat,' he said wearily. 'Bit of a vicious circle, ain't it?'

She couldn't help the tears that spilled on to her cheeks then, even though she tried to brush at them. It would have been easy to do that if her hands hadn't been tied. As it was, she couldn't hide them.

To comfort her, Hugh raised his tied hands and dropped them around her, pulling her close to him. With a shudder, she rested her cheek against his chest as his chin came down on the top of her head.

'*Why* did Sister Maria Madelena do what she did?' Polly asked.

'For love of her country, I expect, and fierce

anger at the French and the way they treated her,' the Colonel replied. He peered at her face. 'Have you never loved something enough to risk everything, even your life, for it?'

'I suppose I have not,' she said, after some thought. 'Have you?'

'Oh, yes,' he said, more promptly than she. 'Perhaps that is why I am a Royal Marine until I die.'

She thought that over, then dismissed the idea. *Maybe I will understand when I am older*, she told herself. 'But why did she involve me?'

'That we will never know, Polly, my love,' he said.

'It's "Polly, dear",' she reminded him.

'I thought I would change the dialogue a little, Polly, dear,' he replied. 'Variety is, after all, the spice of life, or so I am told. I doubt you want a boring, predictable husband.'

She had to smile then. 'When I get home to England, I am going to vie for the attention of an apothecary or perhaps a comptroller.'

'Too boring by half,' he said, his voice light. 'You'll rue it the moment you get in bed with him.'

Startled, she looked up at him, and saw the laughter in his eyes. He glanced over at the bank. 'Uh oh, the Sergeant is watching.'

He kissed her then, pressing his bound hands

against the small of her back and then raising them to her neck. She had never been kissed on the lips by a man before, but she knew better than to draw back or act surprised, not with the Sergeant watching. She returned his kiss, surprised a little at the softness of his lips, since he did not look like a soft man. Their lips parted, and he kissed her again and again, little kisses that made her lean into his hips, to her surprise and embarrassment.

When they finished, he asked in a low voice, 'Is he still watching?'

Suddenly shy, she turned her head to look. Sergeant Cadotte was looking at the water, then tapping his boot with his riding whip.

'You're a scoundrel, Hugh, darling,' she whispered into his neck. 'I'm not so certain he was ever looking.' She laughed then, and stirred in his arms, which was the Colonel's cue to raise his arms and release her.

'Perhaps he wasn't,' he said with remarkable aplomb, 'but at least you are not so unhappy now.'

She certainly wasn't, she reflected, as they travelled into the afternoon of another dreary day. Only the warmth in her middle, which began and spread downwards when she leaned so close to the Colonel, gave her any satisfaction. That she was out of her element, she knew beyond a doubt. So was the Colonel, and for all she knew, despite their hardness, the Dragoons, too. They were captives riding with hunted men trying to get back to their own lines. Sergeant Cadotte must have been a farmer before Napoleon came calling, yet here he was.

'I can't forgive them for what they did to the priest and to Sister Maria Madelena,' she murmured, half to herself, later that day.

'Nor should you, or trust them for even a second,' Hugh said. 'Still, if we had met these men while strolling in Vauxhall Gardens, we would probably just have nodded and smiled. War changes everyone.' His hands tied, he nuzzled aside her hair with his lips and kissed her ear, biting gently on her earlobe. 'Maybe even you, Brandon.'

She looked around, but the Sergeant was not watching them. 'Hugh, darling, you are taking advantage of me,' she said, feeling that warmth again.

'And who would not, in my boots?' he said complacently. 'Polly, dear.'

There wasn't even a deserted village for shelter that night. They dismounted into mud and gravel. When the rains came, Sergeant Cadotte rummaged in his pack for an oiled slicker, which he draped over Hugh's shoulders. Polly shivered in his arms, unable to keep her teeth from chattering with the cold.

She had not complained when the cold rain started to fall. Come to think of it, she never complained, Hugh realised as he held her close. She said nothing about her empty belly, even though he heard her stomach growl and she winced from the pain of it. She had grown quieter and quieter as the hours passed, and Hugh wished with all his heart that he could make her comfortable, even if for only a moment.

They were not in as bad shape as one of the Sergeant's men, a Private gone unconscious with the cold and deprivation. There was no shelter beyond the dripping trees for a bivouac that night, but two Dragoons had put their slickers together and with some sticks, created a rude shelter for their companion.

'Poor man,' Polly said, as she stood in the shelter of Hugh's arms. 'He's going to die, isn't he?'

'Probably. You'll have to ask your brother-in-law why some men are impervious to a little cold, and others succumb. He's the enemy, Brandon,' Hugh reminded her.

'I know. I know. Still…' She let the sentence trail away.

She surprised him by turning around to face

him, burrowing her head into his chest as they stood together, hands tied in front of them. She took his hand and raised it to her breast. 'I don't want to die before I have even lived,' she whispered. 'Don't let that happen to me, Hugh, if you are my friend.'

'I'm your husband, Polly,' he whispered, feeling exactly that. 'I'm proud of you, the way you have borne up under this misery. You're brave and kind.' Unsure of himself, he knew he should make light of what he was saying. 'And an excellent mother to our child.'

She glanced up at him then, her pretty blue eyes so tired and filled suddenly with tears. 'Don't tease me about that, Hugh,' she whispered back. 'I…I don't want to die before I have a child! Don't ever tease me any more about that.'

Words failed him. He raised his bound hands, wanting to pull them free so he could caress away her tears; scrabble in the sparse vegetation to find something—anything—to feed her. In the horror that was São Jobim, he had sworn to protect her with all the fervour with which he had sworn, as a lad of fifteen, to defend King and country. In fact, the two were inextricably bound together in his mind. He wanted to touch her gently until they were content enough in this miserable wilderness where the heavens had opened up. He wanted to assure her that she would not die until she had lived, but he could promise her nothing of the kind.

'No more teasing, Brandon,' he said. 'Don't let me shock you, but I feel exactly the same way about the very same thing.' It struck him then that he understood her completely. 'I...I don't think I have even started to live yet, either, and we know how old I am.'

She hesitated and he leaned closer to her. He thought he knew what she was too shy to ask, this young woman who had been raised properly and carefully, but who must have been aroused as he was aroused when he kissed her ear and then her neck, earlier that afternoon. This was all so strange—no one could seriously fall in love under such conditions.

Or could one? He didn't dare think it was possible. Lord knew he had tried to think of the Brittles' objections to him. But as the rain thundered down, he kissed her with all the fervour of his heart. Because the others were gathered around the dying trooper, this was the most privacy they had enjoyed since the granary. To his joy, she kissed him back, little inarticulate murmurs coming from her throat that made his body yearn for her as he had never yearned for any female in his life. He knew without a qualm that for the rest of his life, he would cherish and protect this woman to the end of his strength. He had sworn to do it, on his honour as a Marine. Was there more? Time might tell, if there was time, and he had his doubts.

He kissed her nose next, then stepped back, shrugged out of the slicker and left it wrapped around his love. Without a word to her, he strode to the circle of Dragoons, calling for the Sergeant. When he had the harried man's attention, Hugh just held out his hands wordlessly. *'S'il vouz plaît,'* he said simply.

Brandon was beside him then, doing the same thing. 'Please, Sergeant,' she said. 'Perhaps we can help your man.'

'And do what?' Cadotte snapped.

Hugh knew that whether seconds or decades would be allowed to pass in the life of his loved one, he would never be more proud of Polly Brandon than he was then. 'I can hold him in my arms,' she said. 'Men are well enough, Sergeant, but women are better. You know they are.'

Cadotte looked at the two of them. Without a word he untied their hands. Polly bobbed a small curtsy that made her look suddenly young. She gave Hugh such a look that he felt his insides begin to smoulder, then shouldered her way through the troop of Dragoons, those men who only a week ago would have raped and killed her, and sat down beside the unconscious Dragoon.

Humming softly, she let one of the men help her lift the dying man into her lap. After only the slightest hesitation, she began to smooth his dirty hair from his forehead. Someone handed her a dry stocking, and she wiped the grime from his face, bending lower over him until her breasts touched his chest. She did it deliberately, wanting the dying man to know he was with a woman.

Hugh watched in humble amazement as his green girl sent her enemy to his death peacefully. She unbuttoned the Dragoon's ragged green tunic and pressed her hand against his chest, stroking him until his eyes flickered open. He tried to speak and she leaned closer.

'Emilie?' he asked, with the smallest bit of hope in his voice.

'*Oui,*' she replied. '*Dormes-toi, mon chéri.*'

With a look of surprising contentment, he died. Polly Brandon closed his eyes and began to cry. As Hugh listened, she seemed to cry every tear that had ever been shed over every soldier in every war since the Lord God Almighty cast Satan from heaven and the trouble really started.

Still enveloped in the too-large slicker, Polly Brandon stood as chief mourner as the troopers buried their comrade. Hugh helped dig the grave, needing the release of hard work to calm the fires in his body. He could have cried at his own weakness, when he had to stop because he was exhausted. No one noticed because all the men, equally starved, were taking turns.

No one said anything over the grave. Polly cried. Hugh held her close, then turned around, walked to the Sergeant and held out his hands, to be bound again. Cadotte shook his head. He pointed to the foot of a large tree. 'Sleep there,' was all he said. 'We ride at dawn. I'll bind you then.'

Without a word, Hugh wrapped the slicker around both of them and sat Brandon down under the tree. His hands free, he pulled the slicker over them, protecting their heads from the rain, and pulled Brandon close. With a sigh, she rested her head on his chest, her arm possessively around his body. In a matter of seconds, she was breathing evenly.

'Please, Polly, I need your comfort,' he whispered, wishing she could hear him.

She did, which humbled him beyond anything. Without a word spoken between them, without even opening her eyes, she unbuttoned her dress. She untied the cord holding her chemise together, took his hand, and placed it on her bare breast with a sigh. It was warm and softer than he could have imagined. He cupped her breast carefully in his hand as his eyes closed, too. He tried to open his eyes when she put her hand inside his tunic and shirt and stroked him as she had caressed the French Dragoon. All he could do was succumb to his best night's sleep in recent memory, as the rain poured down.

Chapter Fourteen

If the burial didn't change everything, crossing an unnamed mountain stream did. What surprised Hugh about saving Sergeant Cadotte's life was the ferocious way Polly Brandon did all he demanded without question. She had the heart of a Marine, and this unexpected discovery bound him to her tighter than the cords shackling them. Not only did he love her; he respected her as a brother in arms.

They had come to the river at dusk one week later. They had been slowly winding their way down to it for most of the day on the precipitous switchbacks that Portuguese mountain passes were notorious for. He knew how terrified Polly was, shrinking back against him as they travelled the dangerous trail, their hands bound and at the mercy of the Corporal, who had roped their horse to his.

One of the Dragoons on the narrow file in front of them had lost his life around a sharp turn when his horse made a misstep and trod upon thin air. The man shrieked all the way to his death. Polly's sharp intake of breath and the shaking of her shoulders told him volumes about her own state of mind.

She had borne up well against the journey. Even the Sergeant had remarked on that to him the night before, when he had tied them to a picket stake and laid down next to them, spreading his blanket over them all, which had touched Hugh.

'I wish matters were different for your lady,' was all the Sergeant said, and it was quietly spoken, as Cadotte turned on his side to sleep, his back to them.

My lady, Hugh thought, as he cuddled Polly close. He knew her body well by now. His acquaintance with it had begun on the voyage from Plymouth, but he had taken pains not to embarrass her, even as they had to manage private functions in sight and sound of each other. She had accepted their constant closeness for her protection. There was nothing missish about Polly Brandon, which eased his plight. When she had so generously comforted him two nights ago, he knew he was in her debt for ever.

He wished she did not continue to chafe about the impulsive gesture that had caused him to jump into the *barco* in Oporto. He knew it still bothered her that he could be safe downriver, and by now, at Ferrol Station, or even in Plymouth. Not even the reality of her probable fate at the hands of Cadotte's troopers seemed to assuage the guilt she felt at endangering his life, because she had insisted upon accompanying Sister Maria Madelena on the ill-fated journey.

'It's my fault you are here,' she told him after the Dragoon fell to his death.

'Polly, dear, life is strange,' he had said, and it sounded so facile to his own ears, something uttered vapidly in a drawing room to impress fops.

Obviously unimpressed with his philosophising, she had said nothing more to him. It chafed him that she felt so alone in her misery. He knew she liked him, but he also suspected she had not invested her heart in him, as she would have if they were actually married, instead of submitting to a great fiction to stay alive. Something told him she needed to discover how much she loved him, if she even did.

They came to the ford of the stream before dusk. The Sergeant sat in his saddle, his leg

across the pommel, in that casual way of his
that Hugh could only envy. Cadotte watched the
stream for some moments, as if weighing the
value of crossing now or waiting until morning.
The mist that had been falling on them for days
must have fallen as rain higher in the mountains,
because the stream boiled along like a river. To
cross now or not? Hugh almost smiled to himself; he knew what command decisions felt like.

'We will cross now,' the Sergeant said finally,
and gestured his men forwards.

'How?' Polly murmured, into Hugh's tunic.

It was a good question. There was little
remaining of the stone bridge that had once
spanned the stream, more properly a river now.
One army or another had blown it into gravel
years ago, leaving behind only stone pillars at
either bank. Some enterprising soul had rigged
a rope across the expanse. Hugh pointed this out
to Polly.

'I suppose we are to grip the rope as the horse
does his best,' he told her, trying not to sound
as dubious as he felt.

'Then the Sergeant had better free our hands,'
was all she said.

The Sergeant seemed disinclined to agree,
which hardly surprised him. What did surprise
him was the way Polly argued with the Frenchman, holding her bound hands in front of her

and then waving them about, which made the Sergeant's face twitch in what Hugh had decided was as near as the man ever got to smiling.

'You insist?' the Sergeant said finally.

Polly stared him directly in the eyes and nodded vigorously. 'I insist.'

'You have no power to make me do anything, Madame Junnit,' he said.

'I know that, but I still insist,' she replied.

Sergeant Cadotte turned to him and threw up his hands in a Gallic gesture. 'Is she always so much trouble?'

'This and more,' Hugh answered. 'Humour her.'

The Sergeant did, gesturing for his Corporal to untie them. The Sergeant had the sapper find him a longer rope and told his Corporal to tie it around their waists, binding them together.

'We would be safer if you didn't fetter us,' Hugh said.

'I don't care about your safety,' Cadotte snapped, obviously weary of decisions and complainers. 'I want you across the river together, or not at all.'

Cadotte sent half his troopers across the stream. Hugh watched as they guided their mounts into the swift-moving water, grasping the rope as the water tugged at them.

'I do not think it is more than four feet deep. I fear the current. Can you swim?'

Polly nodded, her eyes on the water. 'Miss Pym is a modern educationist. She took us river bathing in the Avon.' She glanced back at him, and he saw the worry in her face take on a calmness that impressed him. 'However, the Avon never looked like this. It's rushing so *fast.*'

He kissed her cheek impulsively. 'D'ye know, Brandon, one of the many things that impresses me about you is that you're not afraid to admit you're afraid, but you plug along anyhow.'

His reward was a faint smile and a shake of her head, as if she thought him two-thirds barmy. Perhaps she did; maybe he was. Who understood women?

The Corporal crossed next, holding tight to the rope and calling for them to do the same, as he kept a firm grip on the rope around their waists. The stream caught them, and Hugh felt the mighty pull of the water. Polly whimpered, then was silent as she glided her hand along the rope. He could feel how tightly she gripped the horse's flanks with her legs.

'You'll do, Polly, dear,' he said loud in her ear, to be heard above the sound of the water.

When they reached the opposite shore, he had to coax Polly to let go, finally just twisting her fingers from their death grip on the rope that spanned the stream. Her face was pale and her eyes huge in her head, as the Corporal tugged their mount on to the bank. Only then did her shoulders slump. 'Thank God,' she said simply.

Hand possessively on her shoulder, he turned in the saddle to watch Cadotte cross. No sooner than it took him to blink, Hugh watched as the Sergeant plunged headfirst into the river as his horse stumbled over rocks slippery with moss. He came up sputtering and grasping frantically for his mount, but he was already downstream of any aid.

'Stand up, man,' Hugh muttered to himself as he quickly undid the knot tying him to Polly. 'It's not that deep.'

As he had remarked to Polly before their crossing, it wasn't the depth, but the current that was playing merry hell with Sergeant Cadotte. He retied the rope around Polly and dismounted, his eyes on the Sergeant, who was watching his startled troopers with desperate eyes. He tried to speak as he was swept downstream.

'Polly, I'm going in,' Hugh said as he took off his tunic and gorget and handed them to her. 'Convince the Corporal to let loose of our horse and follow me along the bank with that rope. Get ahead of me and think of something!'

As he unbuckled his shoes he looked back to see some of the men unlimbering their weapons.

Fools, he thought. *And the French think they will win this war?* He dived into the water.

There was no thought in Polly's mind except to do exactly as the Colonel said. Scarcely breathing, she watched him make powerful strokes to the middle of the stream, then let the current carry him towards the floundering Sergeant as he tried to swim. Polly pulled at the rope connecting her horse to the Corporal's to get his attention. 'Let me go,' she shouted. 'Then follow me. And for God's sake, stop them from firing. Hugh is trying to *help!*'

The Corporal must have thought she could do some good. After a spare second to stare at her and mull her demand, he did as she said, untying the rope from his pommel and tossing it to her. Grasping the reins for the first time, she dug her heels into the horse and was rewarded with an unexpected burst of speed from an animal probably as tired and hungry as she was. She could hear the Corporal shouting something to her in French, but she ignored him, putting all thoughts aside of what would happen to her if both men died in the river and she was left to face the troopers alone.

To her relief, she heard the Corporal pounding his horse along behind her. She watched the river, which had narrowed and deepened, and the Colonel, who swam with one arm clasped around the Sergeant now. She urged the horse on until they were nearly parallel to the men in the river. In another hundred yards of pounding along the bank, she was ahead of them.

Once through the narrow gorge, the river widened again and the current slowed. She glanced over her shoulder to see Hugh gradually angling towards the shore, fighting the lessening current. He tried to stand up once, but the river yanked them down again.

Polly glanced back to see the rest of the troopers following the Corporal. Her horse was flecked with foam by the time she came to another ford where the bank gradually inclined to a sandy beach. Throwing herself off her horse, she gestured to the Corporal, who dismounted, too.

'Can you swim?' she shouted.

He returned a blank stare, and she realised she was speaking in English. She repeated her question in French, and he shook his head.

It's up to me, then, she thought. *Oh, I don't like adventures.* She handed him the end of the rope tied around her waist, and told him to hang on tight as she went into the stream, recoiling in shock from the cold, and then struggling to stand upright.

The water came up to her chest and the current knocked her over. She struggled to her feet again, then looked at the bank, where the troopers had dismounted and were helping the Corporal with the rope.

Falling and rising several times, and encouraged by the troopers on shore, Polly fought her way to the middle of the stream where the water boiled around a significant boulder. She heaved herself against the protecting rock, letting it anchor her, gratified to see the rope stretching almost taut as the troopers pulled just enough to keep it level, but not to yank her into the stream.

Eyes anxious, she watched for the men. *Please, Hugh*, she thought, *please, Hugh*. It was not coherent or profound, but as she said his name over and over, she realised there was nothing she would not do for this man. He was no longer a Colonel, a Marine, a man she had only met a few months ago. Proper or not, their trials had bound them together tighter than a trussed Christmas goose. He owed her no more than she owed him.

She waited there, her teeth chattering, as the Colonel and the Sergeant swung around the bend of the river. Hugh quickly saw what she had done, and struck out for the space between her and the bank. He grasped the rope with a waterlogged yell of triumph and clung to it as the troopers on shore dug in against the impact.

The force of two men hitting the rope yanked

her into the channel again, as she had known it would. She took a deep breath and clung to the rope as the current pulled her under and then downstream. His face a study in concern, Hugh tried to reach for her. She shook her head, and held up the end of the rope that bound them to shore, so he would not worry.

She had no reason to fear. Gradually, the troopers pulled the three of them towards the shallow bank. It was just a matter of hanging on now, and she had the rope tied around her waist. She watched in relief as the two men crawled ashore and slumped on the sand, then let the troopers pull her ashore. She sank face down beside the Colonel, pillowing her cheek against the sand. The water lapped at her legs still, until one of the troopers gently grasped her under her arms and pulled her higher up on the bank. She put her hand on Colonel Junot's back, content just to touch him.

When he was breathing evenly again, he heaved himself on to his back and slowly turned his head towards her. 'Words fail me, Brandon,' was all he said, as he closed his eyes.

Suddenly terrified, she crawled closer, then straddled him, shaking his shoulders and crying. 'Don't you dare die right now!' she sobbed. 'We have miles to go!'

She stopped when he grasped her wrists. 'Polly, dear, I am quite alive.'

She collapsed on top of him then, crying, and not moving until he muttered something about swallowing half of the river, and would she please get off his stomach?

She did as he said, helping him into a sitting position, while he coughed until water dribbled down the front of his checked shirt, torn from his rough passage over rocks and past snags of timber.

She thought of the Sergeant then, but the Corporal was already beside him, turning his leader on to his side as water drained from his mouth. Cadotte opened his eyes and he stared at Colonel Junot in amazement.

'*Mon Dieu*, you saved my life,' he said, when he could talk.

To Polly's amusement, the matter seemed to embarrass the Colonel. 'Yes. Well. Of course I did! Do you take me for someone raised by crofters?'

'But you saved my life,' the Sergeant repeated. He lay back, exhausted, his head against his Corporal's leg.

'Let me assure you, Sergeant Cadotte, I have no love for you at all,' Hugh said. 'Not one scrap of affection. But somewhere near Angoulême there are a woman and two children who think you are worth saving. I did it for them.'

With some effort, the Sergeant managed that twitch that passed for a smile. 'You could have saved yourself some money,' he countered, still stubborn.

'I told you I am an officer and a gentleman. Why won't you believe it?' Hugh said patiently, as though he spoke to a child. 'Polly, dear, are you and our little one all right?'

Drat the man. Why did he have to embarrass her? 'Yes,' she replied, her voice steely.

He patted her leg, then rested his hand on her thigh, giving her a roguish grin and daring her to take exception to his fond, husbandly gesture. He glanced at Cadotte. 'I dare you to submit her name for one of Napoleon's new Legions d'Honneur.'

The Sergeant's lips twitched again and he let out a bark of laughter this time that quickly turned into a coughing fit.

'Lord, you are droll, Colonel,' he said, after his Corporal raised him into a sitting position. 'I will give her something better. You two can ride without your hands tied now.'

The Sergeant surprised her again. He reached across the short space that separated them, took Hugh's hand in his and kissed it, then reached for Polly's and did the same.

* * *

There was daylight left, but no one questioned the Sergeant's decision to backtrack to the bridge and move east just far enough to be among the trees and out of sight. There was even shelter of sorts—a gutted stone farmhouse with interior walls remaining, but no roof. Rendered stupid by exhaustion, Hugh allowed Polly to help him from the horse. Her efforts embarrassed him, but all he wanted to do was lie down and never cross a river again.

'If I see so much as a tin bathtub in the next four or five years, I swear it will unman me,' he told her as she helped him into the wholly inadequate shelter of the tumbled stones.

'You're the one who told me adventures really weren't much fun,' she reminded him.

She was as wet as he was, but he let her help him from his shirt and trousers and wrap him in a blanket smelling strongly of horse. Not until he was lying beside a bonfire, built by one of the troopers, did she think of herself. His men were taking care of Cadotte in much the same fashion on the other side of the interior wall, in what must have been the hut's great room in better days. She cajoled another blanket, looked around to make sure none of the troopers were in sight, and took off her dress.

His eyes could barely stay open, but he

watched her stand there in her chemise for a long moment, then sigh and lift it over her head, until she was naked.

'Not a word out of you, Colonel,' she murmured, as she sidled in next to his bare body and pulled both blankets over them. With a sigh, she pillowed her head on his arm, closed her eyes, and slept.

He couldn't help himself. He reached across her body and gently touched her breast. Knowing he deserved a slap to his face, he smoothed his thumb across her nipple, which only elicited a small sigh from her as she burrowed into his warmth. He reminded himself he was an officer and a gentleman as he ran his hand along her rounded hip and stopped there—the spirit as unwilling now as the flesh was weak. He just wanted to sleep until the war ended and he was home again in Kirkcudbright, with his father and sister there to fuss over him.

When he woke several hours later it was dark and Polly was whimpering. Careful to keep the blankets around them both, he propped himself up on his elbow, the better to see her. He watched her expressive face a moment in the faint glow of the bonfire, which had worked its way down to glowing coals, and carefully removed her spectacles. One of the lenses was cracked in the corner now. He set the spectacles on a niche in the wall behind them, a place where a *paisano*'s wife had probably kept her favourite saint.

Polly stirred and cried out, but she still slept. He lay back again, enjoying the feel of her body against his, warm for the first time since he had dived into the river after the Sergeant. As his eyes closed in weariness, he was sure of nothing, except that he relished this woman. How odd it was that in all of his thirty-seven years, he had finally found the woman he wanted like no other, and they were smack in the middle of a war, prisoners, even.

Hugh woke later when Polly stirred in his arms, weeping this time, but still asleep. In his years in both barracks and the fleet, he had heard many a young Marine, newly scoured by battle, do precisely that. His reaction had always been to pat them on the shoulder, so he did that now.

'I'm sorry,' she whispered, as she woke. 'What must you think of me?'

'I think you're magnificent and braver than lions,' he whispered back.

Wordlessly, she turned over to face him and put her arms tight around him, drawing him close as she muffled her sobs against his chest.

'It's too much,' she managed to gasp out, when she could speak. 'Just too much. Is this ever going to end?'

He held her close, cherishing the feel of her breasts against his chest, her hips so close to his. His lust turned to tenderness; all he wanted to do now was touch her shoulder again, as he did his young Marines, and send her back to sleep as he watched over her. It wasn't too much to ask, and God was kind for a moment. She sighed, relaxed, and slept.

He thought she would sleep for the night, but she woke a few minutes later, patting his cheek to rouse him. He looked around in alarm, then settled down when she put her hands on both sides of his face and her forehead against his.

'Hugh, you need to know something,' she told him, her eyes earnest, but with another emotion visible. 'I don't know how you feel about this, but I have to be honest, don't I?'

Mystified, he nodded.

'You may not like it, but I suppose that doesn't matter,' she said. 'How do I say this? Don't let me die without making me a woman.' She put her hands over her face. 'I am so ashamed to say that.'

He took her hands away. 'Don't be. There aren't enough honest people in the world.'

Her words came out in a rush then. 'I know I

am probably asking too much. I swear it won't go any further. I mean, here you are, a Lieutenant Colonel, someone of importance, and we know who I am.' She faltered. 'I just wanted you to know.'

She looked ready to apologise further, but he put his fingers on her lips. 'Stop right there, Brandon,' he whispered.

Her face clouded over, but only until he grasped her shoulders and pulled her close for a kiss. She clung to him, her face against his chest, so he kissed her hair this time.

'Brandon, you're not asking too much. Not at all.'

She raised her head to look at him, and he saw her shyness. 'Hugh, I'm just not sure what to do.'

'Nor am I,' he replied, 'except that everyone thinks we're already married.'

'We look like we are right now,' she pointed out, ever the practical one, which he had decided weeks ago was only one of her many charms. 'My goodness.'

'You're not afraid to give up your virginity to me?'

She shook her head, and her humour came back like a brief candle. 'This sort of thing wasn't covered at Miss Pym's, but I have no intention of going to my death without even a memory of a man's love. I refuse to just take the words of poets and sonnets, even Shakespeare's.'

He doubted he had ever heard a more honest admission in his entire life, even as Polly Brandon's eyes closed. She struggled to open them. 'Drat,' she muttered softly. 'Heroines in novels don't fall asleep at times like this.'

Laughing softly, Hugh cradled her in his arms and watched in amusement and love as she sighed and slept. Exhausted, he did the same.

Chapter Fifteen

At peace with himself after Brandon's declaration, Hugh waited until she slept, then left the warmth of her body, careful to tuck the blankets around her. He found his clothes—still damp—and put them on. At least his thorough dousing in one of Portugal's nameless rivers had cleansed his skin and made his smallclothes less objectionable. He smiled in the dark to think of what his Colonel Commandant in Plymouth would think of his filthy state.

I used to be a bit of a military fop, Hugh thought as he buttoned his trousers, which hung loose on him now. Amazing what three weeks on short rations and then no rations could do. He glanced at Polly. He decided that, as much as he admired her, he preferred the Brandon with more meat clinging to her.

He put his gorget around his neck again, always feeling a relief at having it hanging there, as it had for twenty years now. He knew he should wear it outside his uniform tunic, but there was some comfort from feeling the cold metal gradually warm against his skin, as it reminded him who he was. He glanced at Polly again, as unexpected emotion welled up in him. *I wish I had a ring for your finger right now*, he told himself. *Maybe you are not my actual wife; maybe there never will be one, but you should have a ring. Something eye-popping to impress our lovable Sergeant Cadotte.*

He stood a moment looking down at her, suddenly indecisive. If she should wake up while he was gone, what would she do? He chanced it, because he smelled something cooking in the next ruined stone room. Something told him he and Brandon had nothing to fear now from the Frenchmen. Their Sergeant was alive because he and Polly had acted.

Squatting by the fire, Sergeant Cadotte looked up when he came around the corner. 'You see before you a miracle, Colonel Junnit. I do not refer to myself, although I remain in your debt,' he said.

Food. Hugh felt his stomach contract and then

release its grip on his spine, where he was certain it had cowered and clung for the last week. 'May I have some?' he asked, squatting beside his enemy.

After a glance at his Sergeant, the Corporal ladled what looked like porridge into a tin cup. Hugh took it from him with no preliminaries, scooping up a spoonful and blowing on it.

'One of my troopers went to take a piss by the sheepfold and noticed the stones,' Cadotte said.

'I don't understand,' Hugh said, after he swallowed a glorious mouthful of the bland mixture. It was wheat, probably cracked with the butt of someone's musket and boiled in river water. He knew he would never eat anything so delicious ever again, not if he lived to be a dribbling old man in a kilt in Kirkcudbright.

Cadotte raised his eyebrows. 'I know Portugal better than you. When they do not feel confident enough to build granaries such as you are already familiar with, the farmers dig grain pits and mark them with a cross of stones.' He finished his cupful. 'I cannot imagine how this was overlooked.' He nodded to his Corporal, who ladled out another cupful of wheat porridge. 'This is for your wife.'

Hugh finished his cup. He wanted to ask for more; for a second, he even wanted to eat the small share meant for Polly. 'Delicious,' he said, taking a swipe inside the cup with his finger and then handing it back to the Corporal.

Before he could take the cup for Polly, he heard an unearthly wail from the other side of the wall and leaped to his feet. He ran around the tumbling wall, the Sergeant just behind him, to see Polly sitting up, keening like an old woman from his home parish who had lost her whole family.

She burst into tears when she saw him. Hugh slid on his knees by her, careful to cover her again, and then hold her close. 'Polly, I was just around the corner! Oh, damn my eyes, Sergeant!'

She held herself off from him for a small second, then burrowed into his embrace with more tears. 'You were gone!' she managed to gasp. Hugh doubted any accusation at the eternal bar of God on judgement day would have even one-tenth the terror for him as her plaintive sentence.

He feared he couldn't hold her any tighter without cutting off her breathing, but she kept pressing closer, her tears spilling down her face until he could not help but cry, too, trying to shield himself from the Sergeant so his enemy would not have cause to gloat over his anguish at leaving Polly alone for even a moment.

He did manage a look at Cadotte, when Polly's tears turned into hiccups. What he saw brought tears to his own eyes again. The Sergeant sat cross-legged, elbows on his knees, his hands covering his face. Hugh kissed Polly's head, looked up at the dark sky. The matter had borne itself home to him more forcefully than any emotion of his life that no matter what happened, Polly was his wife. He had vowed at São Jobim to protect her, and he had just failed her miserably.

Finally she lay silent in his arms, worn out and staring at nothing. His face a study in calm, Sergeant Cadotte leaned across the small space separating them and touched her shoulder. 'Madame Junnit, let your husband help you with your clothes and come to our fire. We have food. He had only left you to get you some, too.'

She nodded, but said nothing. The Sergeant got up and returned to the other side of the wall.

'Can you forgive me for leaving you?' Hugh asked, feeling more wretched than the rawest recruit caught sleeping on duty.

'It's…it's the dream I wake up with every night. I was afraid you had left me to the troopers,' she whispered. 'You would never do that. I *know* you would never do that, but I was still afraid. I'm sorry.'

If she had ripped open his back with pincers and poured lime juice inside, he could not have felt worse, but there was only remorse in her voice, and no accusation. He didn't deserve such kindness.

'I'm the one to apologise, Polly,' he whispered back. 'I will never do that again.'

'Brandon, please,' she told him, with a trace of her former sass.

'Brandon only and always, except in company,' he said. 'Polly, dear.'

She tried to chuckle, but it came out in a sob instead. All he could do was hold her until she pulled away from him and let loose of the blanket. Without a word, she raised her arms so he could pull on her chemise, then let him help her to her feet so he could drop her dress over her head in the same way. He hadn't even needed to unbutton it in the first place, because it hung on her. With her hand on his shoulder, she let him help her into her stockings and shoes again. She stood still, a dutiful woman, as he carefully hooked the curved bows of her spectacles around her ears again.

They stood so close together that when her stomach growled, he wasn't sure if it was her or him. 'That is so unladylike,' she said. 'What a relief that I am not a lady.'

Hugh thought to himself that he would some day like to throttle this Miss Pym, who had been so careful to instruct this dear person in the reality of her illegitimate life, and what little she could possibly hope for. Suddenly, he wanted to consult Philemon Brittle, and meet Captain Worthy, and ask them how they managed their wives, these sisters who were unique in all the world.

'You're lady enough for me, Brandon,' he said gruffly, and kissed her.

Her arms were soft around his neck, then her fingers were in his hair, pulling at it, which he savoured more than he would have thought possible, considering his typical fastidiousness. Neatness be damned, he thought, knowing he reeked and his hair was greasy and he hadn't shaved in weeks. All he wanted to do was kiss Polly Brandon, like a brainless schoolboy.

'And for all intents and purposes, we are married,' he whispered to her, his lips still practically on hers.

She didn't hesitate, but what she said had the power to turn him to jelly. Amazing creatures, women. 'Don't you forget that and leave me alone again, Hugh Junot.'

As she sat close to her beloved, warm by the fire and honestly full of wheat porridge that had nothing whatever to recommend it except that it was hot and filled her stomach, Polly felt something incredibly close to happiness. There was no reason she should feel that way, not with the rain starting again, and sitting across from Sergeant Cadotte, the Corporal, and nine troopers—no, eight now, after the fall this morning. Hugh's arm was around her, and she felt safer than she knew she had any right to.

She looked down at her hands in her lap, wondering if the Frenchmen were sound sleepers, because she intended to give herself to Colonel Junot, that orderly, dignified, maybe a little vain, Marine who had become the man she needed now. For nearly two weeks now, they had lived every day as though it was their last on earth. Something burning deep in her body told her she would not willingly surrender her life in the middle of a war without knowing his love. If they only had one night together, it wouldn't be enough, but it might have to do.

Jesting aside, they weren't married and there was no way they could be right now. Maybe she was her mother's daughter, after all, because she didn't care about the niceties, the banns, the seals, the signatures. She wanted the man beside her. What made the matter so sweet was that she thought he wanted her, too. Outwardly, nothing had changed. He held her as close as he ever did, keeping up their subterfuge with the enemy. He called her 'Polly, *chère*,' as he always did around the Sergeant. Maybe it was the way he looked at her now.

She looked at Hugh and smiled, happy to see the relief in his eyes, and a little embarrassed she had frightened him so badly when she had called out and he had come running. So be it. She had been terrified to wake and find him gone. She would make it up to him. She could do no more right then except turn her face into his shoulder and kiss it, which made him swallow a few times and raise his face to the dark sky.

Maybe he knew what she was thinking. Hugh kissed the palm of her hand and tucked her fingers inside his tunic, which almost gave her the giggles, because it reminded her of a portrait of Napoleon she had seen once. When she patted his chest and withdrew her fingers, he got to his feet with a wince and a groan and tugged her up after him.

He released her and held out his hands, wrists together, to the Sergeant. 'No more, Colonel,' Cadotte said in a quiet voice, one that would not carry to his men, who were starting to bed down on the other side of the fire. 'If I cannot trust you after what happened at the river crossing, then I know nothing about character.'

'Merci,' Hugh said, inclining his head in what Polly thought could pass for deference—they were, after all, prisoners. Not even a river rescue had changed that. He turned to her then, and put

his hand against her back. 'Come, my dear, let us go to bed.'

Sergeant Cadotte wasn't quite through. He held another blanket. 'The nights are getting colder,' was all he said, as if daring them to thank him.

She knew what she was going to do that night, but was too inexperienced to even frame a declaration. Tomorrow they would probably be joining the main body of the French regiment, and all chance at either privacy or life would be over. When the Colonel handed her the extra blanket, then walked away—keeping himself in her sight—to finish his private preparations for sleep, she spread out the blanket close to the wall. There was little privacy there, but she felt a certain security in the embrace of old stones and rubble.

Hugh stood on the perimeter of their ruined chamber, his back still to her, just looking into the darkness. He must know what she was going to do; it wouldn't have surprised her. By the time he turned around, she had removed her dress and was kneeling on the blanket, lifting off her chemise.

He watched her, a slight smile on his face. After a quick look around, he was kneeling on the blanket, too, removing his clothing. She could have sighed with relief. She was grateful he did not tell her what a supremely stupid idea this was, because giving away her virginity was a serious matter. She was only going to do it once, and thank God it was going to the man she trusted, to initiate her into an experience that might be brief.

When she was naked and unspeakably vulnerable, he helped her tuck the other blanket over her, his face more serious than she could remember, even after these weeks when little had been remotely amusing. Looking into that middle distance again, he removed his trousers and smallclothes and then lay down with her under the flimsy protection of the blanket.

Wordlessly, Polly moved into his embrace. For a long moment, he just held her close to him, running his hand along her arm, which was prickled with gooseflesh from the cool of early autumn in the mountains. With his other hand, he gently touched her body, seeming to find the most enjoyment in tracing the womanly swoop from her hip to her waist, and then to her breast, as she lay sideways, facing him.

The rhythmic motion of his hand relaxed her, then began to frustrate her as she began to grow almost too warm for the thin blanket. Working up her courage, she took his hand and placed it on her breast.

'Touch me wherever you want,' she told him. 'May I do the same?'

When he removed her hand, and raised up on one elbow, she was struck dumb with mortification until he took the moment to remove her spectacles, reach over her body, and place them in the little niche. He put her hand around his still-peaceful member. 'Share and share alike, sweetheart. It's not that I don't want you to see everything clearly, Brandon—oh, you know what a peacock I am! You wouldn't be disappointed,' he whispered. 'I would hate for your spectacles to fall victim to passion, when they have survived everything else.'

She chuckled, disarmed and relaxed. Tentatively, she began to stroke him, enjoying the feeling, but equally amazed by what was happening to her own body, as she touched his. All the blood in her core seemed to be rushing towards her loins as she stroked Hugh Junot—not a Colonel, not a Marine, not a fellow prisoner, but a man with her best interest at heart—and felt him begin to grow under her delicate touch. It was a power she could never have imagined. For a tiny, delicious moment, as though the thought came from another galaxy, she remembered telling him how much she enjoyed making plants grow.

She realised her eyes were squeezed shut, so

she opened them to see what he was doing. To her increasing warmth and utter gratification, his eyes were closed and he had a slack look on his face, in vast contradiction to his usual military demeanour. She was a total amateur, and this man of experience was putty in her hands.

She kept her touch gentle, exploring him, running her hand next across the junction where his hip and thigh met. Miss Pym had taken them once to a gallery, where she had admired the cool marble men with sculpted bones and muscle. There was something elegant about the way Hugh Junot worked. Why quibble? All bodies had the same hip-and-thigh junction, but to feel another's skin and bone under her probing fingers was a glory she had not anticipated, in her rush to lose her own virginity. Perhaps this was less about her, and more about them, an epiphany that took away her breath for a moment.

She began to breathe deeper then, because he was touching her now. His fingers were soft as he probed into her body, taking his time as though they had hours and privacy and endless freedom to examine the nature of men and women. She had thought his probing, which grew more insistent, might be painful, until she realised that she was turning into liquid.

'Is this going right?' she asked, wondering

for a moment why her mouth didn't work as
well as usual.

'Superbly well, Brandon,' he said. She was
glad to note she wasn't the only one having a
tussle with speech. He sounded less than sober,
slurring his words in a way that smacked of
brandy.

She had been lying on her side, with his leg
thrown over hers. Suddenly it wasn't comfortable; she turned on to her back and put her arms
around him. His swollen member grazed her
leg now as he gathered her closer, kissing her
breasts, and then carefully taking her nipple into
his mouth, which made her sigh.

He kissed her lips next, and then her neck.
'Madame Junot, je t'aime,' he whispered.
'You're the bonniest lass in the universe and I
am happy to be your man.'

She pulled him closer, not sure what to do
with her body. It seemed almost to be thinking independently, as she felt more heat gather
around her loins. *I wish you would enter me,*
she thought, then realised he was probably not
telepathic. 'I wish you would enter me,' she
whispered.

'In a minute, Brandon. Let's have all the fun
we can for as long as we can,' he told her.

In small circles, he began to massage her
mound of Venus, sitting up so she saw his erect

organ and she could watch what he did to her. She could not help thrusting up towards him then, which embarrassed her at first, but not for long. She decided enough was enough, and reached up to pull him down to her again. She clung to him, her fingers splayed out on his spine. She found herself pushing on his buttocks and starting to pant in his ear. She wasn't sure about the protocol, but it seemed a good thing to run her tongue inside his ear and breathe a little harder.

The result amazed her. Who knew that ears were so useful to lovemaking? Not her. Now it was his turn to mutter something indistinct and raise himself directly over her, one hand under her back and the other on his member as he coaxed her legs a little wider apart and slid himself inside.

It wasn't a totally uncontested passage. He positioned her more firmly under him and advised her to breathe deep breaths. It was good advice, because she relaxed after a momentary twinge, then decided on her own to wrap her legs around him, as he went deeper at a sedate pace: no hurry. He must have approved, because it was her turn to discover the delights of a tongue in the ear and reflect—as well as possible, anyway—on what that did to her mind.

And then it was all rhythm, which pleased

her enormously. She had always been musical. The rhythm climaxed into a greater stiffening inside her, then a huge relaxation that filled her with peace, even as Hugh bowed over her body and try to stifle his groans into the hollow of her shoulder. She kissed his hair, sweaty now, and felt them turn into one being.

She would have liked the moment to have lasted longer, but as they lay together, she could almost feel the waves of exhaustion pouring off both of them. She opened her eyes to see his closed, his face a testament to fatigue. 'Oh, my dear,' she whispered, her hands on his hair. Eyes still closed, he smiled and kissed her forehead. Still inside her, he turned carefully on to his back, pulling her on top of him. In another moment he slept, and so did she.

He woke her before daylight, and made love to her again, moving slowly because he had little energy. As dawn came, they went through the entire ritual again, this time with more confidence. Their slow, deliberate pace this time aroused her beyond her ability to refrain from crying out in pleasure, as waves of rhythm seemed to spill from her body into his. He quickly put his hand over her mouth, and kept it there as he bowed his head over her, then put his face into her shoulder to silence himself, as he followed her in pleasure.

When they were more entirely satisfied than she ever would have thought humanly possible, he cuddled her close to his side. 'Brandon, I think Cadotte's Corporal will have to sling us over the horse today like meal sacks,' he whispered, and covered her mouth again when she giggled. 'Can you fathom our potential, if we ever get anything to eat?'

'I wish you would not talk of meal sacks! Lord, I am hungry. Let me remind you we have been married since São Jobim.'

'I feel that way, too,' he agreed, feeling reflective. 'Seriously, you know we have to have someone exhort us and counsel us and remind us that marriage is a remedy against fornication, and we have to sign papers and cry banns, and Lord, I have that all out of order. Maybe I should ask someone for your hand in marriage, but who that would be escapes me. Cadotte?'

She smothered her laugh in his bare chest, then grew serious. 'Nothing's happened in the right order. And please don't think I am angling for a proposal. You have not compromised me because I asked for what you gave.' *There*, she thought. *I am honest.*

Hugh reached over and handed her her spectacles, contemplating her. 'Hold that thought, Brandon.'

He kissed her forehead. It was so chaste, so disarming, that she felt her heart turn over. Polly sat up and put on her spectacles. 'I mean it, Hugh,' she told him quietly.

Again he looked at her in that thoughtful way that she suddenly knew, with a real pang, that she could never tire of. 'Perhaps I should get dressed now,' she said, a little unnerved by his level gaze.

She dressed quietly, and then it was her turn to admire him in the low light. He had not an ounce of extra flesh anywhere, especially now that they were starving, courtesy of the enemy. She wanted to ask him how he managed to maintain such posture; maybe he would tell her that was a requirement of the service. When times were better, she would ask. She decided she had no commentary to make about his manly parts. Maybe Marines were just supposed to be impressive everywhere.

He laced up his smallclothes and put on his black-and-white checked shirt again, tucking the gorget inside, and then doing up the few buttons that remained. The shirt was ripped and well ventilated, and she smiled to herself when he frowned. *You are a vain man, Colonel Junot,* she thought. *Let us hope your hair never dares to fall out.*

She felt no need to look away when he strode to the edge of the ruin laughingly called a room and relieved himself. She felt a sudden breath of fear when he finished and stepped back in surprise. When he did not return to her immediately, she thought he must have trod upon something in his bare feet. He stood there a long while, then backed up a few paces before he turned around.

She wanted to ask him about that, but her eyes were closing again. When he knelt beside her and whispered for her to go back to sleep, she was happy to oblige. He put his lips close to her ear then.

'If I am not here when you wake up, don't worry, my love. I'll just be around the corner, talking to our favourite jailer.'

She nodded, pleasantly aroused again when he ran his tongue around the inside of her ear and took a tentative nibble on her ear lobe.

'Well, well, Brandon, you're a tasty morsel. Let's hope we find some more wheat today, or your succulent accessories might be in danger.'

'You're such a smooth talker,' she said, as the little flame in her body tamped itself down and let her slumber again.

'I am, indeed,' he told her as he lay down beside her once more. 'I'll just rest here a moment.'

He returned to sleep even before she did, to her amusement. Her spectacles were off, so she got as close to him as she could, admiring his face in repose, hoping their children would look like him. She lay back herself then, nearly overcome with the tantalising thought that they might have a future.

And if we don't, at least I have been loved, she told herself, upon reflection. Maybe it took the clear light of dawn to remind her of her place in life. She got up on one elbow to watch him again, knowing she would never tire of her private view, even as she weighed the probability of a real marriage, and not one engineered to fool the enemy into keeping them alive. The realist in her told her such a thing would never happen, no matter what he said when in the grasp of passion. The dreamer in her admonished her to be peaceful and contemplate what she had given away, and received in return.

It was the fairest trade of her life; of that, she had no doubt.

Chapter Sixteen

Hugh hadn't meant to sleep again, not with the Dragoons moving about in the other room. Careful not to disturb Brandon, he raised up on one elbow to watch her lovely face. He lay back for another moment, thinking of his father's letter last spring, admonishing him that it was high time to set up his own nursery.

He yearned to be a father. He had to give Da credit for starting him thinking along concrete lines. His thoughts had begun to solidify at Sacred Name, when he had watched Brandon playing with the little ones in the courtyard. He thought of Sister Maria Madelena and Brandon's promise in the death house of São Jobim to raise João as her own. So be it. They would, and gladly. *There was an old bee who lived in a barn*, he thought, eager for his own father to teach that silly rhyme to a grandson or daughter. Or João. As Scots went, his father was a tolerant man. As Hugh considered it, his father also was dead right about what had ailed him. *I hope I live to tell you, Da*, he thought.

Still, marriage was a serious venture. There was not one thing Brandon had to offer that he could not get from a lady of higher degree, except her own dear self. Lying there next to her, he contemplated his career in ruins, his peers mocking him in barracks and wardrooms around the globe, his sister shocked and his father dismayed. Or not. *We live in uncertain times, Brandon, dear*, he thought, *and I do not mean the war.*

He rose quietly and dressed, gratified that Brandon did not wake up, and joined his enemies. The Dragoons were tending to their mounts, but Sergeant Cadotte stood by the glow of last night's fire, contemplating the coals as he sipped from his tin cup. He poured Hugh a tin cupful of liquid from the pot and held it out.

Ever hopeful, Hugh looked into the cup. It contained nothing more than boiled water, with what appeared to be a thin smear of wheat from last night's poor banquet. He took a taste. Obviously the French had better imaginations than he did. No stretch of his imagination was going to turn it into coffee or tea. Still, the cup was warm in his hands, and the air had a decided chill.

'Colonel, I am sorry we cannot give you and your wife more privacy.'

Oh, Lord. You must have heard us last night, Hugh thought, and felt his face grow warm. At a loss, he took a sip. 'We tried to be quiet,' he said finally.

'Ah, but I am in command here,' Cadotte replied, with that hint of a twitch around his lips. 'As you well know, Colonel, that means I sleep lighter than any trooper.'

'I understand, Sergeant,' Hugh said, and smiled. The Sergeant was the enemy, but he was also a man.

It was time for a massive change of subject, and Hugh had less trouble with that. The Sergeant was younger than he by many years, but every bit as experienced in the ways of war. Hugh knew he could not offer advice, but he also knew how heavy command could feel, especially when there was no one to talk to.

'Sergeant, we are being followed.'

'I know.' Cadotte gave one of those Gallic shrugs that Hugh knew he could never manage, not after all the family's years in Scotland. 'I think we have been followed since São Jobim.'

'I would agree.' Here was the dilemma. Should he say more? Hugh took another sip, de-

ciding that he liked hot water well enough. 'Sergeant, how close are we to the Spanish border?'

He could tell his question had surprised the
Sergeant of Dragoons, perhaps even knocked
him off balance a little, never a bad thing with
the enemy. *You are wondering why I am not
asking you to just let Brandon and me go?* Hugh
asked himself.

Hugh had to give the Sergeant points for
shrewdness, though.

'Colonel, we are close to the border, which
will work in my favour, not yours,' Cadotte replied, regaining his poise. 'When I join up with
my Lieutenant and our larger force—hopefully
today, if not tomorrow—the *guerilleros* who
seem to be content to track us will fade into
the background. I think they are not now strong
enough to attack us.'

Hugh could think of another reason, and wondered why the Sergeant had not. There was no
sense in alerting the man. He went back to the
original point. 'Sergeant, why does moving into
Spain work in your favour?'

Cadotte almost smiled then. 'Colonel, Colonel! You know as well as I do that northern
Spain is still well populated with French troops.
Any hope you have of liberation by your allied
troops are getting smaller the farther north we
ride.' He replaced the threatening smile with

290 Marrying the Royal Marine

something perilously close to scorn. 'We may
have experienced a setback at Salamanca, but—
excuse my plain speaking—Wellington is an
idiot to besiege Burgos.'

Is that so? Hugh thought. Good thing Cadotte
had not been sitting at the conference table in
Lisbon last month, hearing of Admiral Sir Home
Popham's successful raid on Santander, on the
Bay of Biscay. It could be that even as they
stood sparring with each other before a fire in
a battered Portuguese farmyard, the balance had
changed. *Or not*, he had to admit to himself
again. There wasn't much about war that was
predictable. He thought briefly of the happy
times when he knew exactly where he was going
in life, and tucked them away as the idiocy they
represented.

'I, for one, would not mind if you just left me
and Polly here to fend for ourselves.' Surely it
didn't hurt to ask.

The Sergeant was silent, so Hugh finished
his hot water and handed back the cup. Cadotte
shook his head slowly, and Hugh sensed his regret. 'Colonel, I would do as you ask, except for
one reason.' The Sergeant looked at his men,
who by now had bridled and saddled their
mounts. 'Them.'

Hugh understood perfectly, even as his heart
sank. 'Ah, yes,' he said, keeping his tone light.

'How would it look if the leader released his prisoners?'

'What would you do in my position?'

You have me, Hugh thought. 'Precisely the same thing, Sergeant. Excuse me now. I will wake up my wife.'

Still, Hugh had to reflect over the next two days that Sergeant Cadotte was not as confident as he seemed. The Sergeant did not go back on his word to keep them unfettered, which was a relief. They were travelling out of the mountains now, skirting along the foothills, heading for northern Spain. The Sergeant seemed to know precisely where he was going, but he seemed in no hurry to get there, despite the hunger that rode along with them.

'It's odd, my love, but I think our Sergeant is almost daring our invisible *guerrilleros* to attack us,' he whispered in Brandon's ear as they followed the Corporal through the protecting underbrush.

He had told her yesterday of his suspicion they were being tracked, and she had surprised him. 'I thought so,' she had said, in that practical way of hers.

'Brandon, sometimes you amaze me,' he had told her.

'That's good,' she said complacently.

He had let out a crack of laughter at that, which caused the Corporal to turn around in the saddle and glare at them. Sergeant Cadotte even stepped his horse out of line and watched them for a moment, frowning.

'Perhaps he doesn't want us to have too much fun,' Brandon said. After the Sergeant resumed his place in line again, she turned her face into his tunic, lowering her voice. 'What I don't understand is why they have not attacked us.'

'Sergeant Cadotte seemed to think they are a much smaller party than we are,' Hugh whispered back. 'I don't think that's the reason.'

'You think they are larger?' she asked, after a long consideration.

'Much, much larger, my dear,' he had replied. 'I think they are waiting to attack until Cadotte takes them to his Lieutenant and his force.'

'Goodness,' Brandon had said, and nothing more.

Her pointed reminder to him not to underestimate her led him to the only reason for her silence—she knew, or at least suspected, how much more dangerous their situation had become. He could only hug her tighter, aware that she really couldn't know how terrifying a pitched battle would be, when the *guerrilleros* finally decided to attack with overwhelming numbers. Their own chances of surviving such a mêlée were not much better than a snowflake in a furnace, but she didn't need to know that.

The wheat lasted to noon on the second day. By nightfall, Sergeant Cadotte had led his little troop back to his regiment as accurately as a homing pigeon. Before he took them in, he bound their hands again, but not as tight as before.

'The devil we know, dearest,' Hugh whispered in her ear as he settled his bound hands around her again. 'What this will amount to, I have no idea, but we have a new set of captors.'

What it amounted to was a look of amazement on the face of Sergeant Cadotte's Lieutenant, a young man probably in his first command who stared at them, then turned on Cadotte, who had dismounted, along with his troop. After another furious look in their direction, the Lieutenant of Dragoons kneed his horse directly into the Sergeant, practically bowling him over.

'He's an ugly one,' Hugh said into her ear. 'He's never learned what I learned in my first year as a Lieutenant: it's your NCOs who keep you alive.'

Rubbing his arm, Cadotte kept his face impassive as he took the brunt of the Lieutenant's sharp tongue. 'I can't follow what he is saying,' Polly told Hugh. 'It's too fast for me.'

She felt Hugh's sigh. 'It's what you probably think it is, dearest. He's asking our Sergeant why in God's name he did not kill us at São Jobim.'

Here it is, she thought, surprisingly calm. *After weeks it has come to this. Hugh and I will not live to see the sun go down. I only hope to heaven they are quick.*

'Will we die now?' she whispered.

He kissed the top of her head. 'We might. Polly Junot, you've been the best wife a man could hope for.'

His eyes still on the Sergeant, the Lieutenant shouted an order to Cadotte's Corporal, who walked towards them and held out his arms for her. They had done this for weeks now. Hugh lifted his arms up and Polly swung her leg across the pommel and allowed herself to drop into the Corporal's arms.

The Dragoon settled her on her feet, bending close to her this time to whisper, 'Speak only English, Madame Junnit.'

She knew better than to look at him, especially since the Lieutenant was staring at her, his eyes angry, his hand patting his sabre. She stood still, eyes down, as the Corporal helped Hugh from the saddle. When he stood beside her, she whispered. 'The Corporal told me to speak only English.'

'Then trust him,' Hugh replied. 'I have only one feeble card to play. Tally-ho, Brandon.'

Putting himself between them, the Corporal took them by the arms and walked them towards the Lieutenant. He stopped, but the Lieutenant beckoned them closer. When they were standing close to his horse, he suddenly took his foot from the stirrup and shoved Hugh to the ground.

Polly wrenched herself from the Corporal's grasp and threw herself down beside Hugh, who was shaking his head, as if to clear it. Grasping his arm with her bound hands, she tugged Hugh into a sitting position, as the Lieutenant danced his horse around them, almost stepping on her. She glanced at Sergeant Cadotte, noting the dismay on his face, and the two red spots that bloomed on his cheeks.

'I don't think that was called for, Lieutenant,' Polly said, after taking a deep breath. She put her bound arms around Hugh and hugged him to her.

'Parlez-vous francais?' the officer asked, putting his foot back in the stirrup.

She shook her head. 'Through an unfortunate confluence of events, we found ourselves prisoners.'

'I speak French, Lieutenant,' Hugh said. 'My name is Lieutenant Colonel Hugh Philippe d'Anvers Junnit, of the Second Division, Royal

Marines. This is my wife, Polly Junnit.' He hesitated. 'Perhaps you are more familiar with the French pronunciation—Junot.'

Whatever his failings as a Lieutenant, the young officer seemed to have heard of the name, Polly realised, as she watched the man's face. In fact, he grabbed at his reins and stared at Hugh on the ground before him, then dismounted.

'What did you say?'

Hugh repeated himself.

The Lieutenant shook his head in disbelief. 'Junot?'

Hugh nodded. Polly held her breath as the Lieutenant, hands on his hips, glared at Hugh, who smiled back. 'Where *is* my dear uncle Jean-Andoche?'

'Sergeant Cadotte!' the Lieutenant yelled. 'Front and centre!'

Looking almost as amazed as the Lieutenant, Cadotte came quickly to attention, the red spots in his cheeks even more pronounced now. 'Sir!'

The Lieutenant tapped Cadotte's shoulder with the crop. 'Why did you not tell me his name was Junot?'

'Sir, I...' Cadotte began, his voice mystified.

'Help me up,' Hugh told Polly. She did as he asked. He staggered and shook his head again. 'Lieutenant...'

'Soileau.'

'Lieutenant Soileau, it is not your Sergeant's fault. I introduced myself to him as Lieutenant Colonel Hugh Junnit, which is how we pronounce the name in Scotland.'

'Scotland?' Soileau repeated. 'Junnit? Good God. Are you a *spy*?'

'Sir, I am a Royal Marine in his Majesty's service,' Hugh said, drawing himself up and managing to look so masterfully offended that Polly stared, too. 'It happens there is a branch of the family in Scotland, and it is a long story. But tell me, how is my dear uncle? Is he with Clausel or Massena? Does he have his marshal's baton yet?'

Good God, he is amazing, Polly thought. She looked at the Lieutenant, who had the stunned look of an ox banged on the head and ready for slaughter. She watched as he took a moment to collect himself.

'How can I be sure you are who you say you are?'

'Ask my wife.'

The Lieutenant barely glanced at her. 'Bah! She speaks no French, and from the way she is looking at you, she would probably tell me you were the second cousin of Our Lord Himself, if you wanted her to.'

'She is a dear thing, isn't she?' Hugh said agreeably in English. 'Polly, dear, perhaps the kind Lieutenant will untie your hands so you can reach up and unsnap my gorget.' He continued in French, 'My name is engraved on the other side. It's also tattooed on the inside of my left leg.'

The Lieutenant's mouth dropped open. 'The Royal Marines require *that*?'

'Lieutenant, were you never drunk, nineteen, and in a foreign port?'

Lieutenant Soileau shook his head, then gestured to Cadotte to untie Polly's hands. He seemed unaware that the Sergeant's troopers had gathered around, their tired faces lively with interest.

'Thank you, Sergeant,' she said in English, then unbuttoned the top two buttons of Hugh's tunic. He bent down obligingly as she pulled out the gorget he had tucked inside his shirt and unsnapped it from the chain. She held it out to the Lieutenant, who did not take it from her, but read the inscription.

He read it again, aloud this time, and stood another moment in thought. 'As we speak, your uncle is with our glorious Emperor and the *Grand Armée* in Russia,' he said finally, his voice subdued, as though he did not believe his own ears.

'What a shame for me!' Hugh exclaimed. 'I would like to have seen him and exchanged pleasantries. Since the war, family reunions have been impossible.'

Don't press your luck, you scoundrel, Polly thought, as she put the gorget back around his neck and tucked it inside his shirt.

Hugh's lips were close to her ear. 'I'm out of ideas,' he whispered. 'Brandon, this would be a good time to faint.'

With a sigh, she did exactly what he asked. A man couldn't hope for a better wife.

Chapter Seventeen

She must have been convincing. After a suitable amount of time, she moaned and opened her eyes to find herself lying on a camp cot in a tent blessedly warm.

She had known Hugh would catch her on the way down, especially since he had engineered the faint, so never having lost consciousness, it was no surprise to see him kneeling beside the cot, his eyes full of concern, and something else that made her heart leap a little. She touched his face.

She hadn't meant to unman him, but her touch filled his eyes with tears. 'Lieutenant, can you send someone for a little water? Just a sip would be so kind,' Hugh said. He took her hand in his, kissed her palm, and tucked it close to his chest. 'You're better than Siddons,' he said in English. 'Although I suppose after weeks in captivity, it ain't hard to look wan.'

'It's easier than I would have thought,' she murmured to him, putting her hand over his. 'What is this supposed to get us?'

'Some sympathy?' he whispered back. 'Heaven knows, *I* feel sorry for us.'

Lieutenant Soileau snapped out an order and in a moment Hugh was helping her into a sitting position for that sip of water. She took one sip, and with what she hoped was a die-away look on her face, begged her husband to let her rest again.

He did, with a perfectly straight face, and Lieutenant Soileau himself tucked a light blanket about her. He motioned to Hugh and the men withdrew for a brief conference. With a sigh, she resolved to let her husband worry about the pickle they were in, and resigned herself to sleep. At least they were still alive.

When she woke later, Hugh sat in a folding camp chair by her cot, head back, eyes closed. She knew he needed sleep, but she wanted information more, so she put her hand on his thigh and squeezed it. His eyes opened in an instant. He looked wildly around the tent first, as though wondering where he was, then smiled down at her.

'Do we live to fight another day?'

'We do, Polly, dear,' he told her. 'I fear, though, that our good Sergeant Cadotte had to endure a blistering scold for not killing us at São Jobim. I couldn't hear the whole thing, but Cadotte may have even been busted down to Corporal.'

'I *am* sorry for that,' Polly said. 'I should sit up, but for the life of me, I don't want to.'

'Then don't. Lieutenant Soileau graciously consented to your remaining in his tent tonight. He even promised some food, but don't expect much.' He grew serious immediately. 'I think Lieutenant Soileau is taking us along with his force to General Clausel, who had withdrawn to Burgos, where our own dear Wellington is laying him siege. Who knows what will happen then, except that I am so glad Cousin—or Uncle—Junot is somewhere in Russia.'

'You don't even know if he is a relative, do you?' she asked.

'Haven't the slightest,' Hugh replied cheerfully.

'What will Clausel do with us?'

'Probably pass us off to someone else, as Lieutenant Soileau is eager to do.' He hesitated then. Polly knew him well enough to know something else was percolating in his fertile brain. 'I can't gild this, my darling, but I rather think the *guerilleros* who have been dogging our steps will make their move tomorrow. Clausel might be the least of our worries.'

She mulled over that bad news during dinner, which was tough beef in a wine sauce, bread pudding made of hardtack, but soaked in rum sauce with raisins, and excellent port. By the time the meal was over—Lieutenant Soileau had shared it with them—all she wanted to do was sleep.

Lieutenant Soileau had no intention of allowing Hugh to run tame in his tent for the night. So he told Hugh, who translated for her. 'You already know. He is taking me to the detention tent for another of our typical nights in the hands of our enemies, Brandon. I'm sorry.'

She was powerless against the dread of having Hugh Junot gone from her sight. 'Tell Lieutenant Soileau I will go with you.'

The detention tent was no worse than other nights on the trail from São Jobim to this nameless spot in the foothills, and far better than the granary. While Lieutenant Soileau looked askance, Hugh made himself comfortable against a meal sack, obligingly held out his hands to be bound, then patted his thigh. Ignoring the Lieutenant, who refused to bind her hands, Polly sat down beside Hugh and rested her head on his leg, tugging the extra blanket around her. She was asleep in minutes, happy to be where she was.

They were up before daylight, prodded by the sentry, who grudgingly loosened Hugh's bonds so he could attend to his private business and shooed Polly from the tent while he did so. Lieutenant Soileau's blanket around her, she waited serenely in the mist, watching the Dragoons at their breakfast fires. Sergeant Cadotte and his men squatted by their own fires, and she noted with some relief, at least, that the Sergeant seemed to have retained all his rank.

As she stood there, Cadotte brought her a tin cup of what turned out to be chicken broth. She drank it gratefully, surprised there had been a chicken still on the loose in this picked-over terrain. The fowl must have been as determined to live as the Junnits.

'I am sorry we got you in trouble, Sergeant,' she said in French, after looking around to make sure Lieutenant Soileau was not in sight.

He shook his head. 'Junot. Junnit. Good Christ, woman!' Cadotte looked around, too. 'I could not have killed you. It never was the bribe your husband so generously offered, and you may tell him that.'

'Why, then?' she asked, curious.

'That nun was a spy and I did my duty,' he told her. 'You, however, were in the wrong place at the wrong time. God help me, but I don't customarily make war on women.' He looked away, as if contemplating his own family. 'Heartless as I was at Sâo Jobim, God forgive me.'

She handed back the cup. He took hold of it, but did not take it from her. His fingers touched hers. 'Be careful today. I'll watch you two if I can.'

You're my enemy, she thought, grateful for Cadotte. *We owe you so much. 'Merci,'* was all she said.

Cadotte was obviously one of the smaller cogs in the battalion, but he still managed to secure the same horse for them. She noticed he did everything quickly, before Lieutenant Soileau had the opportunity to impose his own regulations. Polly held her hands out to be bound, but Cadotte shook his head. 'Not this time, Madame Junot. Keep your hands low in your lap, and I do not think the Lieutenant will notice. Be watchful and think quickly.'

When he touched his finger to his helmet and turned away, Polly twisted around to look at Hugh, who was watching the Sergeant with his own troubled expression. 'I'm afraid,' she whispered.

'I am, too,' Hugh murmured back. 'Keep your eyes on Cadotte. He'll help us, if he can.'

The column rode into a misty morning, the forest abnormally quiet of birdsong. Although admonished to silence by Lieutenant Soileau, there was no way to totally quieten the creak of harness, clink of mess kit, or the sharp strike of horseshoe against stone. Polly strained for the sound of other horses and men riding on their periphery, but she heard nothing.

The mist gave way to a morning as beautiful as any she had ever seen, the air crisp and the landscape scrubbed clean by the rain that had fallen in the night. They continued their downward path until Polly saw open ground in the distance.

'The plains of León,' Hugh said, and there was no mistaking the relief in his voice. 'I believe we are less than eighty miles from the Bay of Biscay.'

It might as well be a million miles, she thought. Hugh seemed to read her mind. 'Now we will turn east towards Burgos, I suppose,' he said. 'Ah, well.'

Lieutenant Soileau called a rest. When they were in the saddle again, Sergeant Cadotte stepped his horse out of the line and waited a moment until they were beside him.

'This is the last pass to the plains, Colonel,' he

said, keeping his voice soft and looking straight ahead, ignoring them. She barely saw his hands move as he placed a knife in her lap. 'Watch for an opportunity and take it. *Bon chance.*' He touched spurs to his mount and moved up into the line, in front of his Corporal.

Polly could not stop the fear that seemed to ripple down her spine. She took the knife, and cut through Hugh's bonds, as he continued to envelop her in his grasp, his hands in front of her. 'Don't drop the knife,' he told her. 'Do what I tell you when the moment comes.'

It was then that she heard other horses and riders, but they were above them in the pass. Some of the Dragoons were looking up, too, and gesturing. It was just a man here and a man there, standing, observing, dressed in brown to blend in with the dry plains of León. When the column turned, she saw Lieutenant Soileau in the vanguard, his head inclined towards one of his Sergeants, who pointed with some emphasis.

'Lieutenant Soileau is too green for this assignment,' Hugh whispered. 'He is in over his head. He's ignoring his Sergeants. Brandon, it's going to be bad!'

He grasped her around the waist then, his hand tight. At a word from Cadotte, who rode ahead, the Corporal loosed the rope that bound his horse to theirs. Polly snatched the rope, leaning forwards across the horse's neck.

When she tried to rise, Hugh pushed her down again into the animal's mane, and leaned over her. He edged off the path just as the noonday calm erupted in screams and gunfire. 'Get off and slide down the embankment,' Hugh ordered, loosing his grip on her and lifting her leg over the pommel. 'Don't look back!'

She did as he said, as the *guerilleros* seemed to rise like rapid-growing plants from the hillside, and rain down fire. She stood at the side of the road, rooted there in her fear, as the Corporal suddenly slapped his ear, slumped across his horse's neck, then plopped in a heap at her feet, a bullet drilled through his brain.

Polly needed no other encouragement. She slid down the slope, rolling and scrambling up and falling again as the column dissolved in gunfire. Horses screamed and pushed against each other as everyone tried to take cover. Other Dragoons had dismounted, true to their training, and were firing now from positions along the embankment she had slid down.

Scarcely breathing, she watched for Hugh through the growing smoke of the muskets, realising with an ache that he had not been so far from her side in weeks. She began to cautiously climb up the embankment, looking for him. Relief coursed through every fibre of her body as she saw a scarlet tunic and then Hugh as he slid off his horse and tried to follow her down the slope. As she watched in horror, one of the Dragoons pulled out his sidearm and aimed it right at Hugh.

'Hugh!' she shrieked. He had no weapon. She raced up the slope, blotting everything from her mind except Hugh. It wasn't so far, and she suddenly felt strong, despite days of starvation, cold rain, and despair. Suddenly, she knew what it felt like to risk everything for what she loved the most. She understood what Sister Maria Madelena had tried to tell her at São Jobim.

As puny as it was, the Dragoon hadn't expected an attack from the rear. Polly scrambled to her feet and lunged for the horsehair tassel hanging from the man's helmet, jerking it with all her might. It earned her a clout on the shoulder, but he fell backwards, tried to struggle to his feet, then was stopped for ever by a bullet from a musket—friend or foe she had no idea.

Polly sobbed out loud, then shrieked as Hugh grabbed her around the waist and ran down the slope. Not until he found a fallen tree and pulled her behind it did he release his grip.

They lay in a jumble, arms around each other, until the firing stopped. She wanted to say something, but she knew it would only come out as babble, so she was silent, feeling her heartbeat gradually slow, and the tingling feeling leave her arms and legs until she felt as heavy as the log they crouched behind.

'I told you to go down that slope and not look back,' Hugh said finally.

'He came between me and you,' she said, touching his face as though she had never thought to do that again.

He didn't say anything more, but gathered her closer. They lay there, listening, until the voices above them were Spanish instead of French.

'Do you know any Spanish?' Hugh asked.

'Not much. Do you?'

'Precious little.' He sat up cautiously. 'It galls this Scot, but all I can remember is *Ingleses*. I have to tell them I am English.'

'I'm coming with you.'

'You are not!' He took her chin in his hand and gave it a little shake. 'And don't give me that mulish look, Madame Junot! Stay here. I won't ask you twice.'

He sat on the fallen log, brushing futilely at his scarlet tunic, which was torn, stained, and bloody. Most of the gilt buttons hung by threads. He pulled his gorget out of the front of his tunic and settled it where it belonged. He glanced at Polly.

'You're probably going to tell me I'm a dandy and I don't smell very good, either,' he muttered.

'You certainly don't,' she teased, then reached for him. 'Please be careful, my love. My love,' she repeated, enjoying the way it rolled over her tongue.

'Your love,' he mused. 'Brandon, I think—no, I know—your sister wanted you to wait a few years and then fall in love with a solicitor, or maybe a ship builder.'

'Probably,' she replied agreeably, since he was going to be a dunce. 'I will be a sad disappointment to them, but not to me. I never wanted to harm anyone, but Boney gave me no choice. It's my fight, too.'

He looked at her in admiration, then gently pushed her spectacles higher up on her nose. 'I still can't believe they are not broken.' He started up the hill, moving deliberately, his hands up, calling *'Ingleses'* every few feet until he was on the road again. Polly held her breath, fearing a volley of rifle fire, but the only sounds she heard were weapons being thrown on to a pile and the groans of the wounded, followed by shrieks. *Dear God, they are killing the wounded*, she thought. *What kind of men are these?*

When she did not think she could stand it another minute, Hugh came halfway down the slope and gestured to her. She wavered, not wanting to see the carnage on the road, but uneasy to be so far away from her love. Hugh won out, as she knew he always would, and she climbed the slope.

He grasped her arm to pull her on to the road, then held her tight, face against his chest. 'We won't be here long, Brandon. They have no plans to bury the dead or aid the wounded.'

'Are we…?' She couldn't even think of the word. It had been too long.

'Free? Indeed, we are. We are in the hands of General Francisco Espoz y Mina, himself.' He pointed to a tall man, hatless, bending over what remained of Lieutenant Soileau. 'He speaks only Basque, but his Lieutenant, Feliz Sarasa there, speaks Spanish and English.'

She only nodded, her eyes huge in her face, as she watched the killing ground. 'Are they all dead?'

'If they aren't, they soon will be. The *guerilleros* aren't inclined to give quarter. Seems a pity, almost, doesn't it?'

She nodded, unable to take her eyes from the dead, who systematically were being stripped of what clothing might be useful in the guerilla cause, and then rolled unceremoniously down the slope she had just climbed.

Hugh's grip tightened involuntarily. 'Look you there. Sergeant Cadotte.'

She followed where he led, picking her way through the French until the hem of her skirt was crimson. She knelt when Hugh knelt by the side of the Sergeant, who lay with one leg bent in an odd direction, his hands bloody from clutching his stomach.

'He's barely alive,' Hugh whispered. 'What I would give to have your brother-in-law here, except I fear it would do no good.' He put his hands on both sides of the Sergeant and leaned close until his lips were practically on Cadotte's ear. 'Sergeant, can you hear me?'

The dying man's eyes opened finally. Polly could hardly bear to look at him, but when she did, she saw no fear, only weariness.

One of the *guerilleros* knelt beside Cadotte, too, his knife out. Hugh shot out his hand to stop the man. 'No, *por favor*, no,' Hugh said. *'Este...este hombre...'* He stopped, his Spanish exhausted.

'Su amigo?' the *guerillero* asked, a look of incredulity on his face.

'He saved our lives,' Hugh said, leaning over Cadotte, shielding him with his own body. 'Please leave him to me.'

The *guerillero* obviously didn't understand, but shrugged and moved away, looking for en-

emies without friends. Hugh turned back to
the Sergeant of Dragoons and carefully put his
arm under Cadotte's shoulders, raising him up
slightly.

'*L'eau,*' he gasped.

Polly looked around. The Corporal lying
nearby still had his canteen attached to his belt.
Trying not to look at his ruined face, she cut
the canteen with his knife and brought it back
to Hugh. He tipped a little of its contents into
Cadotte's mouth. The water only dribbled out
the corners and from the wound in his neck, but
the Sergeant said '*Merci,*' anyway.

She decided she could not be afraid of this
dying man and tried to think what Laura would
do. She took him by the hand and was rewarded
with the slightest of pressure against her fingers.
It could have been her imagination.

'Sergeant, we owe you our lives, twice and
three times over,' Hugh said, his mouth close
to Cadotte's ear again. 'I remember your wife's
name, but is there a direction besides just
Angoulême where I can send her funds for your
farm? Is there a parish?'

The Sergeant was silent. 'I asked him too
much,' Hugh said in frustration and near tears
himself.

'Lalage.' In spite of his vast pain, Cadotte
seemed to caress the name. A long moment

passed, then, 'Sainte Agilbert.' He smiled at Polly. 'If…girl, name…Lalage.'

Polly raised his bloody hand to her cheek. 'I promise.'

Cadotte nodded slightly and turned his head a fraction of an inch towards Hugh again. 'Cows. A new fence.' He sighed, as though thinking of the farm he would never see again, and a woman named Lalage. The sigh went on and on, and he died.

His face a mask of pain, Hugh gently released the Sergeant and pulled Polly close to him. 'I wish I had not deceived him.'

'Lalage is a beautiful name,' Polly said through her tears. 'We will use it some day, husband.'

He managed the ghost of a smile. 'No one will understand.'

'Do you care?'

He shook his head and kissed her temple. 'When the war is over, we will mend a fence near Angoulême. There will be a lot of cattle for it to contain.'

Chapter Eighteen

⁓⁓⁓⁓⁓

They were in the saddle again in less than an hour, riding at the front of the column now, next to a Lieutenant of Pakenham's division, and dressed like one of Espoz y Mina's ragtag army.

'Wellington has sent a few of us into the hills to ride with the *guerilleros*, Colonel Junot, although I cannot for the life of me understand why,' he said cheerfully as they rode along. 'Good show this morning, eh?'

I wonder what this irritating Lieutenant would do if I suddenly knocked him out of his saddle? Hugh asked himself, his mood sour and his mind dark.

He knew how Brandon felt. As they rode away from the bloody ground, she turned her

face into his chest and sobbed, which only
made the British Lieutenant look at her in
amazement.

'I say, Colonel,' he whispered. 'Doesn't she
understand that we have freed you from the
French?'

Hugh returned some non-committal answer,
knowing it was fruitless to explain to this ninny
that in any war, especially one fought as long as
this conflict, there comes a time where reasonable men and women have had enough. His own
heart was heavy enough, thinking of Lalage
Cadotte and her two sons whom she would continue to raise alone. He didn't want to think how
many sad little families there were in France, in
Spain, in England.

That's it, he told himself, discarding every
reason why the world would think theirs a foolish match. *Polly is my love.* He decided then
that his home with Brandon would not be a sad
one. He longed to take her to Kirkcudbright.
He wanted to walk along the shoreline, watch
the fishing boats, breathe deep of the fragrance
of his late mother's rose garden, and imagine
the delight of a young child skipping along beside him. He knew he was duty-bound to the
Marines until the war ended, at least, but there
wasn't any reason Brandon herself could not be

his proxy, and settle into that lovely life he suddenly wanted for himself.

He looked down at her, wondering if she even knew how much she probably loved him, she who would have killed that Dragoon on the slope. If she did, something told him she would never allow herself to be settled so far away from him. He swallowed as his own heart raced uncomfortably at the idea of such a separation. Scotland could wait, as long as she was safely tucked into his quarters in Plymouth. Even then, he thought it would be hard to kiss her goodbye every morning and attend to his deskbound duties a building away. He wondered if a time would ever come when he would feel easy again without her in his line of sight.

They rode as hard as the French soldiers now lying slaughtered had ridden, in that last pass before the mountains gave way to the vast plain of León. At first, he listened with half an ear to the voluble Lieutenant who rode beside him, learning of Wellington's triumphal entry into Madrid, then the need to move north and invest the stronghold of Burgos. There was hopeful talk of wintering in the Pyrenees and moving on France in the spring, rather than enduring another dreary retreat to Portugal and the safety offered by the lines of Torres Vedras and the Royal Navy close offshore.

* * *

In late afternoon, the *guerillero* leader the Lieutenant called Espoz y Mina stopped the column and rode with his English-speaking Sub-altern along the column, falling in beside the Lieutenant. Through interpreters, he told them his army was taking the road east to Burgos.

'*El jefe* wants you and your wife to continue with a smaller column to the Bay of Biscay,' the interpreter said.

'I won't argue,' Hugh told him. 'After a month in the saddle, this Marine would like to clap his eyes on a fleet.'

'You will, then,' the interpreter said. '*Vayan con Dios.* I will leave you with another inter-preter.' He nodded to the Lieutenant on foot, who gave them a cheery wave and peeled off with the long column. The smaller unit watched until Espoz y Mina's army turned on to what looked like no more than a cow trail, but pointed east to Burgos. The new interpreter, a long-faced Basque named Raul Etchemindy, rode beside them.

The smaller column continued north and turned slightly west, as it sought the relative safety of another mountain pass. 'This area is still patrolled by the *crapaud*,' Etchemindy said. 'That will change, God willing, if your Wellington invests Burgos.' He shrugged philosophically. 'If not, then we fight another year.'

The rains came again as the tired horses plodded into a village Hugh never would have seen from the plains below. Small and self-contained, he wondered if it had been guarding the pass since the earliest days of Roman conquest.

Brandon had said next to nothing through the long afternoon, and he was relieved to hand her off carefully when he halted his horse in the village square. His buttocks on fire, he dismounted with a groan and barely had time to blink before the horse was whisked away down a side street. He looked around. All the horses were gone now, hidden from French eyes.

He put his arm around Brandon, who leaned against him. 'I'm so tired,' she said.

Then it was their turn to be taken in hand by Etchemindy and whisked away into a small, fortress-like house. Chattering in an uninflected language he did not understand, two women pried Brandon from his side and led her away. He stood there a moment, indecisive and uneasy to have her gone, then turned to Etchemindy.

'You are safe here,' his Basque said in good, workaday English. 'In the past four years, we have had English visitors. Sometimes they even bring us weapons, but never enough.'

'Perhaps we can change that,' Hugh said, interested.

'Possibly. We are riding to Santander as soon as your wife is able, *señor*. The fleet has brought more weapons for the Spanish army, but we in the hills need an advocate.'

'We can leave tomorrow, and I can help you,' Hugh told him. 'Admiral Sir Home Popham is my friend.'

Etchemindy clapped Hugh's arm as his solemn expression gave way to a smile. 'It is a doubly good thing, then, that we did not shoot you on sight, and wonder later who the man in the scarlet coat was!'

Etchemindy led him into a heavy-beamed room dark with the wood smoke of centuries, sat him down, and offered him a bowl of soup. Hugh felt his hunger pangs increase at the sight of meat floating in the thick broth. His host handed him a hunk of dark bread, which made a heavenly sop.

He ate too fast, knowing he would suffer for it by morning. He was reaching for more bread when he noticed one of the women hovering in the doorway, beckoning to him. *Brandon*, he thought, alarmed, and rose at once.

The woman whispered to Etchemindy, who turned to him. '*Señor*, follow my wife.'

Outside a closed door, the woman spoke

at length to her husband, who gestured Hugh closer. 'Your little lady is just sitting in the tub and keeps asking for you.'

Hugh let out the breath he had been holding, relieved. 'It is this way, Señor Etchemindy. We have not been separated for some weeks now, and I confess I am feeling lost without her, too. With all due respect and thanks to your wife, may I go in and take care of things?'

Etchemindy nodded. 'Goodnight. If we are not being presumptuous, we can find some fresh clothing in the village.'

'Not presumptuous at all,' Hugh said. 'It's been a long time.'

The wife whispered again to her husband, who laughed. 'She says she is going to burn your clothing, no matter what you decide.'

'Wise of her!'

When the Etchemindys had returned to their great room, Hugh knocked softly and lifted the latch. What he saw touched his heart. Just as Señora Etchemindy had said, Brandon sat in a tin tub, head down to one side, shoulders slumped. Her hair was tumbled around her shoulders, but it was dry. She just sat there, as though too stunned by the day's events to move.

He just looked at her, seeing again how young she was, how utterly spent. She was a woman with the courage of a lion, who would have killed for him, but there she sat. *Do I sympathise?* he asked himself. *Do I tease her? Do I just tell her I love her?*

'Brandon.'

She gasped and looked around, and the relief in her eyes scored him right to the bone. He felt his own heart lift, and he knew he had been hungrier for the sight of her than that whole bowl of stew, as good as it had tasted. A room without Polly Brandon in it was a room not worth inhabiting. It was a simple truth, but deeper than a well.

He was at her side then, squatting by the tub, his arms around her awkwardly. She didn't try to kiss him or say anything, but clung to him, her arms strong around his neck. She was a woman who would never fail him or tease him or play a missish card. She had a heart of oak, first requirement of a Royal Marine.

He kissed her cheek. 'Brandon, I suppose you will have a thousand objections and try to stop me from sacrificing myself, but here it is. Brace yourself. I love you.' It sounded so good to his ears he said it again. 'I love you.'

Her voice was small. 'Enough to marry me?'

'More than enough. Laura Brittle knew. I knew it, even though I didn't dare say anything. And then I tried to change my mind.' He rested his cheek against hers. 'Are you certain you want to splice yourself to a chowderhead?'

'When I saw that Dragoon point his sidearm at you...' she began. She sobbed and tightened her grip.

'Is that a yes?' he asked, cradling her in his arms and soaking his sleeves.

She nodded.

I daren't be a watering pot, too, he thought, *else she will change her mind.* He tickled her knee instead, content to be easy with the lovely body he already knew. 'You know, Brandon, we will return to Plymouth and I will dutifully take my place at the conference table, probably never to roam the world again,' he said into her ear. 'No more adventuring in foreign waters. I shall leave that to the Lieutenants and Captains in my division. You'll be stuck looking at my sorry visage over breakfast and dinner tables. I can't live without the sight of you.'

'I feel the same way,' she whispered. 'As for roaming the world again, you will, but you will be duty-bound to write me long letters!'

She was patient with him as he poured water over her head and worked soap through her tangled hair, digging with his fingernails until she sighed with pleasure. He washed her hair twice more, then devoted his attention to the rest of her.

It was easy to linger over her breasts, which had lost some of their heft, but none of their attraction. He shook his head at the sight of her ribs. Where had his plump Brandon gone? A few good meals would change that. He had no doubt that his cook in Plymouth would not rest until the Colonel's lady was better fleshed.

She stood when he asked, and let him leisurely lather her hips and thighs and the space between. In fact, she began to breathe hard and clutch at his hair, as he bent to the task. She gasped, pressing his hand into her soft folds, making sure he didn't miss a thing. His thoroughness was gentle. She clutched him convulsively, then kissed the top of his head after she found release.

He rinsed her off as she laughed softly, then wrapped a towel around her and moved her closer to the fireplace. As he dried her, he couldn't help but think how it had all started on board the *Perseverance*, and her so seasick. He had cared for her then and he cared for her now.

'Thank you for saving my life,' he said into her bare shoulder, as she finished drying herself. 'What an inadequate statement, Polly!'

'I would do it again,' she said, turning around.

He picked her up and deposited her in the bed. 'You're my hero, Brandon.'

She blushed becomingly, and held out her

hand to him. 'I'd rather just be your wife, and sing lullabies to our children. You can have the adventuring, Hugh. I don't mind.'

'That's fair enough.' He sat beside her on the bed. 'I don't mean to be squeamish, but your bathwater is daunting. Perhaps Señora Etchemindy can get her little Etchemindys— I saw them peeking around the stairwell—to empty this, move it into the kitchen, and fetch some clean water.'

He looked at her. She was asleep, her hand limp on her bare breast. He laughed softly to himself and covered her with the blanket.

Hugh took his time bathing in the kitchen, once the tub had been emptied and moved from the bedroom. Señora Etchemindy had retired for the night, so Hugh entertained his host with the whole story, from his impulsive leap into the *barco* at Vila Gaia to the ambush on the mountain pass. Etchemindy nodded and smoked his pipe.

'That nun at São Jobim was no nun,' Etchemindy said.

'I didn't think so,' Hugh said, soaping up, 'but she had been violated like so many of Portugal's fair women.' He looked at Etchemindy, soap in hand. 'Some women withdrew, some descended into madness, some coped, and some, like Sister Maria, turned it into a great thirst for revenge.'

'No different than men,' Etchemindy commented. 'Sister Maria Madelena passed on valuable information to your navy. She paid a high price.'

Hugh had nothing more than a towel to wrap around his middle when he padded back down the hall, because Señora Etchemindy had taken out everything except his gorget to the burn pit. Her husband assured him that the village wasn't so destitute that it couldn't come up with adequate fabric to hang on his frame, come morning.

The fire had worked its way down to hot coals and a red glow. He breathed in the fragrance of pine oil and pronounced it better than anything he had smelled in weeks. Autumn was well advanced now and the tang of wood smoke reminded him pleasantly of home.

Brandon was sitting up in bed.

'You were supposed to be asleep,' he told her as he discarded his towel and climbed in beside her.

Polly said nothing, but wrapped her arms and legs around him, working her way into his core. She kissed him with a ferocity that stunned him at first, then built a bonfire in his own body. All he could do was show her how much he loved her by easing himself as deep inside her as he could, all the while kissing her open mouth. They were bound up tight in each other arms.

When she cried out, he felt no need to cover her mouth. The walls were thick, and he knew the Etchemindys were understanding. He could have been quieter, too, or maybe not. They had survived; this coupling was a triumphant victory over death, as they told each other of their love and celebrated their survival with their bodies.

Their next coupling at dawn gave them both a chance to watch each other make love. He had never really noticed before that she had a light sprinkling of freckles on her breasts. Maybe, after peace came and he had some free time, he would count each one. He liked the comfortable way she rested her legs on his legs, and massaged his buttocks with her strong fingers.

Drowsy and satisfied, they lay close together later, listening to the Etchemindys moving about in the great room. 'We're going to the coast,' he told her. 'Admiral Popham is there, and we will join the fleet. Brandon, the fleet is big enough to have a chaplain, and when I am on sea duty, my ship is also my parish. Will you marry me there without any further delay?'

She nodded. 'I will probably have to explain a lot to my sisters.'

'I doubt it.' He raised up on his elbow for a good look at her. 'Brandon, do you realize that at every stage of this journey, no one ever doubted we were married?'

She considered it. 'Did we just always seem married?' she asked, caressing him.

'I've felt that way since the *Perseverance*,' he confessed. 'Don't laugh!'

Her hands were soft on his face. He kissed her palm. 'Colonel, you're a looby. You know that's impossible.' She rubbed her nose against his cheek. 'Well, maybe not impossible. I wanted to think along those lines, except that Laura talked me out of it. But I'm young and foolish. How can you explain *your* behaviour?'

He couldn't think of a thing to say. He just cuddled her closer, until Señor Etchemindy knocked on the door, reminded them there was a war on, and invited them to breakfast.

'There is a pile of clothing outside the door,' Etchemindy said. 'I think you will be suitably disguised, Colonel Junot.'

Hugh decided he liked Polly Brandon very well in the ankle-length skirt, white blouse, and shawl of the local woman. He laced up her leather shoes and earned a flick to his head with her finger when his hands wandered farther up her legs than the stockings.

She laughed out loud when he dressed—

courtesy of the village priest—in black soutane, cape, and broad-brimmed hat. The priest had thoughtfully furnished a crucifix for his neck and a prayer book. 'Now you must behave, Père Hugh Philippe d'Anvers Junot,' she teased.

'Let us pray no one needs Last Rites,' he retorted, and frowned at his patched sleeve. 'I look better in scarlet.'

'You are a man milliner,' his love accused.

'Guilty,' Hugh agreed affably. 'It used to be my little secret, but I suppose marriage lays one open to all sorts of charges. Dash it all—everyone in the Third Division knows I am a peacock!'

Polly was generous. She kissed him and murmured something about how grateful she was that he wasn't perpetually clad in a bloody apron like Philemon, or smelling of brine and tar like Oliver, her brothers-in-law. 'I could probably even take you to Bath and show you off,' she told him, tucking her arm in his as they went to the great room, 'providing I felt like parading you about in front of Miss Pym, which I do not. I intend to admire your remarkable posture and creaseless tunic without an audience!'

'I'll even take it off for you,' he whispered, the soul of generosity.

He hoped she would laugh and blush, but she surprised him. Unable to keep the tears from her eyes, Polly leaned her forehead against his arm. 'My love, I never thought we would have a chance to laugh about a future, did you?'

'No, I didn't, Brandon,' he replied, as honest as she was. 'We owe Sergeant Cadotte a debt we can never repay.'

'We can repay some of it,' she said. 'Some day.'

Breakfast was bread and blood sausage, washed down with milk. Hugh just sat and enjoyed the pleasure of watching Brandon eat until she finally had to hold up her hands in protest against one more bite.

Not one to be sceptical of any man's opinion, Hugh still had to ask Raul Etchemindy how an odd couple such as they were now—maiden and priest—could possibly travel north through territory still patrolled by the French.

Raul seemed not at all perturbed. He broke off a piece of bread and dipped it in his jug of milk. 'You're not the only visitors to our village, Colonel. I think I can guarantee you as safe a ride to Santander as you can imagine.'

As it turned out, he did. Hugh decided never again to doubt Providence.

'Wait here,' Raul said. He hesitated at the door, listening intently, which made Brandon tuck her hand in Hugh's and look at him with concern in her eyes. She was even tensed for flight, which told him volumes about her trust for anyone except him.

'Let's see what this new development is, my love,' he told her calmly. 'Raul, don't think I have rag manners, but how *are* we getting to Santander?'

'Would you like a carriage ride with a French-woman?'

Polly shook her head. 'We would not,' she declared firmly. 'No French ever again. I would rather walk to Santander.'

'Polly, let us reconsider your firm stance against anyone of French origin,' he told her, putting his arm around her. He looked at their host, saw the smile in his eyes, and remembered Lisbon. 'Señor Etchemindy, might this lady be of middling height, trim, and with red, curly hair? Young, too? Not much older than my wife?'

Enjoying himself hugely, Raul nodded.

Polly looked at Hugh suspiciously, but he only kissed her hand, so tight in his. 'If this is who I think, I heard of this paragon in Lisbon,' he told her. 'Her name is Madame Felice Sevigny, and she is the answer to more than one of our prayers, actually.'

'The very woman, *señor*. I believe I hear her carriage now.'

Hugh didn't precisely drag his love to the front door of the Etchemindy dwelling, but she

did remind him of his favorite hunting dog—
when a pup—who had to be coaxed towards
open water. 'Trust me, Brandon,' he whispered.
'Our fortunes have turned.'

They were standing in the doorway as a mud-
stained carriage came to a halt in front of the
house and the door opened. Raul helped down
a kindly looking female, not much taller than
Polly and barely any older, whom he engaged
in conversation. The result was several glances
towards them standing in the doorway, then a
bow, rather than a curtsey.

'That's odd,' Polly said.

'Not so odd,' Hugh contradicted. 'Ah, here
she comes.'

The female in question patted her handsome
black hair where a portion of it peeped out from
a bonnet that must have come direct from the
Rue de Rivoli or a Parisian boulevard close
by. She strode across the muddy space to the
Etchemindy's front door, and into the house in
a businesslike manner, forcing Polly, her eyes
wide now, to back up into Hugh's arms.

When she and Raul were inside and the door
shut, she nodded to Hugh, and turned her attention to Polly. With a flourish, she lifted off her
bonnet, which carried away her hair, too, and
bowed again.

'Madam, James Rothschild at your service.'

Chapter Nineteen

Polly stared in astonishment at the young man before her, then clapped her hand over her mouth and laughed out loud. 'Oh, I do beg your pardon!' she said a second later, then turned to Hugh, who seemed to be enjoying her discomfort hugely. 'Husband, you owe me more than an explanation. I think you owe me a lengthy visit to a modiste when we return to England.'

James Rothschild's eyes were merry. 'My dear Madam Junot, I could not resist, so blame me!' He nodded next to Hugh. 'You, sir, seem to know my secret. One for the confessional, eh? Does chastity wear a little thin on a Royal Marine, Père Junot?'

Hugh laughed and turned over his crucifix. 'I attended a secret conference in Lisbon this summer, but never thought to actually meet you. Polly, dear, James Rothschild and his esteemed father in Frankfurt are bankrolling this war through their London office and James's brother.'

'We are, indeed,' Rothschild said. 'Do your fellows know I have set up a house of business in Paris, right under Napoleon's nose? No? I hide in plain sight, Madame Junot.'

'How on earth...?' Polly began.

'Trade secrets,' he replied, shaking his head. 'Let me only tell you I travel back and forth between France and Spain, a little bullion going to the Corsican's generals, but much more to Wellington and his allies.' His smile was almost cherubic. 'We have an excellent record of backing winners.'

And that was all he would say about that, turning his attention and all of his charm upon Polly then. 'My dear madam, although you are charming in that rustic garb, let me give you another dress, so you can travel as my French companion.' He glanced at the Colonel. 'Your husband can continue in his role as father confessor.'

A nod and a word to Etchemindy sent one of the smaller Etchemindys dodging puddles out to the carriage, where he retrieved a travelling case and hat box. Rothschild indicated Hugh was to take it.

'Colonel, assist your wife in changing into something more suitable for this next leg of our journey.' He peered into Polly's face with enough intensity to make her blush. 'Something warm in burgundy, if I have it on this trip. She has such lovely eyes.'

'I tell her that often, so you needn't,' Hugh assured Rothschild, which made Polly accuse him of jealousy a few minutes later, when he was unbuttoning her.

'You have me there,' he said. 'Who could blame me?' He kissed her neck. 'He is right; you do have lovely eyes.'

'Even with spectacles, the bane of my existence?' she asked, then felt immediately embarrassed because she had no experience in fishing for compliments.

'Even with spectacles,' he assured her. 'I like them, actually.' He struck a pose, which made her smile, since he was still dressed as a priest. 'Polly, you know me well enough to know I am not precisely a deep thinker, given to introspection.'

'I could disagree,' she interjected.

He bowed. 'Thank you. With or without spectacles, you're obviously an intelligent female. Think how brilliant and wise you will make me look!'

She gasped and thumped his chest, then

laughed when he caught her up in his arms again. 'That was the most shallow thing anyone has ever said to me!' she declared.

'But it made you laugh and forget our circumstances for a moment, didn't it?' he teased, then turned immediately serious, or possibly half-serious; she knew she couldn't be sure. 'Brandon, the only problem you might have with spectacles is that all of our babies will want to snatch them off your face. Resign yourself to that.'

'Hugh,' she said softly, and it said the world.

There was no burgundy dress among James Rothschild's catalogue of disguises, so she settled for a dark blue wool travelling dress that screamed Paris-made from every discreet, impeccable seam. It was too big, built for a man's shape, but Hugh looped a sash twice around her waist and called it good. A pelisse of similar hue and a straw bonnet completed the outfit and turned her from a Basque *paisana* into a travelling companion for a distinctly average-looking Frenchwoman with impeccable taste.

After hugs for her hosts, Polly let Hugh hand her into the closed carriage and seat her beside Rothschild, who had replaced his wig and bonnet covering his own red hair. He brought out his tatting. 'My mother taught me,' he said, expertly throwing the little shuttle. 'I have made enough lace to trim petticoats for every sister and cousin I have, and I have a lot of them.' He glanced at Hugh. 'You'd be amazed how something as domestic as this deflects any number of questions from guards and sentries.'

James Rothschild played a deep game, and he distracted her with it through miles of uncomfortable travel, telling them of smuggling goods in all sorts of ways. 'My dears, this coach has a false floor,' he told them. 'And my petticoats—trimmed with tatting or otherwise—have deep pockets.'

He was only one in a far-reaching network of couriers and spies that spanned continental Europe and spilled into England, where his older brother Nathan had established a branch. 'Our business is money, so we appreciate the value of enterprise and commerce in a free environment. This war will end eventually, and the Houses of Rothschild will reign supreme in Europe,' he said, then made a face when the carriage hit a larger-than-usual pothole. '*Oi vey!* Meanwhile, our backsides suffer. My Hebrew ancestors would tell you it is hard to start dynasties.'

They travelled through two French sentry posts, both well guarded with troops, which told her volumes about the ever-present threat of *guerilleros*. Rothschild, or rather, Madame

Felice Sevigny, barely looked up from her tatting, and even handed it to one guard while she searched in her reticule for the safe-conduct pass. His audacity took away Polly's breath.

Nightfall found them in León, also patrolled by the French. With remarkable aplomb, Madame Sevigny asked for her usual room and added one for the priest. They ate in a private parlor, but not until the last dish was removed and hot water brought up did Rothschild remove his wig and hike up his skirts, to rest his white-stockinged legs and chic half-boots on a settle. Hugh tugged at his priestly skirts and did the same thing, which made Polly roll her eyes and throw up her hands.

She started the night on a pallet in the same room with Rothschild, clad in a nightshirt, who had taken a yarmulke, phylacteries, and blue-fringed shawl from some recess in his portmanteau and was rocking back and forth, deep in prayer. She watched him, touched at his devotion and wondering how much courage it took for him to practise this huge deception on Napoleon. Madam Sevigny, née Rothschild, may have tried to let them think it was all for business, but Polly knew enough of men now to reckon that even vain ones like Hugh were fuelled by higher motives. *So am I*, she told herself.

When he put away his religious artifacts,

Rothschild climbed into bed and told her good-night. 'I'm certain if you tap on the next door, there is a priest who would probably do you a bout of no good,' he teased. She blushed in the gloom, blew him a kiss, and left the room.

Rothschild was right. Their bout of no good calmed her nerves and soothed that part of her, somewhere under her skin, that seemed to hum with tension. 'This is disconcerting to the hilt, Hugh, darling, but I only feel safe when you are covering me,' she whispered, blushing as she said it.

'Happy to oblige, even though it's *my* sorry ass winking at the ceiling,' he said cheerfully, his breathing still ragged. 'At least I weigh less than when our journey began.'

'It seems so long ago now,' she murmured, drowsy. When he left her body, but continued to hold her close, she kissed his arm and pillowed her head on it. 'How soon will we be at the coast?'

No answer. Her hero slept. He even snored a little.

In two days they arrived at Gijón, where Hugh sighed with relief to see the Bay of Biscay, sparkling in the sun. 'God, I love the ocean,' he said.

'We are less than fifty miles to Santander,'

Rothschild said, putting down his tatting. 'Here is where I trade *haute couture* for rough trousers and a sweater, and take a fishing smack to La Rochelle.'

'You amaze me,' Polly said.

He shrugged, then tied off the length of tatting, which he handed to Polly. 'Sew this on a petticoat and think of me.' Rothschild took out a handkerchief. With a glance at Hugh, he dabbed at her eyes. 'No tears, Polly! You and your excellent husband will come and see me in Paris when this is over. I never knew a woman to tear up over tatting before.'

The plans changed as soon as Rothschild went on board the fishing boat and spoke to the Captain. After that brief conversation, they were all on board to hear the good news that the British fleet was in no apparent hurry to leave Santander. 'The Captain says he will take us to the fleet, Colonel,' Rothschild said. 'You'll be in Santander by morning.'

Bundled against wind and rain, they spent the night on the deck of the fishing smack. Polly visited the rail several times to retch her stomach out, while Hugh came to the rail to look for the first sign of the fleet. 'I'll feel so much easier when we are on board Popham's flagship,' he told her once, when their trips to the railing intersected.

* * *

Morning brought more mist, but not enough to disguise the breathtaking sight of Admiral Sir Home Popham's 100-gun ship of the line, and the frigates and smaller ships, a bomb kedge among them, hovering close by like chicks around a hen.

'Thank God,' Hugh said fervently. 'Polly, we made it.'

They said goodbye to James Rothschild after breakfast, which Polly was wise enough to forgo. After a glance at Hugh, he hugged her and kissed both cheeks, French fashion. 'Be careful, James,' she told him.

Rothschild looked over her head to Hugh in his priest's garments and kissed Polly again. '*Au revoir*, fair lady. We'll meet again in Paris. *Shalom.*' With a wave of his hand, Rothschild returned to his fishing net.

The fishing smack's jollyboat skimmed across the bay to the largest ship in the fleet. Because they approached the flagship as an unknown quantity, they were met on deck by a whole contingent of Marines, bayonets at the ready and commanded by a Captain of mature years who took one look at Hugh the priest and saluted, to the amusement of nearby seamen.

'Colonel Junot! We thought you were dead!'

'A vast understatement, Captain Marten. I

do hope my Colonel Commandant in Plymouth has not replaced me yet.' He glanced at Polly, amused. 'My love, I am about to revert to my frivolous ways and ask Theodore Marten, whom I have known for years, if he has some more suitable clothing.'

'I knew you were a man milliner,' Polly said.

Hugh took her arm and led her closer. 'Captain Marten, this is my wife, Polly Junot, and she is abusing me because I am a peacock.'

Captain Marten snapped to attention again for her benefit. 'Sir, I knew right away after that exchange that she was your wife. Who else would treat you that way, sir? Welcome to Admiral Sir Popham's flagship, ma'am. Colonel, allow me to escort you and your lady to the old man himself.'

To Polly's amusement, the old man was as astounded as his Captain of Marines to see Lieutenant Colonel Hugh Junot—thinner, looking more righteous than usual, but obviously no worse for wear.

''Pon my word, Colonel, we have been scouring the coast for news of you,' he said, pouring them each a glass of Madeira. 'And is this Polly Brandon, risen from the dead as well? There is an anxious surgeon's wife on Oporto who has been pelting me with letters, and an equally anxious frigate captain who should be at Ferrol

Station but who is patrolling this coast, looking for his sister-in-law.'

'It is Oliver,' Polly said with relief. 'I have so much to tell him.'

'And we have much to tell you, Admiral,' Hugh said. 'But first, there is a delicate matter that demands your assistance and your discretion. May we speak privately?'

They could, after the Admiral shooed away his secretary and other crew members. Hugh quickly explained their situation and requested a wedding in the Admiral's great room at the earliest possible convenience. There were no flies on the Admiral; he summoned his chaplain immediately while Hugh procured himself some clothing from slops—nothing fancier than dark trousers and another black-and-white checked shirt. 'I have my limits, Polly,' he told her, as he patted his gorget, which now lay on the outside of his shirt. 'I won't be married in priest's clothing.'

'I still look better than you do,' she teased.

'You always will, my love,' he told her.

I believe him, she thought, a little surprised at herself, considering what a splendid man Hugh Junot was. *I am the most beautiful woman who ever lived*, she thought, watching her husband—in fact, if not by law yet. 'We have been through more than most, my love,' she said, her voice low, but not low enough that Admiral Popham did not hear, and then turn away, muttering about something in his eye, and complaining that his steward hadn't a clue about dusting his quarters.

They waited while Popham demanded one of his Midshipmen to run up the numbered flags that would summon the Captain of the *Tangier* to the flagship immediately. Then they waited a little longer for Captain Oliver Worthy—anxious at the summons and frowning—to gasp and throw open his arms to embrace his sister-in-law, as soon as he came into the great cabin.

'We needed another witness, Worthy. I thought this was one way to get a lick of work out of you and then send the *Tangier* back to Ferrol Station,' Popham said gruffly. He nodded to his chaplain, who stood ready. 'C'mon, man. This won't wait. Splice 'um! There's a war on!'

Admiral Popham dropped his anchor on her when the ink wasn't yet dry on the marriage lines. 'Mrs Junot, take a long look at your husband and give him a kiss. I'm sending him with Captain Marten and his Marines to Burgos with siege guns for Wellington.'

'Then I am coming, too,' she said, as the blood rushed from her face at the Admiral's news, so drily delivered. 'I…I really don't know what I will do if he is not in my sight.'

'That is not possible, Mrs Junot,' the Admiral said, and she felt her heart slide into James Rothschild's shoes, because she knew he meant it.

'I'll take you to Oporto, Polly,' Oliver said. 'Duty is duty and no one knows that better than your husband.'

She looked at Hugh, pleaded with him with her eyes without saying a word, and saw in his glance that he felt precisely the same way, even as he agreed with her brother-in-law.

'I must obey, Brandon,' he told her.

They all looked at her, each man with some anxiety, and she knew why. She was a woman, weak, missish, and prone to tears. This was their world and she had intruded in it from São Jobim on. No matter how much Hugh Junot loved her, and she knew he did, he was a Marine and the world was at war.

I could cry, she thought, *or I could be the woman my sisters have become; the woman I want to be.*

'I know you must obey, Hugh,' she told him. She turned to Oliver. 'I would love to sail to Oporto with you, or even go back to Torquay and Nana, but I would like to remain here with the fleet, at least until I know what happens at

Burgos.' She looked at Admiral Popham. 'I did learn some skills at the satellite hospital, if your surgeon might have need of them. If not, I can stay out of everyone's way.'

'It could be that I must remain in Burgos, or follow the guns, if we are successful, and winter in the Pyrenees,' Hugh said tentatively.

'Or retreat with Wellington to the lines of Torres Vedras,' she said. 'So be it. Just let me know, one way or the other, and I can return to Oporto on a coasting vessel.'

The men looked at each other, and then at the Admiral, whose decision it was. He removed his wig, scratched his scalp, and replaced his wig. 'Done, madam,' he said. 'You may remain with the fleet here in Santander, until we know where this Marine of yours is headed.' The Admiral chucked her under the chin. 'I suppose I am a fool for love,' he told her. 'Let's send Oliver packing, and find you a berth somewhere on this big ship, shall we?'

'Furnish it with a bucket,' her lover and newly licensed husband said. 'She's my darling, but she is no seaman.'

They laughed. Hugh took her hand and kissed it. 'I'm going now to speak with Captain Marten and find out what the duty entails.'

After he left, and before she had a moment to pine, Oliver tucked her arm in his. 'Polly, if you won't come aboard the *Tangier* and let me take you to Oporto, please write a letter to Laura. I will deliver it inside of a week.'

She took a deep breath. 'I have a lot to say to her.'

It was only a brief letter, because the *Tangier* had to sail. It came from Polly's heart, begging Laura's pardon for doing precisely what she had counselled against, but assuring her sister that she knew her heart, even as she did and as Nana did. '"I trust you will come to love my husband as your brother,"' she wrote, choosing each word with care. '"We will be in Plymouth at the Marine barracks, and you are always welcome in our home."'

She showed it to Oliver, who had been given leave to relax in the Admiral's quarters and drink the man's Madeira. He nodded, and patted the banquette beside him.

'I wish I could take you back to Torquay, but I understand, truly I do,' he said, then tightened his grip on her shoulder, at the mention of his and Nana's home. 'I didn't tell you the best news. Nana was confined with our son only three weeks ago. Polly, I was there. I was *there*!'

It was too much. He couldn't say anything else. They were still sitting close together when Hugh returned to Popham's great cabin. He sat beside her, his hand on her knee, and looked at them both. 'Should I be suddenly afraid that my new relatives are emotional southerners?' he asked, his Scots accent never more pronounced. 'Oliver, does it take official wedding vows to bring out the fearful truth?'

'Sister Polly, you have married a Marine, a Scot, and a Lieutenant Colonel,' Oliver said solemnly. 'I am not certain which will give you the most trouble.'

'None of them,' she replied. 'I know this man's heart.'

Chapter Twenty

She slept with her husband that night in quarters off the Admiral's cabin, accustoming herself to the motion of a sleeping cot again. They lay tight as sardines, swinging gently as the ship of the line moved on its anchors. He told her of the letter he had sent with James Rothschild, requesting him to forward it through his secret channels to his brother Nathan in London. It was a request for a tidy sum from his banker to be sent through James in Paris to Lalage Cadotte in the parish of Sainte Agilbert.

'Providence sent us the only man in Europe who could actually get that money to our Sergeant's widow before this war ends,' he told her. 'We will still go and see her later, but at least we know she will soon have what we promised her husband.'

'Bless you,' Polly said. 'And João at Sacred Name?'

'He'll come to Plymouth with us, just as we promised his mother in São Jobim, my love.' He turned towards her, his hand inside her nightgown now. 'Give a Marine some comfort,' he whispered, his lips on her breast. 'You're my only girl in a port, and I can't waste a moment. Time management, wife.'

Admiral Sir Home Popham and his Captain commanding kindly allowed her access to the quarterdeck, where she stood at the rail for long hours, looking south towards Burgos. She had said an appropriate farewell to her husband belowdeck as the circumspect wife of a Lieutenant Colonel should, but came above deck to watch the Marines and seamen, aided by brown-suited *guerilleros*, move three eighteen-pounders from the fleet to be used as siege cannon at Burgos. After they were out of sight, she longed to tug at the lace on Sir Home's sleeve and demand to know how long the men would be gone. Instead, she chose discretion and kept her own counsel, as Hugh would want. She passed her nineteenth birthday alone, her mind and heart on her husband, adding his own mantle of duty to her shoulders. She was strong enough to bear the weight of it, and had not a doubt of her own courage.

To her relief, the Admiral had no intention of pulling up anchor until he knew what had happened at Burgos. The rains gave way to unexpected sleet in mid-October and a choppy anchorage, which sent her belowdeck, white-faced and trembling, to kneel over the bucket in her quarters.

Less than a week later, the detail returned, but without the cannon. Even Admiral Popham stared in surprise to see them. ''Pon my word, Mrs Junot,' he said, handing her the glass and pointing. 'There had better be an adequate explanation!'

There was, and it was delivered by one of Wellington's aides-de-camp, looking decidedly out of place among his naval brethren. 'The General sends his compliments, Admiral Popham. I am to tell you that he has lifted his siege and is returning to Portugal. Your guns are no longer required.'

'Admiral, General Wellington sent his ADC to us when we were still fifty miles from Burgos,' Hugh added. 'He couldn't sustain a siege and he decided it was time to retreat to Portugal.'

Popham frowned and deliberately looked all

around the deck. 'Then where, Colonel, are my flaming guns?' He stared down his long nose at Captain Marten, his chief Marine officer on the flagship, who had accompanied the guns, too. 'Sir? Did they take wing?'

Captain Marten blushed. 'No, sir, not at all. Colonel Junot suggested we give them to General Espoz y Mina and his *guerilleros*, who so ably assisted us in the transport.'

'Hmm,' the Admiral said, returning his gaze to Hugh. 'I trust you have an excellent reason why this was a good idea?'

'I do, sir,' Hugh replied, not ruffled at all by the stare from an Admiral of the fleet. 'The rain was bogging down our own retreat, and Espoz y Mina can find good use for the guns in his operations here in León.' He glanced at Polly and smiled. 'Polly and I have seen him and his troops in action, sir. I think his army is worth three of any bona fide Spanish army. I take full responsibility.'

'Good of you,' Popham murmured, but with no malice.

'Sir, if I may, any muskets, rifles, and materiel you have not handed over to the regular Spanish army should be given to the *guerilleros*,' Hugh said, pressing home the point. 'Do this, and León will be pacified before winter ends.'

Admiral Popham nodded. 'You guarantee

these ragged men can do what a Spanish army cannot?'

'Admiral Popham, no man can guarantee that. My advice is to trust him. Espoz y Mina's brand of hit-and-run war may become a standard of warfare, in future.'

'I doubt that very much, Colonel,' Popham said, after a long pause and much scrutiny of Colonel Junot, who did not squirm. 'Care to make a wager?'

The tension on the quarterdeck vanished when Hugh gasped theatrically. 'Not with my wife standing here, Admiral! She will give me a regular bear-garden jaw, if I gamble away my pay chit.'

'I wouldn't, you know,' she told him later, when they stood on the deck of the frigate *Aurora*, which had peeled off from the fleet towards Oporto with them aboard. 'The Admiral will think I am a shrew.'

Hugh kissed her check, and wrapped his borrowed boat cloak tighter around both of them. 'No, no. He's a married man, too.' He sighed then, and gently rubbed his thumb under her breast, more for comfort, to her way of thinking, than any greater design. 'I don't know what I accomplished during this sojourn in the Peninsula, as far as military matters go. I have a wife—

the best one imaginable—but the notes I took from all those interviews must be scattered from here to breakfast. My conclusions about the *guerilleros* will be met with scepticism—you heard the Admiral—because no one understands this kind of warfare yet.'

'You can still write a report about that,' she pointed out.

'I can. I can also urge my Commandant Colonel that our Marines be used here and there among the *guerilleros* as liaison. They'll be better than that ninny from Wellington's army. Certainly more flexible.' He pulled her closer. 'Is it enough?'

'Probably not for you,' she said. 'Will you be content to sit at a desk in Plymouth now and make policy?'

'And not go gallivanting off to the Peninsula?' He kissed her fingers. 'Aye, Polly, dear, because I know that when I come home each night, you will be on the other side of the door.'

She had no resistance to that. After a quick scanning of the deck, she turned around in his arms and kissed him, pressing against his body so brazenly that she was glad his cloak enveloped them both. *Better get the man belowdeck and roger him royally*, she told herself. She knew that as soon as the frigate began its dance on the Atlantic rollers, she would be kneeling by that bucket again, with love a long way from her mind.

He kissed her back with some fervour, but then he sighed, and rested his chin on her head. 'Brandon, I have to tell you something.'

'That you love me?'

Hugh held her off a little, his face serious. 'When we were fifty miles from Burgos, where the ADC joined us, so did El Cuchillo.'

She thought a moment, then tensed. 'Dear God. Sister Maria Madelena's brother?'

'The very same. He came right up to me out of the shadows and stood practically on my shoes. What could I do? I didn't know whether to fight or run, but then he clapped his arms on my shoulders and kissed me on each cheek.'

Hugh couldn't help himself then. He sobbed out loud, trying to smother the sound in her hair. Polly held him closer. 'She spared you!' she said fiercely. 'I'll remind you of that whenever you need to hear it!'

She wiped his eyes, kissing his lips and neck until he could speak again.

'That was what he told me, too, my love. We didn't know it, but the deacon at São Jobim witnessed the whole wicked turn of events from the choir loft. He carried the tale to El Cuchillo, and it was El Cuchillo who took word to Oporto that you and I were still alive. He…he just wanted to assure me he knows the truth.'

'Poor man,' she murmured. 'Did…you tell him of our plans for João?'

'Aye, and he gave me his blessing again. Polly, I want to be a good father.'

'You will be,' she said, running her hand along his face, caressing him. 'And to all our other children,' she whispered.

'Is that an announcement, Polly, dear?' he asked, and he sounded so eager.

'No. It's just a fact,' she said. 'I even predict that when we get to Oporto, my sister will give you a hug and a kiss.'

'I doubt that,' he said. 'She doesn't like me.'

'She will! Philemon will be our advocate, Hugh. Did you know it was Philemon who delivered that letter you so incautiously wrote to me?'

The frigate began its Atlantic roll. He walked her carefully to a nearby hatch and sat down, his cloak still tight around her. 'He did tell me that, and gave me some reason to hope.' He glanced at her. 'Polly, do you think you and I will disagree on things, as the Brittles do?'

'I think you can count on it,' she told him. 'I have a brain; so do you. How could we possibly see eye to eye on everything?' She moved herself into his embrace, wrapping her arms around him. 'I never told you this, but I wrote you a letter, too, only I never sent it. You can read it, when we get to Oporto.' She sighed. 'It's not cheerful reading.'

'It's not a cheerful war. You know that better than any female, Brandon. We're returning to Stonehouse Barracks and I am going back to boring desk duty, where I will write that report—as much as I can from memory—and strenuously argue for the Marines to be used as liaison with *guerrilleros* like Espoz y Mina.' He twined his fingers through hers. 'Maybe there will be time for you and me and João to visit Scotland, but I doubt it.'

'What will I do?'

He kissed her hand. 'You can begin by decorating my quarters. I'm embarrassed for you to see them now, but that can't be helped. And just think—you can spend leisure time playing "There was an old bee" with João.'

'I can,' she agreed, feeling impish. Either the waves weren't rolling too high yet, or she was finally developing those mythical sea legs her Marine spoke of. More immediately, she saw a future belowdeck in a sleeping cot with her husband. *I used to be a lot more circumspect*, she thought, as she leaned closer to him. *Thank goodness that passed.* 'I have a version of my own for you. "There was an old bee…"'

'Brandon, you scamp,' he exclaimed, even as he made no effort to stop her pointing finger, which was more of a caress than a circle, and targeted south of his stomach. 'No one's ever done the bee like that before. No, don't stop.'

"'…who lived in a barn,'" she continued, not even bothering with the circle any more, but touching him where she knew it would do the most good, considering her designs on her husband. She began to undo the buttons on his trousers. "'He carried a bagpipe…'" she began, but he stood up then.

"'…under his arm,'" he continued, as he kept the cloak around both of them and started with her for the gangway. 'So glad you remember that little ditty, except that I may never be able to look at it in the same way again. I believe you are a rascal, Brandon.'

Thirty minutes later, he was deep asleep, cradling her in his arms, as he had protected her from Plymouth to Santander, and apparently back again. She thought about looking for her nightgown, but that was more effort than she deemed strictly necessary. Besides, she might just have to take it off again, and she knew how Hugh, darling, felt about effective time management.

As Colonel Junot slept the good sleep of

the thoroughly rogered, she pillowed her head against his chest. So much had happened since early summer, when she had left Plymouth as a green girl. Autumn was almost winter. Wellington and his troops were slogging back to Portugal. The war was her companion, but no war lasted for ever. Duty called her Colonel, and always would, but she expected no less. In the grand scheme of things—where armies marched and tyrants decreed—perhaps nothing had changed. In her heart, everything had. She listened to the ship's bells, content to watch over him.

* * * * *

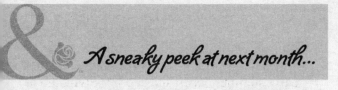

A sneaky peek at next month...

HISTORICAL

IGNITE YOUR IMAGINATION, STEP INTO THE PAST...

My wish list for next month's titles...

In stores from 6th April 2012:

☐ The Scandalous Lord Lanchester – Anne Herries

☐ Highland Rogue, London Miss – Margaret Moore

☐ His Compromised Countess – Deborah Hale

☐ The Dragon and the Pearl – Jeannie Lin

☐ Destitute On His Doorstep – Helen Dickson

☐ His Californian Countess – Kate Welsh

Available at WHSmith, Tesco, Asda, Eason, Amazon and Apple

Just can't wait?

Visit us Online

You can buy our books online a month before they hit the shops! **www.millsandboon.co.uk**

0312/04

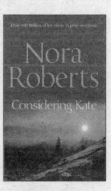

The World of Mills & Boon®

There's a Mills & Boon® series that's perfect for you. We publish ten series and with new titles every month, you never have to wait long for your favourite to come along.

Blaze®
Scorching hot, sexy reads

By Request
Relive the romance with the best of the best

Cherish™
Romance to melt the heart every time

Desire™
Passionate and dramatic love stories

Have Your Say

You've just finished your book. So what did you think?

We'd love to hear your thoughts on our 'Have your say' online panel
www.millsandboon.co.uk/haveyoursa

- 🌹 Easy to use
- 🌹 Short questionnaire
- 🌹 Chance to win Mills & Boon® goodies